Wolf in Tiger's Stripes

Wolf in Tiger's Stripes

Victoria Gordon

FIVE STAR
A part of Gale, Cengage Learning

GALE
CENGAGE Learning

Detroit • New York • San Francisco • New Haven, Conn • Waterville, Maine • London

GALE
CENGAGE Learning

Five Star Publishing, a part of Gale, Cengage Learning.

Set in 11 pt. Plantin.

Printed on permanent paper.

LIBRARY OF CONGRESS CATALOGING-IN-PUBLICATION DATA

Gordon, Victoria, 1942–
Wolf in tiger's stripes / Victoria Gordon. — 1st ed.
p. cm.
ISBN-13: 978-1-59414-844-6 (alk. paper)
ISBN-10: 1-59414-844-9 (alk. paper)
1. Women journalists—Fiction. 2. Thylacine—Fiction. 3. Wilderness areas—Tasmania—Fiction. I. Title.
PR9619.3.A22W65 2010
823'.914—dc22 2009037807

First Edition. First Printing: January 2010.
Published in 2010 in conjunction with Tekno Books.

Printed in the United States of America
1 2 3 4 5 6 7 14 13 12 11 10

This book is for those who believe in Tasmanian tigers.
And the Sasquatch, and maybe even unicorns.
And romance, of course.
We know why we do it.
It's because we must.
And because we should!

1

The conversation seemed to hover like noxious smoke over the long, oval dining table, the words indistinct and, to Judith, irrelevant. She stared down at the incinerated contents of her plate, idly wondering how a woman who cooked as badly as her American-born but now thoroughly Tasmanian cousin, Vanessa, could even dare to hold a dinner party in the first place.

Judith prodded gingerly at the charred remains of what had once been prime rib steak, wishing she had the nerve to feign a headache, nausea, anything to avoid having to actually try to eat this burnt offering. But with the dinner party ostensibly in *her* honor? No, not a chance.

She wasn't comfortable at being the supposed guest of honor, either. Her cousin, goodhearted as she was, had absolutely no compunction about blatant matchmaking, and on this occasion Vanessa had outdone herself. It was seriously unnerving for Judith to find herself partnered at dinner with a man so splendidly masculine that under normal circumstances she'd have been blessing her now-Tasmanian cousin with every bite.

Bevan Keene, Judith had decided from the moment of seeing him for the first time, was the quintessential rugged Australian stockman—the physical manifestation of countless romantic and adventure novels. He was tall, lean, ruggedly handsome, but also urbane, clearly well educated, witty, dangerously charming, and too damned close for comfort.

And you don't believe in love at first sight. Not even lust at first sight. Well . . . usually.

But there was nothing usual about the effect Bevan Keene had created merely in being introduced to her, and sitting beside him now, Judith could almost feel the physical current that flowed between them. He wasn't touching her, never had, but . . . Judith's tongue flicked across her lips just thinking about what she'd like to do with the man beside her. Under normal circumstances!

These were not, however, normal circumstances. Here, now, Judith wasn't interested in any man, not even one so attractive and charming as Bevan Keene. So Judith had ignored Keene from the very start of the evening, or at least as much as she *could* ignore him without being outright rude.

None of her current antipathy toward men was *his* fault; it was all because of Derek Innes. And at the very least, there was no sexual baggage involved there, not on her part, anyway. But not really Derek's fault, either. Not entirely. *Your own fault, Judith Theresa—all your own fault.*

Judith was honest enough with herself to admit that, just as she admitted that Bevan Keene was turning her on just by sitting there beside her and assaulting his overdone steak with perfect teeth. He was himself edible in every way she could think of, except that she wished *not* to think of such things. Fat chance!

Try as she might, Judith couldn't stop herself from imagining those strong, tanned, capable hands touching her, that mobile mouth caressing her own lips before moving on to caress other parts of her body . . .

Tuning back into the hubbub of conversation, she had to give herself a mental shake. *No wonder the table talk is so overwhelming. They're all talking at once just to avoid having to eat. Lord love us, but I cannot understand why a vegetarian should ever be allowed to even try and cook meat, presuming of course that this ever* was *meat, which I'm beginning to doubt.*

Judith's own taste tended to huge, thick steaks that hit the plate kicking and bellowing. Quite early in her Australian sojourn she'd heard a Queensland local in an upscale restaurant proclaim, "Just cut off its horns and wipe its bum and put it on the plate." She had cringed at the vulgarity but secretly applauded the sentiment.

Now, glancing round the table while still ignoring the conversation, she noticed suddenly that she wasn't alone in her opinion of cousin Vanessa's so-called cuisine. Even Vanessa's husband Charles, the advertising executive known to be totally enthralled and totally smitten with what he termed his "imported wife," had barely touched the offering in front of him. Vanessa herself hardly appeared to have eaten anything, but then she had the excuse of soon-to-be-delivered twins.

Poor kids. You'll probably grow up without ever knowing what a good steak tastes like. Nessie will have Charles fully converted by the time you're weaned, and she'll raise the lot of you on bean curd and lentils. Judith couldn't escape the thought when it struck her mind, or the frown that accompanied it.

"This tucker's a bit overdone, but not that bad, surely." The voice was low, not quite a growl.

Judith almost leapt from her chair as the remark penetrated her self-imposed solitude but failed to touch her understanding.

"I'm sorry," she replied, turning to the speaker. "I was . . ."

"You were looking as if you had a toothache, or more likely a stomachache," was the reply from Bevan Keene, and it was accompanied by a scathing glance at the charred scraps on his own plate. He had done better justice to the meal than she, but not by much.

"It wasn't the food," she replied, her lips curving in what she hoped would emerge as a grin. "Although it could have been, couldn't it? No, I was thinking of . . . something else."

"Some thing, or some *body?*" he replied, softening the query with a smile. "I wouldn't want to be him if it was a person you were considering. The look on your face suggested hanging would be too good for him."

She'd been thinking of Charles and children, but his question thrust her mind back a notch, to Derek. "It would be," Judith replied briskly. "Drawing and quartering would be preferable, I think. I'd like to watch him suffer."

Bevan Keene's hooded gray eyes sparkled to match the gleam of white teeth that flashed a quick smile. The gesture made the ends of his heavy mustache quiver, giving him a bold, almost flamboyant air. A pirate, disguised as a prominent Australian grazier.

"Pretty fierce talk," he said. "Is it just because he done you wrong, or is there a helping of hell hath no fury in there?"

Wrong question. Judith felt herself going cold inside, could feel the barrier lifting between them like an icy curtain. She didn't reply, merely turned her attention back to her charred steak. Bevan Keene watched her for a moment; she could feel his eyes as his gaze strayed across her features in a bold, if not blatantly sexual, appraisal.

It was as if he'd physically caressed her—she could actually *feel* his touch on her cheek, her lips. But then he accepted the rebuke without further comment and turned to speak to the person on his other side.

Judith returned to her reverie, all too aware that she might be visibly trembling at the intensity of the feelings his incautious questions had aroused. Done her wrong? Derek had done worse than that. He had virtually destroyed her career as an environmental journalist—that's what he'd done! What she now felt had nothing to do with being scorned. It had to do with her shame and guilt at having been so easily manipulated.

So here I am, ten thousand miles from home, out of a job, probably blacklisted in the entire industry. All because of my own stupidity! Judith shook her head angrily. *Because Derek was just so damned smooth? So damned plausible? Or just because I'm what's known as a natural victim?*

Judith stared blindly at her plate, wondering, not for the first time, how she could be smart enough to know her weaknesses, yet so stupid as to have let Derek manipulate her in the first place. Of course, with hindsight, she shouldn't have let herself be led astray by Derek's seemingly solid principles. The rising star of the Queensland environmental movement, he was, of course, relevant to her own work. But having trusted him was nothing short of stupid, and she'd known that even as she walked wide-eyed and innocent into his idealism-baited trap. Professionally questionable. Personally, little short of outright foolhardiness.

Right from the start, there had been a question of who was using whom, an issue Judith had idealistically assumed she could handle. Derek, as she now realized, had handled it better. He had used her right from the beginning and, worse, had always intended to!

He'd been handsome (not that it mattered because she hadn't been attracted to him sexually), charming, persuasive, charismatic—and as crooked as a dog's hind leg. Behind the façade, he was cunning, devious, and manipulative, a man so self-centered he would use anybody and everything to achieve his objectives. For Judith, it had been a monumental disaster, the ensuing story so blatantly and obviously rigged that it had given her New York boss—who'd been trying for two years without success to lure her into his bed—the excuse he'd been looking for to fire her on the spot. Derek had come out looking triumphant; Judith had emerged jobless and looking a fool.

And now here I am in Tasmania, of all places, licking my wounds and hiding from the world like a wounded animal. Good one, Judith Theresa!

She found herself thinking of the North American wolverine, an animal that habitually fouled whatever it could not use itself, just to be sure no other animal could use it. She had once playfully told Derek the wolverine should have been dubbed the original political animal. Now, she realized, Derek himself was the classic wolverine, the consummate politician. A user, no more and no less.

It was the name of another animal, however, that brought her out of her fugue and back to the present with an almost visible start.

". . . Tassie tiger? Well of course they're extinct. It would be nice, of course, to believe otherwise, but really . . ."

"It's not only the greenies that believe they still exist," said Phelan Keene, the brother of Judith's dinner companion. "A lot of genuine bushies and graziers—people who *should* know—believe it too. Even the top scientists who've studied the Thylacine believe it *might* still exist."

Or might truly be extinct, Judith thought. The Thylacine, more commonly known as the Tasmanian tiger despite being—technically—a marsupial wolf, was a conservation icon both in Tasmania and in the rest of Australia. The weirdly doglike creature with its tawny striped coat and distinctive gaping "yawn" was a much larger cousin to the Tasmanian devil so grossly miscast in cartoons, but had never quite gained international recognition in the same way. "And every year, some weirdo gets on his favorite hobby horse and starts things up again." This came from the other end of the table. "And of course the media leap onto the bandwagon, and we're off and running. *Tasmanian Tiger Sighted!* It's a load of old cobblers, if you ask me. Damn it, Phelan, if tigers do exist, why don't we get reports of them from somebody responsible? Like Bevan, or some other knowledgeable grazier, for instance."

"Because no sane property owner would ever admit to seeing a Tassie tiger within a hundred miles of his own property," replied the sandy-haired man seated beside Judith. In a voice that, while soft, seemed to reverberate through the sudden quiet in the room, he added, "If he did, he'd be overrun by government boffins and politicians and bloody journalists."

A boffin is a so-called expert. Judith made the mental translation while almost tasting the acid in Bevan Keene's final word, "journalists." Not a new response to her, but seldom had she seen such a pronounced antipathy from a person who seemed otherwise calm and rational.

"Not to mention being held to ridicule and quite deservedly being called a liar and a damned fool," came from the other end of the table, and Judith actually *felt* the tension that ran through her dinner companion, like some strange current of static electricity. Bevan Keene seemed to freeze in a posture that suggested he might leap to his feet and commit mayhem.

He replied with a quick and ready grin, but his tension was obvious enough, at least to her.

"That too," he replied in that deceptively soft, growly voice. And Judith noticed he was looking not at the obnoxious speaker, but at his own brother. And the look was alive with warning.

Too late. Even as Judith began trying to interpret the subtle signal between the brothers, Phelan Keene was halfway to his feet and glaring across the dinner table at the man who'd mentioned fools and liars.

"A damned fool, maybe," Phelan said through clenched teeth. "But I'd go easy about calling people liars, if I were you. Bevan might accept it—he's a peaceful soul and he's a grazier, after all. He can't, as he said earlier, very well go around admitting he's seen tigers more than once in his short life. But I've seen them too, and my temper is a bit less gentle than his."

Judith could hardly believe her eyes and ears. It was like being transported back in history to a time when duels were fought. Phelan Keene had visibly flung down a challenging gauntlet and was poised for a fight—a startling transformation from the man who only moments before had been trading tax collector jokes with his stunning, relatively new wife, a woman who worked for the tax office and seemed quite used to her husband's teasing her about her work.

"Settle, boy." Bevan's voice was still low, but somehow it penetrated the now-hostile atmosphere at the other end of the table. The older brother at her side was, Judith felt, of a much less volatile nature than Phelan, but no less dangerous for all that. Probably even more dangerous. But for now his calmer temperament stood out as he spoke to defuse the issue. He spoke to the man who'd upset Phelan, but his eyes and attention were locked on his brother.

"I've seen a pink elephant or two in my time," Bevan said with a deprecating grin, "and a flying pig, too—once. But I wouldn't reckon any of them, or the circumstances, are subjects for discussion in polite company. We ought to change the subject."

Which, Judith realized, was a casual but deliberate way of telling his younger brother to drop the subject and do it now. Bevan Keene's apparent relaxation might seem real at the other end of the table, but she could feel the tension that remained in his large, muscular frame. Their elbows touched, although she didn't think Keene was aware of it—his concentration was elsewhere. But she could feel his muscles flexing, could see the taut tendons in his neck and jaw.

It was like being next to a wild animal poised to pounce, and without thinking, Judith reached out a hand and laid it on his thigh, seeking to calm him.

Not a good move! Because it wasn't his muscular thigh that

her fingers encountered, but his lap. And because her touch didn't reduce *any* tensions, merely created tension of a different sort entirely!

Judith froze, strangely unable to obey the instinct to let go, move her hand, flee the encounter—maybe flee the entire scene! It was as if her fingers had been coated with glue, and when he turned to capture her startled gaze with his own, that only made things worse.

Keene's wonderfully mobile mouth curved in a grin that could have been amusement or sheer satisfaction. It didn't matter because Judith was transfixed by it, could only sit there, stunned as a tiny prey animal confronted by its nemesis predator.

She blushed—couldn't *not* blush, couldn't *not* be aware how her fair, freckled skin and copper-red hair made the blush impossible to hide. But she couldn't speak, couldn't think, and—worst of all—couldn't seem to let go of him!

Her mind had gone into idiocy mode. All she could hear in her head was a nonsense rhyme about the dreaded one-eyed trouser snake, and she wanted to laugh and didn't dare, wanted to let go of this *thing* that writhed and squirmed beneath her fingers, but couldn't do that, either.

She could only meet the amused stare from the softest gray eyes she'd ever seen on a man, could only fix a death-grip on what little composure she could still claim, could only nod in response when Bevan Keene finally spoke.

"Well," he said, "that certainly got my attention."

2

Six words only, but enough to break the spell. Judith snatched her hand away as if Keene's lap were a glowing stovetop. Somehow, she also tore herself free of his gaze. But she couldn't summon the clarity of thought it would take her to formulate a reply or—first choice!—leave the table without making a total spectacle of herself.

And then things got even worse.

Judith had been warned about the Keene family by her cousin and was half surprised that sister Alana, also at the other end of the table, hadn't leapt into the fray as well. The Keenes loved nothing better, she'd been warned by Vanessa, than to engage in familial slanging matches that to outsiders seemed uncommonly fierce.

But it wasn't the diminutive and lovely Alana that stirred the possum again. It was—and this, Judith thought, she ought to have expected—her own dear, severely pregnant cousin, Vanessa.

"Well *I'm* certain that Tasmanian tigers aren't really extinct," Vanessa said, beginning innocently enough. "Not that I've seen one, of course, although I'd love to some day. But if you and Bevan have seen them, Phelan, I know Judith would just adore to talk to you about it. Being an environmental journalist, she'd be absolutely fascinated, I'm sure."

Fascinated? No, dear cousin—more like MURDEROUS! If a Tassie tiger walked into this room right now, I'd feed you to it! How COULD you?

Judith could have cheerfully crawled under the table, she was so mortified. Her journalistic career, post-Derek, was non-existent, and Vanessa not only knew that, but had been specifically told that it was an off-limits subject. Worse, the change in focus that Nessie's naïve comment had created was worse—if anything *could* be worse—than her feelings of embarrassment. Phelan Keene positively glowered at her from his end of the table, and she'd distinctly heard a gasp of surprise from his sister Alana. And beside her . . .

Judith looked up to meet gray eyes now the color of wet Tasmanian mudstone, eyes that only an instant before had been laughing, had held the texture of gray velvet, even while visibly bemused at her predicament. No longer. Now they were hard, accusing, almost frightening in their intensity. Bevan Keene was looking at her as if she'd just crawled out from under a rock, and Judith's temper, matching her copper hair as it so often did, was poised to explode. Her own blue-green eyes flashed at the challenge in his gaze. She met his gaze fiercely, but in total calm, waiting for him to make the expected disparaging remark.

But he said nothing. They sat there, each now oblivious to the dinner party around them, eyes locked in some strange form of combat for which Judith didn't even know the rules. It seemed at first as if everyone around them was waiting, impatient for the explosion, but then somehow her surroundings faded, leaving only his eyes, his face with its beaky, high-bridged nose, his abundance of curly, sandy hair. Until finally she was compelled to break the unnatural silence because his eyes were changing even as they held her. His expression softened, the hostility melding into something else, something equally dangerous, but much less obvious. Now there was a sort of slyness there, strangely predatory.

There was a warning, too, of some kind, but it wasn't strong enough, or alarming enough, to quell Judith's seething defensiveness.

"You have something against journalists?" she heard herself asking, and then, unable to bear the silence, added, "Or is it just *female* journalists?" before he could possibly have replied to the first question. Then she waited and continued to wait as Bevan continued to look at her, his gaze now leaving her own and patiently, deliberately, stalking across her face, her lips, her throat, and down the slender lines of her body as far as he could see. Then back to meet her stare boldly, blatantly, challenging in its intensity.

His gaze was that of a great predator assessing prey, until it suddenly changed—as did his eyes. At least they seemed to, although common sense said it wasn't possible for them to flash in the instant from dove gray to a deep, menacing yellow shade. Wolf's eyes. Tiger's eyes. Predator's eyes!

And this time, when he used them once again to assess her body, it was with an almost tangible touch. She felt the caress that began in the hollow of her throat, shivered as it traced a circuitous track down to the cleft between her breasts. Her nipples literally sprang to attention as invisible fingertips plucked at them. In her tummy, thankfully hidden by her napkin, she felt an awesome tingling, almost a humming sensation. It was as if she'd gulped too much air and bubbles were floating there, bubbles which occasionally burst.

When he did speak, it was in a voice so low that only she could hear, and that barely. His voice didn't carry past her, couldn't possibly have been heard across the table.

"You're overreacting."

Only the few words from his lips, but his eyes—miraculously gone back to gray again—spoke volumes. All in a language Judith didn't want to hear, didn't want to know, didn't dare try to even comprehend. *I want you,* those eyes said. Loud as a shout in her suddenly feverish brain. *I want your body and I want your mind, but your body first. And I'll have it, too. When I'm ready.*

"Or is it *environmental* journalists you take such an immediate dislike to?" she challenged, having to force out each word against a heart that thumped in her breast like some great drum, making it hard to breathe, harder still to think. Overreacting? Well of course she was overreacting, but now that *he'd* mentioned it, damned if *she'd* admit it, anymore than she'd admit the incredible sensation of a caress that began at one kneecap and slowly, deliberately, crept up the inside of her thigh.

Judith had to force herself not to look down, not to acknowledge the weirdness of it all. Because both of Bevan Keene's hands were there on the table before him, in plain sight. And they had been all along. She was certain of it. Well . . . nearly certain.

Bevan raised one eyebrow, his eyes again light gray, gleaming like wet, radiant jewels. Laughing at her—she knew it. And she hated it!

"You're awfully defensive," he finally said. "This is me, remember? Not whomever you were thinking of before."

"As if there were any relevant difference," Judith said with a sneer, her mind somehow freed by the sound of his voice. But her heart still thumped like a wild thing caged, and she could feel his gaze, a caress upon her skin. Was the entire dinner party watching this bizarre exchange, she wondered? And, if so, what on earth would they make of it?

She shivered, then fought the shiver before it could radiate to her very core.

"Oh," he said in that soft, curiously gentle voice, that distinctive Tasmanian accent. "There's a difference all right. And you know it, too. Even a female . . . environmental . . . American . . . journalist could figure out that much," he added, stretching out the words, deliberately provoking her without raising his voice much beyond a whisper.

"Not this one," Judith snapped, again wishing she could just crawl away silently under cover of the table, or disappear in a puff of smoke. Anything that would allow her not to have to continue this farcical debate, a discussion all the more ridiculous because it had been she who started it. Because now that they'd clashed, now that they'd made more than just polite social contact, Bevan Keene could no longer be ignored.

Not that she wanted to anymore. Quite the opposite. What she *wanted* was—

"You're just cranky because I didn't react like you expected me to," he said with a quiet chuckle. "You wanted me to go all feral and insulting, just so you'd have somebody to vent your spleen on." He shook his mop of sandy curls. "That bloke who done you wrong sure did a number on you. Top job. He's turned you off men and got your liver in a right royal snit at the same time."

It might have been funny, had it been true, but it was nonetheless far too perceptive. And it might have been even funnier, had she not, just a moment earlier, had her hand in his lap without having the faintest idea how or why.

None of which explained why this man could somehow look at her and turn her insides to mush. She was saved from having to reply by a demand from farther up the table that they pass up their dinner plates to make room for dessert.

It gave her a welcome opportunity to hop up and help with the job, and to scold Nessie when the two were alone in the kitchen. Not *much* of a reprimand—how vigorous could one be, after all, with a woman due to birth twins at any moment?

"I'm sorry . . . I'm sorry . . . I'm sorry," her cousin pleaded before Judith even got warmed up. "It just slipped out. It wasn't deliberate." Then Vanessa retreated into her own viewpoint, once she had realized she was safe in her advanced state of pregnancy. "What harm did it do, for goodness' sake? I noticed you and Bevan getting on like a house on fire."

"More fire than getting on, Nessie," Judith replied, thankful she could steady herself against the kitchen counter because she felt strangely weak in the knees. "Which isn't the point! The point is that we had agreed—AGREED, DAMN IT!—not to mention my job. My *former* job, Nessie. I'm not any kind of journalist right now, except the unemployed kind. That's why I'm here, in case you've forgotten."

"Oh, come on. You'll have your job back soon enough. Or a better one. *Much* better, if you can get on Bevan's good side and put this Tassie tiger story together," Nessie said in what Judith considered her cousin's usual blind naïveté.

"For goodness' sake, Nessie. There *is* no tiger story, and if there were, Bevan Keene would be the last man on earth to give it to me. And the last one I'd ask, if you want to know the truth. Why on earth did you have to saddle me with *him* tonight, anyway?"

"Apart from the fact that he's devastatingly handsome, charming, rich, and *available,* I hate uneven dinner parties," Vanessa replied calmly.

"You hate dinner parties, period! Anyone could tell that by your so-called cooking," Judith muttered as she turned to shuffle slices of store-bought lemon meringue pie onto serving plates.

"Now you're being catty, Judith Theresa," her cousin replied. "And that isn't at all like you. The Judith I remember would have been cutting up Bevan's meat and feeding it to him by hand if it meant a crack at a fair-dinkum 'tiger' story," she concluded, lapsing into the lingo of her adopted country.

"I'd need a chainsaw to cut up any meat you'd cooked," Judith snapped, her already fragile and aggravated temper betraying her. Of absolutely no consolation was her memory of a comment from her old friend Jeremiah Cottrell, a British magazine publisher, upon hearing of her sacking and anticipated trip to Tasmania to lick her wounds and recuperate. Jeremiah hadn't offered her a job—that would have been too easy. He'd left her to her suffering instead, but with a bit of salt for the wounds.

"Turn me up a new slant on the Tasmanian tiger saga—with pictures, of course—and I'll almost let you write your own ticket," he'd said. Joking, of course. He had to have been joking. The reality was what had been said at the dinner table. About once a year somebody resurrected the saga of the Tassie tiger and gave it another stroll down the proverbial garden path. Because—and she'd have been the first to admit that—it was such a *wonderful* story!

An animal known to have existed right into modern times, but now presumed to be extinct. Except for the fact that people kept reporting having seen live specimens, even if no real evidence was ever produced. No validating pictures, or scat, or guaranteed tracks, or hair, or even—especially important—a recently dead tiger carcass. The last wild specimen of the Thylacine, the marsupial wolf called Tasmanian "tiger" because of its partially striped coat, was accepted as having been shot in 1930, and the last specimen in captivity died on September 7, 1936.

But people kept seeing them. Or saying they did. And for those who investigated such matters, the sightings provided a provocative mystery. Most reports were from bushmen, farmers, or rural residents who should have known what they'd seen. Others held somewhat less credence, but every year there were sufficient reports to keep the legend alive.

Because people *want* the tiger to have survived, Judith thought. Just as they want there to be a Sasquatch, and a Yeti, and an Elephant Graveyard. Like the best of her professional colleagues, Judith was a confirmed skeptic, and yet . . .

"So," said Bevan Keene when she returned—having run out of plausible excuses to delay any longer—to sit down beside him, her temper somewhat cooled but her defensive armor fully in place and mollified not a whit by his politely rising to hold her chair. "What are *your* feelings about Tassie tigers, Miss Bryan? Do you believe, or do you consider them in the same class as the Dodo and the Passenger Pigeon? Or . . ." and he grinned, ". . . your American Bigfoot, or Sasquatch."

His grin nearly did her in. It was a predator's grin and the grin of a happy child and the smug, self-satisfied smile of a winner—all in the same package. But there was something else in that package, too, something sexual and sensual that struck her like a bolt of lightning. Once again, she felt her knees go weak and was immensely pleased he was holding the chair she collapsed into.

"I'd like to believe they still exist," she said, fighting to hide the raggedness in her voice. "It's not that many years since they were known to be alive, and according to rumors on the conservation front, there's been more than one shot since then, too. It's just that nobody's been prepared to admit such a thing. People want them to exist, want to believe in them. That's why I think this latest suggestion that they try to clone one is going to fail, even if it were to succeed. People don't want a clone. They want a symbol!"

Like Bevan was a symbol . . . of everything masculine. This man wore his masculinity like a second skin, not blatantly, but with a total, powerful self-assurance that threatened and promised at the same time. And he was focused upon her now with a frightening intensity.

His expression seemed to reveal surprise. "You've studied the subject, obviously."

"It's an environmental issue, and I am—was, actually—a journalist who specialized in such things." Her reply was carefully worded, cautious. So was her reaction to Bevan Keene. She hardly dared meet his eyes, lest they lure her into inappropriate thoughts. *Enjoyable* inappropriate thoughts.

My God! Did I just think that? I couldn't have. But I did. And I do!

Judith suddenly realized she was avoiding Bevan's gaze by looking at his lap. Worse, her hand was following her glance, moving as if possessed of a separate will. She yanked it back before he could notice . . . she hoped.

"*Was?* That isn't what Nessie said."

"Nessie is prone to putting her own interpretations on things even when she isn't . . . in her present condition," Judith said, then hurriedly corrected herself. "No, let's be fair. It's got nothing to do with Nessie. Okay . . . I *am* a journalist, and I did specialize in environmental matters. But I'm . . . between jobs right now. There, does that satisfy you?"

It didn't satisfy *her!* She was physically holding her right hand with her left, willing it to stop this nonsense. But she couldn't stop her imagination, much less the frisson of excitement that single word—*satisfy*—sent tingling down through her tummy.

Some sort of emotion flashed across Bevan Keene's face, but it was too fast for Judith to interpret. Then he was looking directly into her eyes, and his speculation was all too obvious.

"I'm not easily satisfied, when it comes to some things," Keene replied enigmatically. "Although I guess everybody needs their dreams. Even journalists. So tell me about your dreams, Ms. Bryan. Not the ones about the scoop of the century. I've no interest in that. But your *real* dreams."

And he spiced the question with a smile so devastating it nearly took her breath away, if only for an instant. This man was too clever, too perceptive. What would he reply, she wondered, if she told him straight out that he both fascinated and terrified her and she wasn't even certain why?

"Not a dinner subject, I'm afraid," she said as calmly as she could. Lying and astonished she even *could* lie. "I'd rather discuss tigers."

"Oh, I'm sure you would," was his reply. "I'm sure you'd like nothing better than to write a scintillating article about a prominent grazier who says he sees them regularly in his back paddock." And again there was that devastating grin, only this time tinged with cynicism. Surprisingly, though, he didn't wait for a reply. "Or, better yet, some reliable, responsible observer you could report as having seen tigers in one of the areas the greenies are trying to save. Wouldn't *that* be a coup?"

More than just cynicism, now. His voice, his entire demeanor, sparked with a sarcasm that bespoke a deeper anger. Obviously, he didn't like activists.

"Not without proof," she said. "*Real* proof, I mean. Without concrete, unassailable evidence, it would be nothing at all. Unless, of course, a politician claimed it, in which case it would be *less* than nothing."

Bevan Keene raised one eyebrow. "Why, Ms. Bryan, do I detect a note of genuine cynicism there?"

"Realism, not cynicism," she replied. "Politicians are like bananas—they can be green or yellow or rotten, but they always hang together in a bunch and they're always bent. That's not *my* quote, but one I've found to be pretty accurate overall."

He didn't so much as flinch. Never registered even a flicker of surprise.

"My goodness. We've found common ground after all," Keene said. And grinned hugely. "I was beginning to despair." And he grinned again, this time a predator's grin, smug and self-satisfied. Like the wolf in Little Red Riding Hood.

He looked calmly around the table as if about to ask how

everyone else felt about politicians. And he smiled again.

My, what big teeth you have, Grannie, Judith thought. *The better to tell lies with, perhaps. Common ground? There is absolutely nothing about you that's common.* Again, Judith had to mentally recoil from Bevan Keene's devastating charm, suddenly worried by just how easily he turned the charm off and on to suit his purposes.

"It is my firm belief that there is nothing so perfect in this world that it can't be totally stuffed up by a bit of political intervention," he said, and the bitterness in his tone was there to taste, to smell. It was tangible, given life by his voice. Then he shook his head, and bowed his mass of sandy curls almost apologetically.

"Forgive me," he said, and appeared to be genuine. "I was just reminded of the time-honored rule that religion and politics ought never to be allowed in dinner party conversation."

"And sex. You forgot to mention that," Judith said, the words out of her mouth before she realized she was thinking them.

"How could I?" His words slid past a grin so deliberately wicked she might have laughed had he not followed up with "Merely put on hold, my dear Ms. Bryan. There is a time and place for everything."

He never touched her, but his glance was like a physical caress that began at her copper-red hair and flowed slowly downward, gently stroking her eyelids, touching the sensitive spots behind her ears, forcing her to lick at her lips to see if she could taste it. By the time the caress got that far, her nipples had hardened in anticipation, aided by an apparent inability to draw a decent breath.

Merely put on hold? she repeated silently. *I'll give you "on hold," you smug, arrogant bastard.*

Keene's tongue flicked sensually across his lower lip, then—almost apologetically, she thought, though that made no sense—he looked away and reached down to spear a piece of the lemon meringue pie, giving her a chance to recover.

But he was waiting for her to say something, so she let fly with the first nonsexual comment that popped into her head. "Have you really seen a Tasmanian tiger? I mean . . . really, truly, alive and walking around?"

"Would I lie to you?"

It was a strange response, subtly out of context, definitely evasive, she thought. "I rather expect you would, in this case," she replied honestly. "Although I don't know why you'd bother. I've told you, I'm not working, not looking for any sort of *scoop*, which is an outdated word, by the way. I'm just curious."

"Ah, yes, so I noticed."

Bevan Keene's words held both acceptance and accusation. Then he lapsed into silence. He just looked at her, his gaze once again moving across the terrain of her face as if he were attempting to memorize it. And the wry twist of his lips said it all. He didn't believe her for a New York minute.

" 'Ah,' what?" she was finally forced to ask, knowing it was a stupid question even as the words left her lips, knowing there was no valid answer, only one that would take advantage of the opportunity she'd now given him to heap insult upon injury. To get even.

Bevan Keene just shrugged, although there was a slight twist to his lips when he finally did speak. "I was walking through North Hobart one day," he said, "and I saw a dog there. He was a blue heeler crossed with mastiff, or Rhodesian ridgeback, or pig dog of some kind, or all of the above. And he had stripes in just the right places, and just the right type of head, and the light was just right, and for an instant, there—right in the middle of the city—I could have *sworn* I'd just seen a tiger."

The calm, calculated evasiveness served only to infuriate Judith. She had asked her question in good faith, and now he was laughing at her.

"Well, pardon me for asking," she snapped, and turned away, glaring down at her dessert, wondering if she'd be able to resist the urge to make Bevan Keene wear it.

"Now don't get cranky," he said with a broad grin. "I wasn't playing word games. I was only making the point that there are times we see what we want to see, or maybe just what we hope to see. I can't explain it better than that, and I realize it makes no sense, since obviously I wouldn't *expect* to see a tiger in the middle of Hobart, would I?" Then he sighed and continued. "In my whole life, I've seen what I thought was a tiger three times. The very first time Phelan and I were together and we both saw it. Or did we? We were only boys then, and although we both knew the bush and would have been considered competent observers, at least in some circles, we were still just boys! Did we see a tiger? Or just what we wanted to see, expected to see, hoped to see?

"Because at that age, of course, we were both total romantics. We wanted to believe, so we did believe."

He chuckled, a low, growling sound that rippled with humor. "Of course Phelan's still a romantic, which is why he got all frothy there when the discussion was getting heavy."

"And you're not? A romantic, I mean?" Judith asked the questions without thinking about how it might be interpreted, her mind solely on the subject at hand despite the intense attractiveness of the man she spoke to. But once the words were out, so were the implications. And again she felt that insane compulsion to reach out, to touch him, to dare to let herself drown in his eyes, to succumb to the inappropriate thoughts scheming in her mischievous brain.

Bevan's eyes and wry grin answered the innuendo even as it emerged. He looked into her eyes, then deliberately allowed his gaze to caress her cheek, her lips, her throat. It was as if he'd used his fingers; she felt her skin begin to tingle, felt a strange, hollow feeling that started in the pit of her stomach and flowed in waves of prickly heat to tauten her breasts, throb at her nipples and groin.

"Not about tigers. But in other areas, I'm . . . open to persuasion," he responded. "Although as I said before, there is a time and place for everything and this, Ms. Bryan, is really not either one." And his eyes danced with laughter.

Judith retreated from them, turning her attention to her dessert and the sweet, sticky dessert wine in front of her. She had already drunk too much—*that's my excuse and I'm sticking to it*—but was obsessed by the need to do something, anything, to check the developing situation.

Bevan Keene clearly felt no such compulsion.

"You're going all cranky again," he said, reaching out to lift her fingers in one huge hand, his touch seeming gentle for the size of his hand. The gesture was so totally unexpected that Judith froze, then mentally cursed herself for losing the opportunity to escape, or snub him, or . . . ? Because suddenly she was aware only of the touch of his fingers like thistledown along her wrist, tracing the pale veins that now throbbed to a cadence he was creating, controlling.

This was worse than when he'd looked at her, when he'd seduced her with his eyes. Much worse! Now the seduction was as much physical as mental. And she was under *his* control. His fingers talked to her in a private, secret language known only to the two of them, in a conversation unnoticed by the others at the table, incomprehensible to them if they did notice. It was different—totally different—from her touching of him or his earlier flirting.

This was far more serious, far more dangerous.

"Yes, you'd believe in tigers," he said aloud, literally sighing the words. "You'd have to, I reckon. You couldn't help yourself."

"I'd like to believe they still exist, yes," Judith answered, her voice trembling with the shudders of sensation he was creating with his fingertips. "But you're not helping. If you've really seen them, why won't you tell me more about it, help me to believe?"

His chuckle was halfway to being a laugh.

"You don't need *my* help to believe," he said. "I've just told you that. I also told you, if you were listening earlier, that no sane property owner would admit to seeing a tiger—especially to a journalist!"

"But you've already admitted it."

"I have? Methinks, my dear Ms. Bryan, you'd best clean out your shell-like, virgin ears. All I said—and under duress I'd deny saying even *that*—was that I *thought* I saw a tiger, and that I was but an impressionable lad at the time. And that another time I thought I saw a tiger, but it was in the middle of Hobart, which makes the statement ridiculous from any viewpoint. No story in either, sorry as I am to disappoint you."

Sorry—my ass! You're not one damned bit sorry. You're enjoying yourself, and you're enjoying making me look and feel like an idiot. Well damn you, and damn your Tasmanian tigers, too, Mr. Bevan-bloody-Keene.

But what she said was, "I'm only disappointed I'm here on such a short visit. I'd have liked the chance to see a Tasmanian tiger for myself. In fact there are a lot of things I'd like to experience here in Tasmania, but I guess I'll have to give most of them a miss."

She threw Bevan Keene her most haughty sneer, yanked her arm free, rose from her chair, and flounced from the room. Time to help Nessie in the kitchen, and this time she *would* plead a headache.

And she did. It was easier than trying to forget Bevan Keene's parting remark, softly spoken in a voice that was half threat, half promise.

"You'll keep," was all he'd said, but it echoed through her real or imagined migraine and, eventually, into her dreams.

3

The first dream Judith ascribed to drinking too much wine and eating too little food. It crept into her mind that very night, padding softly on Tassie tiger feet.

She was in a dense, subtropical rainforest. Running. Running from a myth, from a specter of her imagination. And she was naked, or nearly so, her nightgown torn and rent almost to rags, hiked up so she could run faster, could more easily clamber over huge windfall logs, scramble between the immense, old-growth trees that hid the sky.

Slitted, sly yellow eyes peeked from the blackness of the surrounding night, then suddenly became gray as Tasmanian mudstone as the dream swirled and whirled with no obvious sense of direction. As *she* swirled and whirled with no sense of direction, she only had a sense of being followed, of being watched, of being prey!

As if from the stygian darkness above, she somehow watched herself doing a tuneless dance in a tiny clearing, could see the watching, terrifying eyes—feral and yellow, then foreboding and gray—but not the creatures they belonged to, saw only the vaguest of shapes, the shifting light patterns that suggested stripes, the flashes of ivory that bespoke gleaming fangs.

And then she saw herself fall, and felt—rather than saw—the leap of the Tassie tiger as it pounced. Whereupon it all changed again, and the tiger wasn't a Thylacine, and the eyes weren't those of a Thylacine, but those of Bevan Keene—not that this made them any less powerful in their effect on her.

She was in her own body then and saw, even recoiled slightly as she saw, his gleaming teeth bared in something between a smile and a snarl, his generous, expressive lips moving to her throat. She felt the touch of his teeth, but only for a second. Then the touch was replaced by the delicate touch of a lover's fingers against the pulse in her throat.

And those same fingers then magically journeyed across the terrain of her half-naked body, pausing to tease at a nipple, bringing it to a turgid erectness, a painful tenderness, then to play a silent tune across the flatness of her tummy, the fingertips able to drum up butterfly sensations inside.

Were these Bevan's fingers, then, which stroked and tickled and stimulated her to the edge? Which made her body arch to lift herself against their touch? Which suddenly went from tender to fierce as they lifted her passion higher and higher and then, ruthlessly, threw her into overdrive, ignorant and uncaring of the uncontrollable bucking and thrusting of her body as . . .

They were, Judith discovered when the spasms of passion had ceased and her eyes were suddenly, almost frighteningly, wide open to the reality of the bedroom around her, not Bevan Keene's fingers, but her own body twisted in the sheets.

She lay there, sleepy and wide awake at the same time, staring at the ceiling but seeing Bevan Keene's face, Bevan Keene's eyes, even hearing—in her half-awake memory—Bevan Keene's voice. Until it changed from predator's growl to the maniacal shrieks of kookaburras laughing up the dawn.

Judith didn't believe in omens or even in coincidence, but it was a challenge not to. It was as if the conversation from what she thought of as the incineration dinner had itself ignited and now seemed destined to spread unchecked. A tiger sighting was reported from near Diddleum Plains, northeast of Launceston, followed by another, less believable sighting by some tourists who had managed to get lost in their attempt to reach Holwell Falls, to the northwest.

There was nothing particularly relevant about either report except the excuse for every newspaper in the state to bring out all the hoary old theories and pictures from their files. The various conservation groups leapt onto the bandwagon with quite predictable speed, demanding that yet another area be locked away from all development, exploration, or public access.

"Except from the bushwalkers, of course," Judith found herself remarking wryly to her still-pregnant cousin Vanessa. "It's really quite amazing how all these conservation groups believe that their own people are so pristine and lily-white, but everybody else is some sort of villain."

"You really are getting cynical, dear," Nessie replied calmly. "You want to watch yourself, or you'll have no credibility left unless you're prepared to lie down in front of a bulldozer somewhere."

"I will NOT! And, I would remind you, cynicism is part and parcel of being objective about these things. Environmental journalism is a highly emotive subject."

Judith's horror at the suggestion wasn't even remotely feigned. She was herself a conservationist but had always prided herself on being a *reasonable* conservationist. She had little time for the radicals who chained themselves to trees or—worse!—deliberately spiked trees, putting honest forestry workers at risk just to make a political point. As for lying down in front of bulldozers, she felt that backing extremist views with extremist actions did nothing but give the entire conservation movement a bad name.

Her own journalistic credibility had been solidly founded on a staunch neutrality and a fair presentation of every side of the issues until she'd been led into treacherous waters up in

Queensland by Derek *damn-his-soul* Innes and discredited in the process.

"I doubt if I've got any credibility left anyway," she admitted to her cousin, equally an admission to herself that she had now faced up to the situation and accepted the reality of it, if not the unfairness. "What I ought to do is go looking for a job selling shoes or something," she mused aloud. "I really don't think there's much left for me as a journalist."

"You're wrong, and what's more, you know it," Vanessa stated with typically naïve conviction.

And was proven correct not five minutes later when the telephone rang to connect Judith with Jeremiah Cottrell in England.

4

"Just setting up this final bit of the operation has kept me on the telephone for three days. I assume you do know about the time difference between here and the antipodes? It is an ungodly hour here right now; let me assure you of that much."

Jeremiah's voice registered weariness, but it was a weariness tempered by satisfaction. The smugness traveled better than his ferocious Yorkshire accent.

"And I must say, Judith, that your conservation types there down under are a strange and motley crew. They are positively bilious with distrust for each other. I've had the devil's own time getting an agreement about who's to be involved in this little project."

"What project? I'm sorry, Jeremiah, but I have no idea what you're talking about." Judith was frantically signaling to her cousin for some paper and something to write with. She knew only too well how abrupt Jeremiah Cottrell could be, not to mention his propensity for assuming he'd told people things that had never left his own devious little mind. That mind had made him a multimillionaire, but it didn't make him any the easier to converse with. He might have been an educated Yorkshire man, but his *real* degree was from the school of hard knocks, with no courses in elocution.

"The Tasmanian tiger project, of course." He replied brusquely, then softened his tone. "I'm sorry, my dear. I forgot you haven't been told yet, although it seems you must be the only person involved who hasn't. So I shall start at the beginning and promise that from now on, you shall know everything—everything!—because you'll be my official Johnny-on-the-spot, won't you?"

"I will?" Judith tried to hide the note of caution she knew would be creeping into her voice with only those few words. Jeremiah Cottrell was notorious for hare-brained schemes and initially simple projects that ended up complex beyond all belief, although usually—and astonishingly—profitable. More seasoned journalists than Judith had—having survived one of his projects—tossed aside their jobs with Jeremiah and considered their lives vastly improved for having done so.

"But of course you will, Judith me old love. It's the chance of a lifetime for you and of course you'll accept. You'd better, because I doubt if I could pull this one off without you."

"Accept what? And I will *not* accept, Jeremiah—not just like that! Not without you telling me a good deal more than you have." Judith tried to force some calm into her voice. Already, it all sounded too good to be true, which she had found often to be the case, initially, with Jeremiah's ideas.

The publisher's own voice, as always, registered supreme confidence as he went on to explain how he had arranged for funding from one of his companies—translation: a major advertiser—for a three-month expedition to seek reliable, positive evidence about the Tasmanian tiger's existence. "*New* evidence, my dear! And there will be some, no doubt about it." He chuckled enthusiastically. "There might not be much, but whatever does come out will have to be acceptable and accepted, given the credentials of the people involved."

"Who are . . . ?"

This, to Judith, would be the crux of the issue. Over the years all sorts of expeditions had been mounted to search for and find the elusive, allegedly extinct Tasmanian tiger. Some quite respectable scientists and naturalists, but also some—in her cousin's words, "ratbags and rum'ns"—had embarked on extensive but fruitless tiger hunts in the Tasmanian wilderness.

Among the most credible had been Stephen J. Smith of the National Parks and Wildlife Service, Tasmania, and Dr. Eric Guilder of the University of Tasmania. They had separately conducted serious but inconclusive searches in the early 1980s, using World Wildlife Fund money. Others, ranging from serious amateurs to raving lunatics, occasionally turned up on usually ill-founded and underfunded projects. Many had taken quite unique approaches in a bid to prove the non-extinction of the animal, but hard evidence was harder yet to establish.

The first names Jeremiah mentioned were unknown to Judith, but she dutifully wrote them down. Reg Hudson, Ron Peters, and Jan Smythe. All, apparently, locally known die-hard conservationists, but with impeccable credentials.

"And of course your old friend Derek Innes will be in joint command, which ought to please you," the publisher continued, apparently—or deliberately—oblivious to Judith's involuntary gasp of astonishment and dismay. Jeremiah plunged on relentlessly before she could get out the words to reject him, his project, or anything else that might involve dealing with Derek Innes.

"Of course the real coup was getting a chap called Bevan Keene to lead on behalf of the local establishment," Jeremiah continued, thankfully unable to see the effect *that* had on Judith's already shattered composure.

She was so shaken she could barely hold the pencil to write down the other names he spieled off—Roberta Jardine and Ted Norton—both, apparently, rural people in Bevan Keene's establishment circle. What Jeremiah said next was even more astonishing, and she nearly dropped the phone from a hand that suddenly went sweaty and trembling.

"And of course I've you to thank for bagging Keene," Jeremiah added, his tone of voice suggesting he would actually be doing it only as a favor.

Me? Thanks for bagging Keene? What did I do? Judith only just managed to stifle her alarm.

"It wasn't until I mentioned you that he softened enough even to discuss the proposition, really," Jeremiah said. "I gather he wasn't overly impressed at having to be involved with Innes, or maybe it was just being involved with the greenies in general. He really gave me the third degree about you, though, and it made a tremendous difference."

"Which means you lied." Judith spoke without thinking, only then realizing that Jeremiah would know every rancid detail of her fall from grace; he hadn't become what he was in the publishing world without knowing such things. He'd obviously had no trouble tracking her down here in Tasmania, which must have been some Herculean task, she thought. Judith sighed and shook her head.

"I may have laid it on a bit thick," the publisher admitted, a chuckle in his voice. "But it was no more than the truth. I couldn't have him believing I'd hire somebody who was less than the best available, could I?"

And then there was a pause—one of those pauses referred to as a *pregnant* pause, Judith thought, and she normally would have laughed outright at the thoughts that created when she looked across the kitchen at her cousin Vanessa. Normally, but not this time, because this time she didn't dare put words into the pause because they wouldn't come out of her mouth, wouldn't even line up properly in her brain with any sense of sanity.

Jeremiah had described her to Bevan Keene as available. *Well, I guess that's one word for it.* And this time she had to choke back an hysterical laugh.

"What did you tell him?"

"Well, I had to mention your . . . uhm . . . situation with young Innes."

The publisher's voice showed no sign of apology for it, either, and Judith's heart dropped to her stomach. He didn't know—couldn't know—that there *was* no *situation* with Derek, that the so-called situation was the only reason she was available for this insane proposal in the first place.

And the reason she would have to refuse it.

So now what to say? Judith decided to brazen it out. Nothing else would serve any purpose.

"Derek Innes and I don't have a situation," she said. "Never did. Nothing even close!"

"Doesn't matter," Jeremiah replied, dismissing the issue. "I merely mentioned it to Keene so that he wouldn't feel he was being set up or anything. Of course, I told him you were so professional it wouldn't matter a whit even if you were actually *cohabiting* with young Innes, and he accepted that, I'm sure."

Cohabiting? Not if Derek was the last man on earth! The words screamed in her mind, but stayed there. Except . . . how would Bevan Keene think about it?

"How sure?" The words were out even as she thought them, out and hovering in the air before her like smoke from Hades, some omen of worse to come.

"Oh, quite sure," was the expectable reply. "He said it wouldn't make a skerrick of difference, wouldn't matter a bit."

"Ah," Judith said, keeping her voice light despite the giant rock that was actually growing in the pit of her stomach. She could feel it, visualize it, almost touch it as she made the mental translation: *skerrick = iota*. "He said that, did he? In exactly those words."

"Well no, not in those exact words. But he thanked me for being so candid about it, and he certainly did imply that it wasn't any issue at all. In fact, he seemed to just disregard it as an issue once I'd mentioned it. Did the same about the details of your . . . little problem . . . with your previous employer, as a matter of fact."

"You told him about that?" Judith was certain the rock inside her now made her look more pregnant than Vanessa, was positive she ought to back away from the kitchen counter just to make room for it. And the rock was cold, slimy, putrid—just like the knowledge that Jeremiah Cottrell had discussed her disgrace with Bevan Keene.

"Didn't have to tell him. He knew. Just wanted my take on the situation is all."

And then, while Judith was framing polite words of refusal, the publisher began speaking words of money—British pounds sterling, American dollars, Australian dollars even, should she want to be paid that way. The refusal exploded in a diffused vision of bills marked "PAID" and bank statements printed in black ink for a change, and the rock in her belly began to soften and diffuse.

"I . . . I . . ." Judith wanted desperately to say she needed time to think, time to try and rationalize the whole thing. But Jeremiah Cottrell, she knew, wouldn't give her that time. He'd already determined she was the one he wanted for the job of *Official Recorder* for his expedition, and any hesitation would be taken as a sign of weakness. One didn't show weakness in front of Jeremiah—not even on the telephone.

"What are the major problems, right off the top of your head?" he asked abruptly. All business, now, the accent thick with impatience.

"I'm not comfortable about Derek Innes," she began bravely. "He's not a person you can trust, although I suppose you already know that. And he would be quite capable of turning your expedition into something different than you've bargained for."

And I didn't cohabit with him, or anything even close! I wouldn't trust the bastard as far as I could throw him!

"Such as?"

"Such as the springboard for his personal campaign into the national or even international level of the conservation movement. In fact, I'd be astonished if he didn't."

"More to it than that," her new employer growled with surprising perspicacity. "And you're hedging."

Hedging? Of course I'm hedging. Do you think for one minute I'm going to spill out all the sordid details of my "situation" with Derek, which is what I'd have to do—and might, yet—if I'm going to persuade you just how dangerous a move it would be to let Derek Innes take charge of anything so potentially valuable to Derek?

Derek Innes would, Judith knew, use anything and anybody to further his ambitions, and Jeremiah's project was tailor-made for him.

"Derek has some pretty big plans for himself," she finally said. "He wants to be the next Bob Brown, or the next David Bellamy, or David Suzuki—or to be seen as being that significant, at the very least. At the political level, especially. It will almost certainly lead to some serious conflict of interest."

"Which you will duly record and publicly document. I daresay this Bevan Keene will be able to keep him in line," was the reply. "What are your feelings about *him,* while we're on the subject?"

"I don't know anything about him, really. I've only met him once, at a dinner party."

Lies, damned lies, and statistics. You know him better than you know most of the men in your life, or at least more intimately. Or you want to. Or wish you did. Or worse . . .

"You must have made quite an impression," Jeremiah said.

"He certainly took the trouble to find out all about you. Might I suggest you return the favor? You're going to know him quite well, I expect, before this is over."

Judith nearly choked, suddenly stricken by terror at the accuracy of her new boss's assessment.

"I know enough to be sure he's very much his own man, and likely able to cope with Derek." She got the words out without spluttering and was sure they sounded honest enough despite her own misgivings. Bevan Keene exuded a solid, basic honesty that might be a handicap when dealing with Derek Innes. Derek, she knew only too well, was intrinsically shifty and devious, the type who always knew all the rules and how to bend them to best advantage.

"No doubt of that in my mind," Jeremiah replied. "And no doubt you'll be able to keep them from each other's throats, provided you don't go making yourself the catalyst for real trouble. You're not involved with this Keene, too, by any chance?"

Damn you, Jeremiah.

"I'm not involved with anyone!" *No lie, that!*

"Well, see that you keep it that way. We don't want a repetition of . . ." He let the rest of it drop into an unintelligible mumble, but Judith knew exactly what her new boss meant. Knew it through and through, and hated herself—and him—for the need to bring it up at all. The publisher feigned clearing his throat, then continued as if he'd never paused in the first place. "I'll have the contracts in the mail immediately and you can start work now, if that suits."

And even if it doesn't suit. I wonder if anybody's ever said, "No" or even, "Not yet" to you, Jeremiah. I doubt it, somehow.

"Innes will be down from Queensland within a fortnight, and Keene already has most of the information you'll need to start the publicity machine rolling. I mentioned, of course, that you'll also be wearing the publicist's hat?"

"Are you absolutely sure you want to publicize this project before it produces any sort of results, before it actually begins? What if it turns out to be a complete and utter disaster? This sort of thing doesn't have a great track record, you know."

"It'll pay for itself in advertising and P.R. even if it does fail, which it will not."

No doubt in his voice, nor any sense of caution. Was that how one got to be a multimillionaire, Judith wondered—throwing caution to the winds?

"Jeremiah, you are the world's greatest optimist. Or have you been listening to Derek Innes too much already? I have to say this: Bevan Keene told me straight to my face that no sane grazier or farmer would ever admit to having seen a tiger. And he meant it, and I'm sure he's right, too."

There was a grunt from her new employer. "He told me the same thing, but he was only talking about such sightings in relation to people's own property. That, of course, would be nothing but common sense. But this search will be on government land."

"It still doesn't promise much hope for cooperation from the rural sector."

"That is Keene's role, or one of them. And a £100,000 reward for hard evidence ought to help."

"There has been a one-hundred-thousand *dollar* reward in force for years," Judith replied, her brain scrambling to recall the details. "Put up in 1983, if I remember correctly, and nobody's ever claimed it. The best thing it accomplished—the *only* thing it accomplished, really—was to force the government here into legislating a substantial penalty for anyone who caught a tiger. I don't know if that's still in force, but I expect it would be, and that might complicate your little project a bit."

"Do not be defeatist, Judith. Is there something else I should know about, or can I return to work now?"

I know Derek Innes is a liar and a crook and an utter bastard, but I'd hardly need to tell you that. And I know he and Bevan Keene will be about as friendly as two tomcats in a sack, but I probably don't have to tell you that either, since you'll have researched both of them more thoroughly than I ever could. And I know that Bevan Keene and I . . .

"I'm just a bit leery of publicizing the thing too heavily in case it all comes apart before we really get started," she finally said. "And that's presuming we can generate much publicity. Tiger stories aren't given much credence here, except as human interest fodder. Fluff. To get any serious coverage outside your own stable, you might need more than just a highly credentialed expedition. Honestly, Jeremiah, the majority of informed opinion is that the tiger really *is* extinct."

"The advertising dollar is not!"

Which ended that little sortie rather nicely, she thought, and abruptly changed the subject. "May I ask exactly what role this contract you're sending will specify for me? I mean, am I to be a journalist, or some sort of P.R. person, or what? 'Official recorder' seems a pretty vague sort of job description."

"You'll be *my* official representative, and all those other things as well, my dear. As you well know, so stop being tiresome. It's the best deal you've been offered in several years, and certainly the best you're likely to see just now."

No mistaking *that* message, even without the hard edge of Jeremiah's voice. Time to change partners again.

"Well, I still have a few reservations, Jeremiah. You don't know Derek like I do . . . did. And I simply cannot see Bevan Keene coming to the party on this without some agenda of his own, either. There's more to his involvement than meets the eye."

And that is no lie at all. I know exactly what his agenda is likely to be—and I'm on it!

"Indeed. I just hope it isn't something with red hair," the publisher replied coldly. "You just remember that while each of them is in charge of his own contingent, and in joint control of the expedition as a whole, you are the one directly responsible to me. You have the final word. Your young man Innes is no more than a figurehead, in many ways, and well he knows it."

"He knows it? And he's agreed?" Judith didn't like the sound of that. It was as questionable as Bevan Keene's acceptance. Had Keene agreed to similar conditions?

Jeremiah Cottrell chuckled, and it wasn't the sort of chuckle that implied humor. It had a thin, nasty tone that made Judith perk up her ears.

"He most likely anticipates being able to manipulate you, my dear. And I didn't think it my place to, let us say, disillusion him. Keene, of course, has a different agenda, but they're only men, Judith. You'll have them both toeing the line before the first camp is established."

"You are not a nice man, Jeremiah. Has anyone told you that lately? Because they should!"

"Jeremiah *Sir,*" he reminded her quietly. But his voice made the point. Jeremiah had reached the stage of severe impatience.

"Yes, Sir," she replied. "I shall await the contract, Sir. And your orders, Sir."

"First off, go and buy a cell phone, assuming they have them in Tasmania, and assuming one might expect such technology to operate in the antipodean wilderness. Be sure it can reach me here, and make sure I know the number so that I may reach you. Second, just do your best, Judith. And please don't let your personal feelings get in the way."

"You can be certain of that, at least." And she meant it, too, although she wished she felt as confident as it had sounded. Derek wasn't going to be an issue, but she was far less certain about the suddenly too-agreeable Bevan Keene. What on earth had prompted him to link himself to such a project, and use her name in the process?

Damn it, Judith, at least be honest with yourself. He wants exactly what you want, and it has nothing to do with tigers and everything to do with plain, old-fashioned lust!

5

Judith was still having misgivings about it all when she returned from the city the next afternoon from a research expedition that was less successful than she'd hoped. But she mentioned only the project issues to her cousin. No way was she going to mention her personal difficulties at the prospect of having to try and work with Bevan Keene, much less her extremely confused feelings about the man.

"I shouldn't let it bother me, and I know that," she told Vanessa. "It's Murphy's Law, that's all. Everybody who's anybody at the museum and the university just happens to be unavailable right now, when I need them the most. I got some research done at the library, of course, but still . . ."

"You should have asked me in the first place," her cousin replied, drumming pudgy fingers on a belly Judith could have sworn had doubled in size overnight. "You've only got to talk to Bevan. He has probably the most extensive library on the subject anywhere."

"Why am I not surprised?" Judith asked the rhetorical question, then abruptly snapped her mouth shut. Bad enough that she felt ridiculously drawn sexually to Bevan; she also had this insane, yet equally illogical feeling she should avoid him until she had absolutely no other choice.

As if she *could* avoid him! Vanessa might be flighty beyond belief, sometimes, but she could also be frighteningly observant. Indeed, it wouldn't surprise Judith to discover that her cousin knew exactly what had transpired between Bevan and her at the dinner table.

"You really got off to a bad start with Bevan, didn't you?" Vanessa asked after a long silence in which she fixed Judith with a blue-eyed stare of clearly feigned innocence. "That's funny, actually, because I honestly thought you'd fancy him like crazy," she added in the vernacular of her adopted home.

"Just because you do?" Judith replied with a sarcastic tone, then instantly relented. "It isn't that he's not fanciable, if that's a word. But really he isn't all *that* impressive." And she winced inside. Lying wasn't one of her strong suits.

"Oh, bollocks! You're just off all men because of that 'greenie' you were involved with, the one who led you down the garden path and then dumped you in the you-know-what."

"I was *not* 'involved' with Derek Innes. But okay . . . I might be a bit gun shy. That much I will admit to. But honestly, Vanessa, men are terribly overrated anyway. I mean, what are they *really* good for?" Then she glanced at her rotund cousin and couldn't repress a smile. "Except of course to you. You couldn't have gotten into your situation without a man somewhere in the picture. I'll grant you that."

"Without the *right* man," Vanessa retorted, patting herself gently on the belly. "And don't think there haven't been days recently when I've wondered if there was any sense to it at all. Charles may think pregnancy is the most wonderful thing in the world, but he doesn't have to carry this lot around with him all the while."

"If men had to bear the children, humanity would die out in a generation," Judith said sarcastically, then brightened. "And I don't know why I'm complaining, either. You're the one who's going to have to do all the work. My role is to provide you with moral support, and now I'm getting paid while I do it. Although," she added somewhat ruefully, "I'm not sure the job will be anywhere as cut-and-dried as Jeremiah thinks."

"Does it matter? You still get your Tasmanian holiday, only much extended, and you get paid for being here."

"Yes, it does matter. I already have that fiasco in Queensland to live down, and now I'm getting involved in a hunt for the Tasmanian tiger? That's even more ridiculous, by almost any standard. Not to mention my having to try and be a buffer between Bevan Keene and Derek, who's a total bastard. It isn't going to be an easy task."

"I doubt very much that Bevan needs your help to deal with this Derek person." Vanessa looked thoughtful, an expression that in her case could, and often did, prove deceptive. "You might have lucked into a wonderful position to get revenge on Derek," she ventured, eyes brightening at the prospect of witnessing such activity.

"Not on your life. I am not a vengeful person. All I really wanted was never to see or hear from him again as long as I lived, and I certainly didn't get that wish."

"That was your choice, wasn't it?"

"It was my red-ink bank account's choice."

Vanessa beamed. "Someday, Judith Theresa, when I'm not in such a delicate condition, maybe you'll condescend to tell me truthfully whether this is all about finances or maybe just a wee, tiny bit because Bevan Keene's involved. In fact, you could tell me now, if you like. I'm robust enough to handle it, I think."

"Well, I'm not, so you can just wait." Judith wondered—not for the first time during her brief stay in Tasmania—if she would ever truly understand the national sense of humor, not least the pastime of stirring the pot just to provoke a reaction. "And just now, I'm not half as interested in the man as I am in his library."

I am such a poor liar. But what else can I do? Admit that I fancy Bevan Keene like crazy, to use Nessie's words—but it's all physical? Or is it?

"You can ask him about that tonight," Vanessa said. "After all, you're supposed to be working on this project together."

It took a moment for the implication to strike, but when it did, Judith felt a curious little hollow forming in her stomach. Or maybe not a hollow place—maybe just the beginning of another huge rock.

"What do you mean, *tonight?*" she asked abruptly.

"When you go to Launceston with him, of course. I told you. Oh, no, I didn't actually *tell* you, I wrote you a note. I . . . oh dear, oh *shit,* oh dear . . . the note's in your room, and of course you haven't seen it yet. Oh, Judith, I'm getting so scatty I hardly know what day it is. I'm sorry."

"Don't be sorry," Judith snapped. "Just tell me what you've got me into this time—presuming you can remember." Then she stopped and hung her head, astonished at her own temper. "I'm sorry, Nessie. This whole thing has got me flustered too, I guess."

"No. It's my fault. Honestly, I meant to tell you as soon as you walked in the door, but when you did, it just flew out of my mind. Nobody told me being pregnant was going to make me totally scatterbrained."

Judith refrained from suggesting the pregnancy had only exacerbated an already-existing condition. Instead, she laughed at her cousin, then went to read the note before it disappeared in a puff of smoke or something equally ridiculous. She read it, looked at her watch, and suppressed the immediate urge to go back out and throttle her scatty cousin. The note said there was a lecture being given in Launceston that very evening, that Bevan Keene knew she'd be interested, and would be picking her up—

"In fifteen minutes! Nessie, you . . . you . . ." Judith swallowed the rest of her rant as she caught her disheveled reflection in the mirror. There was no time for throttling, not even enough time for a verbal dressing-down—not that either would do any good. Quickly stripping off her soiled clothes, she fled to the shower.

Less than five minutes later, her short, crisp, coppery hair glistening with droplets of water and her slender body wrapped in an oversized bath towel, she rushed just as swiftly back to her room. She dressed quickly in a white wool sweater and snug dress slacks in British racing green. Medium-heeled shoes to match, a quick touch of lip gloss, and she was ready for anything, she thought.

Then the doorbell rang to announce Bevan Keene's arrival, and she realized with a start that her preparedness was only physical. Mentally, she was totally, completely, thoroughly, and frighteningly unprepared.

6

Keene said nothing at first. He just stood there on the stoop and looked at her, his gaze roving along her body with an almost studied insolence. It wasn't until he'd looked her over quite thoroughly that the tall grazier deigned to speak, and when he did, his voice somehow managed to hide more than it revealed.

"You look quite, quite splendid, Ms. Bryan," he said with a slow smile. "Very professional. I assume you're ready for what may turn out to be a long and hopefully interesting evening."

"Ready when you are," she replied, unable to match his cool, but game to try. And quite prepared to spend a moment of her own on simple physical assessment—fair's fair, after all.

Bevan was dressed much as she would have expected, in expensive but casual clothing that suited him perfectly. A soft flannel shirt tucked into sharply creased slacks over gleaming boots; a subdued but expensively tailored Harris Tweed sport coat.

"You'd best bring a jacket of some sort," he said, and his voice was gruff enough for Judith to wonder if he resented being given the same sort of onceover he'd bestowed upon her. "It might turn fairly cool before we get back," he added.

Unwilling to argue, Judith obeyed without comment, and after a brief farewell to her cousin, she allowed Bevan to escort her to his vehicle. Or at least to the footpath outside Vanessa's home, where Judith took one look at Bevan's transportation and stopped dead in her tracks, unable to believe her eyes, unable *not* to believe them.

"It isn't mine, and you're not thinking anything I haven't thought a dozen times over," her companion growled, clearly not amused by her reaction, but sharing it. "Mine's in for a service and couldn't be got ready on time, so I had to borrow *this* from my tame mechanic."

"Tame?" The question escaped before Judith could think. What awaited them was a flashy, American-style pickup truck, all glitz and chrome and perched so high above the street on custom suspension that she thought it might require a stepladder just to get into the thing. A monster truck, and that was only the half of it!

"Tame as any woman could be," he muttered. "She's a good mechanic. The best. But I shall never understand her taste, assuming taste is the word." Bevan said with a shake of his head, "Is this, or is this not, just about the most ghastly contraption you've ever seen? Gives a whole new meaning to the term 'Yank tank,' I'll tell you that."

"That," Judith said as they stood together staring at the apparition, "is putting it mildly. A monster truck—how cool!"

The customized F-150 was a vision in gleaming black duco and chrome, with the addition of what could only be considered a fantastic imagination gone awry. Flames poured up over the hood and from the wheel-wells to frame dynamic scenes of sword-wielding warrior women in bloody combat with incredible monsters, while spaceships and ringed planets hovered overhead. There was no arguing the talent of the airbrush artist who'd done the work—it was truly splendid. But as for taste . . .

"You said *her.* This really belongs to a woman?"

"And a beautiful one, on the rare occasion she sluices off the grease and grime and changes her mechanic's overalls for a dress," Bevan said, this time with a wry grin. "A top mechanic, if a bit of a feminist. I think she considers this truck some sort of definitive statement, but I've never worked up the nerve to ask her what it is she's trying to say."

He helped Judith clamber up into the vehicle, where she found the interior just as impressive as the outside, with plush velvet fittings, inch-thick carpeting and a dazzling array of sound equipment. And when Bevan turned the ignition key, the machine responded with the throaty growl of an angry living creature. Bevan laughed as Judith flinched at the rumbling sound.

They maneuvered their way northward out of Hobart, heading—as Bevan explained over the burbling of the beast's breath—for the Mud Walls Road and eventually the Midlands Highway to Launceston. It was, he said, perhaps a two-and-a-half-hour journey, although "*She* swears I could do it in one if I pushed this animal to its limits. Fat chance of that," he said with a scowl.

Judith became increasingly amused at how Bevan seemed embarrassed by the borrowed vehicle and its outlandish appearance but couldn't resist letting himself enjoy it just a little, too.

"I'm not sure we'll have time for tea—that's dinner, to you—before this damned lecture," Bevan muttered as yet another youthful motorist *beeped* in recognition. "Every copper in Tasmania will have this beast on his list, and we'll likely get stopped a dozen times once we hit the proper highway."

Judith couldn't be certain whether he was avoiding mention of the dinner party incident or merely saving his comments for a better time. She didn't stay uncertain for long.

"Speaking of which," he said when they stopped at the first red light he encountered, "I sincerely hope you're intending to play fair tonight, at least while I'm driving."

"Play fair?" she asked, playing for time.

"Don't be obtuse," he said, a grin softening the abruptness of his remark. "It means no groping while I'm driving. If you absolutely can't keep your hands off me, just please say so and I shall stop and take care of your animal desires."

"I . . . you . . ." Judith knew she was stuttering but couldn't make her mouth work properly. "You don't honestly think I'd . . ."

"I wouldn't have thought you'd do what you did during dinner the other night," Bevan said in a voice that seemed infuriatingly calm. "Not that I'm complaining, mind you, merely reminding you that the time and place for such antics is not while I'm driving somebody else's vehicle. Your time will come." And there was a threat and a tension there she couldn't ignore, dared not ignore.

He relaxed visibly as they left the suburbs and began their way north through the dry grazing lands of the Coal River valley, and when they moved into the sweeping curves leading up to the Craigbourne Dam, north of Campania, he seemed to be enjoying himself, pushing the powerful vehicle to sports-car–like exertions.

Conversation, however, was difficult when not impossible. The burbling growl of the exhaust turned to a fierce, resounding bellow whenever Bevan stepped on the accelerator. Judith welcomed the lack of conversation and used the respite to study the passing landscape and—when opportunity presented itself—the man doing the driving.

Bevan unexpectedly slowed at one point to indicate with a forefinger the shape of a homestead in the distance. "My baby sister lives there," he said. "You met her at the dinner party, I think. I *could* stop there and trade this thing for a civilized car, but she and my mechanic are good mates, so it would only get me into heaps of trouble with both of them. Something," he added somewhat ruefully, "I'd just as soon avoid."

Judith couldn't resist a reply. "I have great difficulty seeing you worrying about a thing like that," she said, but her attempted levity fell flat.

"Because you think I'm the ultimate male chauvinist pig," Bevan muttered over the burbling exhaust sound, even though he didn't bother to turn and look at her. "Which I am, perhaps. But the fact of the matter is that one is stuck with one's relatives, but really good mechanics are worth their weight in gold."

With which profound if enigmatic comment he returned his attention to the narrow highway and his driving, leaving Judith free to ponder the scenery—*Could there really be this many sheep in the world?*—and wonder if taking on this job had really been such a good idea after all.

Close in to Hobart, the landscape had been relatively lush and green, but the farther north they drove the more dry and sere it appeared. And the sheep weren't white, either. In some places they were as rust-red as the seemingly barren paddocks on which they wandered. Once they reached the Midlands Highway, she found the bizarre vehicle—whatever its aesthetics—could truly get up and move, and once settled more or less on the speed limit, the acoustics improved to the point where conversation was actually possible, presuming anybody wanted that. Judith decided she did.

"You never actually explained where we're going, or why," she finally ventured. "Am I to presume it has something to do with this project we're to be involved in?"

"If I'd just wanted a date, there'd be easier ways of going about it," was the reply, and she thought she saw the glimmer of a smile forming around his generous mouth. So difficult to tell, though. Until now she had thought him almost brutally direct. His reply had been neither answer nor question, and she found it difficult to continue her inquiry without sounding as if she were deliberately probing. Which, beyond argument, was just what she intended, although she'd hoped to be a bit more subtle about it. If only he would give her something to work with, some concept of how he really felt about the three-month task ahead of them.

And how you feel about me. No way you can be this casual about what happened at the dinner party. No man could be.

But it seemed Keene was more comfortable than she with long silences. He let considerable time elapse before saying, "There's an academic type giving a lecture at the Queen Victoria Museum tonight on research he's done into some aspect of tigers. Judging from the title, I doubt he'll touch on anything very relevant to our 'project,' as you call it, but you never know. And it's a nice evening for a drive, if nothing else."

If nothing else. Judith found her mind floundering for the right words to keep the conversation alive. Jeremiah's comments had made it seem likely that Bevan had only become involved in the project because of Judith's own involvement, which made no sense at all. Unless, of course, he had in mind retaliation for her impulsive, quite improper behavior at the dinner party.

She glanced over at Bevan's profile, again noting the strength of his features—the fierce, hawk-like beak of a nose, the sun wrinkles that flowed from the corners of his eyes, the generous, mobile mouth, half obscured by his pirate's mustache.

All her feminine instincts prickled at the sheer machismo of the man, but she couldn't find the right words to search for the answers she wanted. And clearly he wasn't going to make it any easier for her.

They sped north in the flamboyant pickup truck, but Bevan kept his silence, answering her occasional direct questions, and those only briefly. He kept his eyes on the road and his hands on the wheel, and Judith wasn't totally sure if she preferred it that way or not.

As they reached the outskirts of the northern city, he glanced at his watch before turning off one secondary road and onto another. "We've got time for tea after all, if we're quick. Chinese okay?"

"Whatever," she replied, and wondered what he'd have said had she objected, because he was already slowing to park near a restaurant named the City Pearl.

"I don't know if this is the best of its kind in Launceston," he said as he silenced the growling vehicle. "But I found it by accident a year or two ago and somehow never got round to trying any of the others. Good tucker."

He must, Judith decided, have been a fairly frequent customer ever since, judging from the way the staff made them welcome. This early on a Wednesday evening, the small restaurant was nearly empty, which ensured them speedy and efficient service, but Bevan was greeted like a long-lost friend.

Bevan made a point of sitting well out of her reach, softening the reminder with a slow smile when he was sure she'd got the message. He ordered a bottle of dry white wine by name without bothering to consult the wine list, then offered to guide Judith through the extensive menu.

"You choose," she said. "I'm like a goat. I eat anything that's put in front of me."

"That might be fun," he said with a perfectly straight face, then proceeded to order a sampling of several starters including squid fritters, honey chicken wings, and Chinese sausage, before going on to the main courses.

"We'll share everything," he told the smiling waitress. "And"—with a raised eyebrow and a fanciful glance at Judith—"we'll use chopsticks, please."

"Is this some sort of test?" Judith found herself inexplicably prickly about his decision, though she had no valid reason, and knew it. "Some designation of how civilized a person might be, perhaps?"

"Test? No," he said. "I just think a girl eating with chopsticks is sexy, that's all." And he said it with such a straight face, such a bland, straightforward innocence, that it took Judith way too long to catch the devilish gleam in his eyes. By which time, of course, it was too late; she'd already nibbled at the bait and both of them knew it.

When their food began to arrive, Bevan attacked his with chopsticks dexterously manipulated. Judith found herself fumbling, her fingers made clumsy by his unexpected comment. It was worse than embarrassing. Bevan cast an air of sensuous intimacy over the meal. His even white teeth teased at morsels of chicken, but his eyes said they were nibbling at Judith's earlobes. His gaze roved across her face and neck and shoulders and breasts with the same anticipation and appreciation he devoted to the meal.

She barely took her eyes off the recalcitrant chopsticks in her clumsy fingers, ever conscious of his glances, ever certain she was about to drop something gooey down the front of her snowy sweater. The food was delightful, but her enjoyment was increasingly hampered by the treacherous reactions he so easily aroused in her. His every glance and gesture was a caress, an invitation, a promise.

It was so blatantly, deliberately sexist that under any other circumstances she might have found it either amusing or enraging, but now—perhaps because it was so deliberate and blatant—Judith could only fume at her inability to combat his tactics. And at her own body's betrayal. Mentally, she knew she was being led down the proverbial garden path, but her nipples throbbed at the touch of his gaze, and her tummy fluttered with empty anticipation despite the food she was desperately forcing into it. The wine did not help.

By the time they reached the museum and the lecture, she was in no mood to be entertained by the antics of the lecturer, a pudgy, long-haired, bearded academic from Melbourne. The essence of his talk, which was punctuated by bursts of static as he flamboyantly strode between lectern and overhead projector, kicking the microphone cord as he moved, was that the long-defunct Launceston City Park Zoo—with at least forty-six specimens—once had the largest collection of tigers ever in captivity.

Well, I know that. Everybody knows that!

The man's arm-waving style seemed to Judith somewhat overdone. His audience of some forty souls was immune to his occasional attempts at humor, attending his every word with a reverence that was almost humorous in itself. But it was an interesting lecture overall, if primarily one designed to provide the speaker with possible assistance—in the form of government grant money—for his attempts to continue the research along his selected route.

The information sheet accompanying the lecture provided a wonderful illustration of how the tiger had been looked at during the history of the beast as a living entity in Tasmania—ranging from near werewolf status to legend in only a few years. The lecturer had provided a handout containing nine excerpts from scientific journals and popular newspapers of the day, asking his audience to determine which were the scientific and which the excesses of overzealous journalists.

Judith could feel Bevan's gaze on her as she read through the astonishingly florid excerpts, all of which portrayed the animal as a bloodthirsty, vampire-like slayer in the most colorful language. She took savage, if minor, satisfaction when the lecturer revealed that only four of the nine—and these the least colorful—had come from journalists of the day. She enjoyed his allusions to the scholarly pretensions of the era, but found his insight into the politics of the times hardly surprising or unusual and little changed in the present.

Only at the end of the two-hour performance did she perk up

her ears when he commented somewhat pretentiously that he thought it ridiculous to suggest the animal had escaped extinction, given the thousands of wallabies, possums, and wombats—logical prey for the tiger—that died on the state's roads every year without a single tiger ever suffering a similar fate.

Would Bevan rise to this challenge, she wondered, then quite unexpectedly found herself thinking of how he might rise to *her* challenge, of the way he might feel beneath her fingers. She squirmed in her seat, hoped he wouldn't notice, and was equally certain he did.

They stayed for coffee, and while she noticed that Bevan was obviously known to some of the audience, he didn't seem disposed to spend much time exchanging more than simple greetings. Sooner, rather than later, they were inside the monster truck and en route back to Hobart in the dark of night, driving in a subdued silence that soon lulled Judith into a half-sleep populated by weird'n'wonderful visions.

7

The velvet interior of the vehicle had magically become a lush rainforest, silent but for the hollow rumblings of some distant thunder. And, as in her earlier dream, she was naked and fleeing . . . something.

Only this time she wasn't alone, and this time she wasn't human, either. Beside her loped a solidly built male Thylacine, and she knew without having to think about it that she, too, had been miraculously transformed into a Tassie tiger.

Side by side they moved through the shadowed, damp forest, alert to the night sounds, aware of the distant thunder but not fearful of it, more alert to the sounds nearer to them—the thumping sounds of wallaby and 'roo dispersing through the dense underbrush but leaving behind distinctive scent and sound trails that revealed each individual's fitness, age, and potential to become the Thylacines' next meal!

Then, unaccountably, the big male beside her stopped dead in his tracks and turned to regard her with gleaming yellowish eyes that somehow answered their own question without it even being asked. She was nudged—at first gently, then not so gently—by paws at her shoulders, her hips. She writhed against the male's touch . . . or perhaps in response to it, was helpless to resist as the male reared up from behind to cover her, her own body responding.

But her response wasn't that of a Thylacine. Instead, she felt an all-too-familiar fluttering in her tummy, felt the quiver of tender nerve endings, the blushing rush of sensation as it flowed from the core of her up through her body and down along her legs in blunt, harsh bursts of energy that quickened her breathing, forced her fingers into fists.

Then came the scream, but it wasn't from her . . . nor was it from the thrusting male Thylacine of her dream. Judith woke to find herself thrashing against the confines of a car rug that had been tucked around her as she slept, the police siren still echoing in her ears as she looked around in confusion at the aura of blue police lights that pulsated in waves from behind them.

Bevan bit back a curse, although not quickly enough that she didn't catch it, and she'd have smiled at his word choice had she been further awake. But even as he pulled the exotic F-150 over to the side of the highway, Judith's mind was struggling to catch up.

She listened as Bevan exchanged words with the policeman, returned to the *now* of the situation in astonishment at how calm Bevan seemed. The two men didn't seem to know each other, but there was no sense of tension or conflict, none of the hostility she'd have thought normal had the traffic stop happened in New York State.

It was, she thought, all extremely civilized.

The first time.

8

The best entertainment of the entire evening, Judith thought later, was having Bevan stopped *three* times—two of them for breathalyzer tests—by the police along the Midlands Highway. Nothing specific was said, of course, but it was obvious the flamboyance of the pickup truck was a major factor.

One policeman looked almost disappointed when Bevan blew 00.00. The cop then spent several minutes checking over the vividly painted pickup truck, looking at headlights, tailights, and tires with increasing frustration and skepticism.

Bevan took it all with good grace the first time, even laughing as they left the scene. But the second time they were stopped, this time by a policeman obviously doing random checks, Bevan's temper was visibly being restrained. And the third time . . .

"I've a damned good notion to change mechanics," he growled, ignoring his earlier comments on the subject. "Bad enough she's a bloody woman, but I'm beginning to wonder how anybody who'd drive a thing like this should even expect to have credibility."

Judith wanted to laugh out loud at his chagrin and the contradictions in attitude, but thought better of it. Her amusement must have shown, however.

"Go ahead and laugh, if you're prepared to get out and walk," he snarled into the uncomfortable atmosphere inside the rumbling vehicle.

Judith's amusement turned to anger at his overdone reaction.

"I've done it before, for better reasons," she retorted. Then, recklessly, added, "But if anybody should get out and walk, it's you. I'm not the one who's complaining."

They were on the Tasman Highway now, between Cambridge and the city proper. Judith didn't believe Bevan's threat, but if he did insist, she knew it would be no great problem to get home, despite the fact it was long past midnight. Still, it wasn't a prospect she relished. Nor did she have to. Bevan lapsed into a silence that he maintained until the truck was parked at her cousin Vanessa's curb, and when he did speak, it was to offer an apology of sorts.

"I'm sorry. I get a bit cranky when I'm pushed," he said gruffly. "Especially with a full moon like this. That idiot lecturer would probably say I had a bit of tiger blood or something."

"You're mixing your metaphors," she replied without thinking. "Full moons go with werewolves."

"Okay, werewolves." And there was a curious new note to his voice that caught Judith by surprise. She turned to face him, to see in his shadowed face something that wasn't the provocative chauvinistic sexism she'd expected.

A glimmer. For an instant. But then it was gone. For that fleeting instant, she thought—wished!—he would lean over to kiss her. But he didn't, even though she was certain he noticed her wish, was more than aware of the way her mouth was set to receive that kiss. But her mouth instead opened to spill out the question that had been lurking there since her telephone discussion with her new boss. "Why are you getting involved with this insane tiger project anyway? What's in it for you, Bevan, or aren't I supposed to be asking that?"

"You can ask. It's a fair enough question. Let's just say I have a kind of vested interest. I know, for instance, what's in it for your boyfriend Innes. And I know what's in it for the other greenies. My side is just involved to try and keep the bastards honest, if you like. And," he added in a slightly different tone of voice, "I think I know what's in it for you."

Then he chuckled, and it was a sound that held memories of Jeremiah's similar cold chuckle over the telephone. "I even know what's in it for the tigers, presuming we find any," he continued. "And *that,* my dear Ms. Bryan, is what really bothers me!"

Judith, caught between her own curiosity and her desire to speak out, to deny the reference to her relationship with Derek Innes, had no chance to speak.

"The big problem in this whole thing," Bevan went on, his voice lazy now, but oozing a strange sort of menace, "is that it's only the tigers who have any credibility at all. If they exist, that is. The rest of us all have some axe or other to grind."

"I certainly don't think I do," Judith responded, keeping her voice calm, uncertain whether or not he was having a go at her. His voice said no, but his words were open to almost any interpretation.

"Never let the facts distort a good story," he said. "Especially now that you're a fair-dinkum journalist again."

"That's to be expected, I suppose, knowing your opinion of journalists in general," she said. "But it's also unfair. You don't know anything about me."

His laugh boomed through the carpeted cab of the truck. It was mocking, almost cruel laughter, and it carried with it the message Judith had forgotten—Jeremiah's "chapter-and-verse" discussion about her, admitted by the publisher himself and now confirmed by Bevan Keene.

"I know all I need to know," the man himself replied coldly as he leaned across to flip open her door for her. It was a quite unsubtle way of making his statement. He wasn't even going to be a gentleman and get out to hand her down from the high-slung vehicle.

Judith, fuming but unable to find the words for her feelings, took the hint. She turned away and slid down to land precariously on the footpath, stumbling as she did so. Then she righted herself and leaned forward to peer at him through the still-open door. “Thank you for a lovely evening,” she said in as sarcastic a voice as she could muster. She started to slam the vehicle’s door, then thought better of it.

“But I don’t know why you dislike this truck so much. I think it suits you,” she said. And walked away without a backward glance, deliberately swinging her hips as she did so. It was all an act and did little to make her feel better once the burble of the truck’s exhaust had faded and she was left standing on her cousin’s veranda in the small hours of the morning with no more chance of sleeping than of flying to the moon.

Inside her own room, the sleeplessness became intolerable, and Judith found herself in Charles’s office, staring at nonsense computer images as she scanned the Internet in search of information she didn’t really need and wasn’t totally sure what to do with.

Until she found what she needed. Then it was just a matter of writing down the details and firing off a lengthy, detailed e-mail to an old friend in New York who dealt with such matters. It took her friend a few hours, but by dawn, Judith had her plan together and the results dubbed onto a CD.

9

"What on earth is *this* all about?" Vanessa's belly entered the kitchen before she did, and the woman herself had her hands over her ears as the sound of Gretchen Wilson singing "Redneck Woman" reverberated and Judith, groggy from her lack of sleep, rocked along with it.

"This is one of the better ones," Judith replied. "I've got a whole CD of this stuff." She stopped the music long enough to pick a different selection—the first on the CD—and Alan Jackson's voice growled out his version of "It's Alright to Be a Redneck."

Vanessa remained unimpressed. "Are you trying to *force* me into labor?" she asked.

"Now there's a thought." Judith paused to make a third selection, and her cousin was treated to Jeff Walker's "Redneck Mother." "There you go—just for you," Judith said with a giddy, overtired laugh. "Although I didn't have this collection put together for *your* benefit, dear cousin."

"Well, that's nice to know." Vanessa moved to turn down the volume. "I guess your trip with Bevan didn't work out so well?"

"I don't even know what happened," Judith mumbled across the breakfast table. "Talk about striking sparks! It just seemed like no matter what either of us said, there was instant lightning."

"Be careful. Charles and I started off that way, and now look at me." Vanessa patted her enormous tummy, her face radiant.

"It's hard *not* to look at you. Are you sure you haven't got your dates all mixed up, Nessie? It would be just like you, and I've never seen anybody quite as thoroughly pregnant. If the dates are right, then it must be triplets, not twins."

"They're twins, and the date is exactly right. The ultrasound does not lie."

"Then what has it told you about the sex of these jolly little pumpkin seeds?" Judith persisted, unable to resist teasing her cousin as a sop to her own foul mood. "Come on, dear cousin. What's it to be? Boys, girls, or one of each?"

"I don't know."

"But you must know. That's what ultrasound is for."

"Its main purpose is to determine the health of the fetus. Yes, I could have been told about the sex of my babies, although some experts say you can only tell if it's a boy, and only if it's in exactly the right position, but I chose not to know."

Judith paused to put a curb on her tongue. This, she realized, was no time for teasing. When she did speak, it was in a quite different tone of voice and attitude.

"I can understand that, I think," she said soberly. "That element of surprise is something that probably shouldn't be taken away from a pregnancy. I think you made a sound choice, if you'll pardon the pun."

"Well, I just hope you make good choices when it comes to surprises in your own immediate future," was the reply. And no pardon with it; clearly Vanessa wasn't in the mood for such frivolity. "Because I warn you, Judith Theresa, don't go judging Bevan Keene by any standard you've used for that greenie bloke, or any other man, for that matter, because if you do, you'll be in for a helluva shock, let me tell you."

"Judge him? I haven't been judging him, for goodness' sake. I've barely been communicating with him, much less judging. And really, Nessie, I'm old enough to know the danger of making idle comparisons between men."

But Vanessa, who'd endured Judith's soul-baring in the aftermath of her firing, was not to be so easily put off.

"You've never even *met* a man like Bevan, my girl," she said, shaking a forefinger in a gesture of admonition. "I know you, and I know how stubborn and downright contrary you can be. You get to warring with him—as you're already on the way to doing!—and there'll be a lot more than sparks flying."

"I don't intend to go to war with him," Judith insisted. "It would be silly anyway. How could I do the job I'm supposed to do if I'm at odds with both the key men in the project."

"Which is an admission you're expecting problems with Derek Innes, in case you missed hearing your own words. And I'll bet anything you won't find Bevan Keene any easier to deal with. I think he rather fancies you, which is just guaranteed to complicate things."

"Fancies me? He thinks journalists are the scum of the earth. You wouldn't say that if you'd been with us last night." Then Judith collapsed into a mixture of tears and laughter as she related the hapless adventures of Bevan Keene and his borrowed pickup truck.

"And in the end I stomped off in a mighty snit, which accomplished nothing, and then spent half the night organizing this CD on the basis that if he wanted to act like a redneck I'd at least acknowledge it. Or rub salt in the wounds." Judith shook her head and moved to silence the music. "I won't be able to give it to him, of course, unless I catch him driving his mechanic's truck again, and I somehow doubt that will happen."

"And you forgot to even ask about accessing his library," said Vanessa.

"But of course. And if I did it now, I can imagine what his reply would be. He'd probably—"

Judith was cut off by the ringing of the telephone, which

Vanessa answered, then handed to Judith with a positively wicked grin.

"You forgot to ask about my library." Bevan's distinctive voice rumbled in response to her hello.

Spooky. Too spooky, like you're reading my mind.

Judith didn't—couldn't—answer immediately. He didn't sound even remotely concerned about the events of the night before. If anything, his deep, powerful voice held overtones of some curious laughter, as if he was deeply pleased at having this excuse to mess with her mind.

"You're awfully sure of yourself," Judith finally managed to reply. "What makes you so certain I was going to ask about it? No, don't tell me. You're a mind reader."

Which was so ridiculous, but somehow believable. She didn't really want to know the answer. Not really.

Now his laughter was open, unconfined. It rumbled through the telephone with the same burbling sound his borrowed truck had made last night—alive, almost infectious.

"Because this dossier I've been collecting on you is quite specific about how thorough a researcher you are," he said. "And since I have the most exhaustive collection of Thylacine data all in one place of anyone in the country, it seems obvious you're not going to be happy until you've had a chance to look through it. Simple logic, not mind reading."

Dossier? That word alone still tumbled around in her brain when Bevan finished speaking. And continued through the silence that followed while she searched for words. Just how much did he know? It wasn't that Judith felt she had any deep, dark secrets—the humiliating details of her being fired and Derek Innes's involvement with it notwithstanding—but she instinctively felt it could be dangerous to let Bevan Keene know any more about her than he already did.

Knowledge is power, she thought, and shivered inwardly at

the implications. There was just too much truth in that simple statement. It made her decidedly uncomfortable to accept that Bevan knew more about her already than she wanted him to know.

"Hey! You still there?"

"Yes. I was just . . . thinking," she replied, noting the sound of satisfaction in his voice. He'd shaken her all right, and he knew it, and she now realized he'd intended all along to do just that.

"Well, how about thinking about coming up for dinner tonight? And, more to the point, you might also give serious thought to staying over for a couple of days at least," he said, then continued without seeming to worry about how she might react to such a blunt invitation. "The first of the equipment for our little junket has arrived already, and I could use a hand sorting things out."

"You could? And this is somehow, I gather, what you consider to be my role in the expedition? Sorter-outer?" Judith could hear for herself the challenge in her voice, could feel the totally unjustified anger that Bevan must be hearing, but she could do nothing about it. It was as if someone else were scripting her replies.

"I thought you might be interested," he said, voice calm, revealing nothing of his feelings except to register a coolness that hadn't been there a moment earlier. "I was informed you were to be the official recorder, whatever that is, for this wondrous expedition."

"Which is not the same as being official sorter-outer," she reminded him, wincing at how blunt she must sound, but still unable to find the right words to say it gently.

"Well, you're going to have a helluva time recording all this gear if it *isn't* sorted out," he replied, voice definitely cold now, almost concealing his irritation.

Judith took a deep breath, fighting more with herself than with Bevan. What was it about this man? Why couldn't she even talk to him without sparks flying? At this precise instant, she realized, her defensiveness was almost entirely a result of his mentioning that damned dossier, but it went further than that. He was getting under her skin. And the worst part was that she wasn't at all certain he was even trying!

"You're right, of course," she forced herself to say. "But this business of staying for several days . . . ?"

"It's a damned long drive, otherwise," he replied bluntly. "You'd spend more time driving than working, and time's getting short. Your boyfr—your little mate Innes will be here next week, and from the sound of him we can expect he'll want to go bush right away, which means being ready when he gets here."

Judith felt a shiver along her spine at his reference to Derek, not to mention his too-innocent, too-deliberate fumble over the word "boyfriend." It had been, she was positive, far more deliberate than innocent, and she resolved not to let him know he'd scored.

"I expect Derek will want to 'go bush' right away," she said calmly. Then added, "But what about the rest of our party? Surely it isn't expected that you and I will be doing all the preparation."

"Ted Norton, who—okay—*should* be doing the quartermaster's work, is off bush someplace himself and won't be back before Friday. And Roberta's not going to be free until Monday, not that it matters especially because she's always totally organized, and will be no matter what Innes decides. As for the greenie contingent, I still have to find them, so I've no idea what help they're going to provide in the preparation."

If any, he might as well have said, although the tone of his voice did it for him. Judith found herself wondering again just how harmonious relationships on this project were going to be.

"I see," was all she could think to say. Then found herself forced to add, hurriedly, "Well all right, then, I'll come."

What choice, she asked herself, did she really have? True, her contract from Jeremiah hadn't yet arrived and wasn't expected for the better part of a week. But he had said she'd be on his payroll beginning with that first phone call, and her research successes to date hardly justified the magnificent salary she was theoretically drawing.

"I'll come," she repeated more emphatically.

"I expect you will," Bevan replied, and the sexual innuendo that replaced the coldness in his voice was no great improvement. "Are you going to be all right about finding the place?"

"I should hope so," she snapped, now inexplicably on edge without being certain why. "I'll need, oh, an hour to pack, I suppose. And . . . what? . . . two hours to get there?"

"More like three, assuming you don't get lost. No great fuss, anyway. I won't start cooking tea until you actually get here, and you'll have all afternoon to do that."

"And you expect me to stay for how long?" she asked through gritted teeth.

"Oh, three or four days should do us unless a whole lot more gear arrives in the meantime. Which it probably will. You might as well come prepared to make a weekend of it, and that way we'll be ready to launch if your boy comes in Monday morning and wants to start things off with a hiss and a roar."

Not without time to organize a press conference, he won't, Judith wanted to say, but didn't. Instead, her mind switched topics.

"You do realize that Vanessa is due next Wednesday?" she asked. "And I hope you also realize that I don't intend to miss that occasion. Not for you, not for Derek Innes, not for all the fictitious Tasmanian tigers in the entire state!"

Or the real ones, for that matter. Ignorant man! I suppose you think I'm here in your precious "Island" state just to hide from the real world. Well it ain't so—I'm here to support Nessie—first, last, and foremost. Not that I'd expect you *to recognize anything that simple.* And she scowled at the thought, more than half angry with him despite not being entirely sure he deserved the anger.

"I would expect nothing else," Bevan said with a soft, surprising chuckle. "And you shall be there, too. That much I can promise."

10

It was Bevan's promise that kept floating in and out of her mind as she made the long drive north to his property in the southwestern foothills of Ben Lomond. He had pointed out the highway exit during their journey the night before and given her more specific directions over the phone, so she thought it would be impossible to get lost.

And she was right. She found the property easily after a trip that lasted just two and a half hours door-to-door.

The laughter shared with Bevan on the phone had vitally changed her mood. His sense of humor, she had decided, might be decidedly quirky, but it matched her own sufficiently to be appreciated. And, more important, it seemed to be genuine. Not like Derek's, which she had found increasingly dependent upon other people's misfortunes and shortcomings.

Judith emerged from her rental car and stood looking up at the massive sandstone house. The sound of dogs barking furiously at some distance continued until a disembodied voice commanded them to stop, but nobody came out to meet her.

She walked over to knock at a magnificently carved front door but paused before doing so as she realized the front door of the house was apparently not in use. The stoop was covered in pots of flowering plants which appeared to have lived there for some time.

"You'll have to come round this way," said Bevan's distinctive voice from behind her, and she turned to find him watching her, a half-smile on his generous mouth.

This was yet another Bevan Keene—the working grazier, dressed in work boots and khaki pants and shirt, his sleeves rolled up and the shirt open halfway down his broad, muscular chest. It was strange, she thought, that with his wet-sand colored hair and mustache and the khaki clothing he didn't look sort of nondescript and washed-out, as so many outdoorsmen did. With Bevan, the khaki clothing only seemed to intensify his pale gray eyes, and the gleaming whiteness of his teeth as he smiled at her.

"Am I too early?" she asked with deliberate innocence. "I drove a bit quicker than perhaps I should have, but I didn't want to find myself getting lost without time to find myself again."

Utter and complete bull—and Bevan clearly realized it, from his grin.

"You're just in time to peel potatoes, actually," he said. "But come in and have a drink first to fortify yourself against such nonjournalistic labors."

He guided her around to the rear door, explaining that the formal entry to the immense house hadn't been used since the family had bought the property some years previously.

"Typical, here in the country," he said. "I expect it only got opened twice in the history of the previous owners, too. When they bought it and when they sold out."

Inside, having entered through a gigantic kitchen that had been modernized without diminishing any of the house's traditional elegance, Judith found herself carrying a very large glass of red wine as she followed Bevan on what he called "the two-bob tour."

The house was as gracious as she might have expected. It was sparsely furnished, but each piece of furniture was clearly chosen with good taste and great care. His, she wondered? And remembered how Bevan's much-younger sister had exhibited a similar quality of taste at the incineration dinner party.

"Alana was some help in getting the place fixed up as far as we've got," he said, and Judith had to hide her flinch at the way he seemed to read her mind. "There's a way to go yet before it can ever approach the way it once was, and will be again. I've sort of slowed down now because the rest of the work is getting into that personal taste area that requires a lot of thought."

And somehow, without his even mentioning the word, Judith found herself thinking it. *Wife!* The house clearly didn't have one, a fact she found annoyingly satisfying, but such redecorating as had been done had been halted just at the point where the personal taste of whatever woman would live here simply had to be considered and consulted before anything further could be done.

The original builder had clearly been a person of vision. The house was sited to face the most-used rooms north and east, providing both winter sun and a wonderful view of the imposing bulk of Ben Lomond as it loomed above with an air of solid protectiveness. Impressive plantings of both native and European trees provided for summer shade and year-round privacy from the property's work buildings and yards.

But for Judith, the crowning highlight was the library, a large, well-lit room absolutely alive with books and atmosphere. Everything was neatly displayed, but the entire room seemed to shout that it was a *working* library, that every book was there to be read, enjoyed, cherished. The room and its contents seemed to have a life of their own, a total personality that cried out to Judith. She felt her fingers itching to open first this book, then that, and then yet another. So enchanting was the wondrous mixture of novels, research books, records, and other works that she could happily have stopped right there and stayed, all else forgotten.

But the tour didn't stop at the house.

"You might as well see it all," Bevan suggested. "We'll have a good wander round, work up an appetite for dinner."

Judith was thankful for having dressed appropriately in jeans and a sweatshirt, not to mention comfortable jogging shoes. By the time they'd toured the outbuildings, the neat and well-maintained yards, met the dogs in their individual runs and inspected the denizens of the "hospital paddock" she was more than ready for dinner.

As they returned to the house, she found herself evaluating Bevan Keene in the light of his home, the way his animals appeared to be treated, and the way he seemed to fit his surroundings as if born to them, which it turned out he had been.

"Our family settled originally around Ouse," he told her during their walk. "That's a little place out west of Hobart, in the Derwent Valley. The old man was a rum'n—what you'd call eccentric. Some would have said he was mad as a meat axe, but he knew what he was about, and by the time I was half grown he had fingers in so many pies I don't think even *he* knew the entire picture. He had land holdings everywhere, and the worst record-keeping system you can imagine."

Then Bevan laughed, and it was a generous, genuine, comfortable laugh.

"Caused us no end of hassles just before he died. Got into strife with the taxation department because of the way he'd organized the family holdings, this one among them. I wasn't much impressed, but Phelan was the one that really got done over. He ended up with his share, but he got a wife to go with it."

As he related the tale of his brother and tax officer sister-in-law Vashti—both of whom Judith had met at the dinner party—Judith found herself warming more and more to Bevan. It seemed as if all the prickles in their relationship had dissolved during their walk, for which she was extremely grateful.

Until he finished the tale by saying, "I think Phelan and Vashti have finally forgiven little sister Alana for her part in the whole sorry tale, but I haven't forgotten and I'm not about to. So kindly remember if you get to talking to her that she is not to be trusted. Not a single inch!"

A roundabout, but hardly subtle way of reminding her that he wasn't looking for a wife and wouldn't welcome his sister's intrusions into such affairs if he were?

"In fact, I considered aiming her at your little mate from Queensland," Bevan continued, confirming Judith's last thought. "Alana would keep him so confused and off-balance he wouldn't know which way was up, and that might be a good thing for our little expedition."

And he looked at Judith directly, his eyes flickering with unholy lights that she interpreted as a warning of worse to come.

"Except I suppose you mightn't think much of that idea." And now his grin was that of a predator, some crouching jungle cat just waiting.

"I quite liked your sister," Judith replied after too long a silence. "Whatever she's done, or you think she's done, she doesn't deserved being *aimed* at Derek Innes. She couldn't possibly deserve it. Nobody could!"

Carefully and quickly thought out, but her verbal reply was wasted. Bevan had clearly made up his mind about her relationship with Derek, and wasn't going to let facts get in the way, as he said, "Rather keep him to yourself?"

Bevan didn't even bother to look at her, simply threw the remark in as a sort of aside, making it neither question nor direct statement. Deliberately baiting her. Making no bones about it.

"I'd rather he stayed in Queensland, and I expect you'll feel much the same once you've had to deal with him for very long," she said. And then, patience strained, she added, "In fact I really don't know why you're involved in all this. The project is ridiculous and we both know it."

"If it's so ridiculous, then why are *you* involved?" he countered. And now he did look at her, but there was virtually no expression in those pale eyes. No warmth, no discernible hostility, just a sort of deep, fathomless emptiness.

"I needed the job," she admitted, making no attempt to either dress up the issue or evade it.

"Ah."

He made a veritable meal of that tiny, single word, seeming to roll it around in his mouth, savor it, taste it. As if he was savoring, Judith thought, his ability to make her most thoroughly uncomfortable with this accusative inquisition.

As he did so, his pale eyes roamed the terrain of her face. Then his gaze roved even farther afield, drifting down the line of her neck, lingering with intent on the fullness of her breasts, then returning to meet her gaze—mocking her, and doing so quite deliberately.

"My needing a job seems a far simpler reason than any you're likely to have," Judith protested. She could see the wry downturn at the corners of his mouth, could palpably feel the disbelief he was registering.

"Certainly does seem so," he replied enigmatically, then quickened his step because they were nearly at the door and before she could even think, he was opening the door, holding it for her, bowing her inside with exaggerated formality.

"I think it's time for another drink," he said. "And while you're getting around that, I shall bring in Madam's baggage, properly park her car, and"—whereupon he smiled broadly—"promise to stop rousting on her until after dinner."

"You can roust on me all you like," she said. "But yes, it would be nice if you'd feed me first. I can get very, very cranky on an empty stomach."

"Hah! One thing, at least, in common," he said with a genuine attempt at a friendly grin. "That's probably what's wrong with both of us. We're hungry and starting to show the effects."

Judith didn't answer that one. He was certainly correct in her case, but she didn't think his was quite so simply explained away. It was obvious Bevan was leading her toward something, and she wasn't certain she liked the direction.

The vocal silence lengthened as he built them each a fresh drink. Then he handed hers over with a bow and said, "Right, that's a start. Now I'll get your bags and then excuse myself for long enough to throw my body beneath running water, if you don't mind. We won't be dressing for dinner, but I'd like to be a bit more civilized than this."

Judith wandered into the library after his departure, and although thoroughly entranced by its contents, she was also uncomfortably aware of the man himself, the man whose presence fairly haunted the large room. It was a haunting ultimately enhanced by the faint sound of his voice as he sang—and sang quite well, too—in a distant shower. She couldn't distinguish the words, but the tune sounded vaguely familiar.

When he returned, he'd changed to comfortable, casual clothing, and smelled ever so slightly of tangy aftershave. His curly hair was still damp and springing back from a cursory attempt to tidy it.

"Now come into the kitchen and keep me company while I chef," he said. "You'll be safe enough, I promise. I was only joking about making you peel the spuds."

"I don't mind," she said, but he shook his head.

"Not in my house. I don't invite people for dinner and then expect them to work, or even sing for their supper. Speaking of which, I was quite taken with your choice of driving music, although it nearly blasted me out of the seat when I started your car."

Judith could only gasp. She had quite forgotten that she'd driven all the way north from Hobart under the influence of the redneck song album she'd put together with the intent of giving it to Bevan Keene as a pointed reminder of his earlier behavior.

Is he joking? Or has he been reading my mind again, and knows exactly what I intended, and why, and even that I chickened out?

Such thoughts took up her attention as she sipped her drink and watched as Bevan—having donned a ridiculously conventional apron—kept up a totally innocuous conversation as he peeled potatoes, poured a smidgen of oil into a huge, cast-iron frying pan, then started cooking the biggest, thickest, steak-fries Judith had ever seen. He took her by surprise a moment later when he turned, suddenly, and said in a mock-serious tone, "I warn you this is a test with only one correct answer. How do you want your steak cooked?"

The Queenslander's words leapt to her lips, but she stifled them, imagining Bevan's reaction to such a crude description. *Oh, why not, Judith Theresa? Then he'd be certain of your redneck tendencies.* She almost laughed aloud at the thought, and it took her a moment to regain control.

"Three moos," she finally said, deliberately meeting his eyes to check his interpretation. They were smiling, perhaps even laughing—and *with* her instead of *at* her, for a change.

"One when it steps into the pan, one when it turns over, and the third when it steps out onto the plate," he replied without batting an eye. "I'll pay that one. Wins you diner of the year award and makes it a lot easier for me. I always have trouble arranging things so the spuds and meat are done just right at just the same time, and it's easier if we're both having our steaks cooked to the same degree."

"Which makes two things in common," she said without

thinking about it. "We'd best be careful or we'll wind up being compatible after all."

To which he didn't reply, except to turn and look at her with an expression in his eyes that told her absolutely nothing, and yet far, far too much at the same time. When he turned back to the slowly browning steak fries, Judith couldn't help feeling she'd been quietly observed walking on very thin ice by somebody who had no intention whatsoever of warning her.

It served only to intensify her awareness of him. She found herself cataloguing all sorts of things—the way he moved, the texture of the sun-bleached hair on his arms, the way his mustache flexed when he smiled, the various expressions that came into being in his incredible gray eyes. An extremely self-contained individual, she decided, and realized this was only in keeping with all her earlier impressions of him.

He was certainly at home in his own kitchen, which he had quite obviously organized to suit his own way of doing things. A truly gigantic spice rack held about twice the variety Judith ever used, and she had already been shown the large walk-in pantry with its racks of condiments in jars and tins.

As the steak fries began to near readiness, he delved into a large refrigerator and emerged with a platter containing the steaks themselves. And, rather to Judith's surprise, they weren't the expected two-inch-thick T-bones, but rather smaller noisettes that were as thick as they were big around.

"No objections to venison, I hope," he said, and the look in his eyes told her there was only one correct answer to this question.

"Certainly not," she replied, trying at the same time to smother a small laugh of satisfaction. If it had been a test of some kind, the ploy had failed. Bevan Keene would have to seek new ways to shock or surprise her.

What did you expect me to say, I wonder? "Oooh, I couldn't pos-

sibly eat Bambi"?

Her reaction, if it surprised him, didn't make him reveal the fact. Indeed, he was so engrossed now in the intricacies of his cooking that he didn't have time even to keep up a dialogue. His large hands were continuously busy, shifting the rounds of potato, moving the noisettes of venison careful around on the griddle section of the pan, stirring in rounds of onion, setting out a decanter of red wine to go with dinner.

And almost before she realized it, dinner was there on the table, served with a casual élan that ignored the rather tricky timing she knew had been involved. Bevan whipped away his apron and graced her with a flamboyant little bow before seating her, then himself across the table from her.

"I guess I'm safe enough here," he said. He glanced down at his lap, and grinned hugely when Judith, caught by surprise, scowled, then dropped her gaze.

You cunning bastard. I'll bet you planned that one the whole time you were cooking.

Still grinning, he poured two generous glasses of wine and lifted his in a salute.

"And what shall we drink to?" he asked, only to continue without waiting for her to reply. "To tigers, or absent friends, or conservation—or just to us?"

It was a blatant challenge. Everything about the gesture said so, none more so than the devilish gleam in his eyes. Judith was tempted, but restrained herself from stepping into the obvious trap.

"I intend to drink to the chef," she replied in a voice as calm as she could make it. And met his eyes only long enough to make her point before returning her attention to the meal in front of her.

Bevan accepted the gesture with a modest nod, then murmured, "You'd best at least taste that before making such a compliment." But he clinked glasses with her and sipped his wine with appreciation before lifting knife and fork to assault his venison.

Thereafter, they ate in a shared silence, a time of heightened senses, of appreciation, and . . . of anticipation. Bevan made the meal an astonishingly sensual experience without saying a word. His eyes spoke for him, his gestures enhanced the unique, silent conversation.

When he sipped at his wine, his eyes told Judith it was in this way he would sip at her lips, her neck, her breasts. When he savored the unique taste of the venison, his eyes told her his tongue had other, even more pleasant uses. He watched her lips as she ate, and when he licked at his own, it was like a caress, a promise. All in relative silence, all in a sort of atmosphere that was invisible, yet unquestionable, unspoken, but tangible. And all of it enhanced by the sheer wonder of the simple but somehow amazing meal.

Judith had tasted venison before, but only in restaurants, and only in portions adulterated by complicated sauces and preparation. Never had she been subjected to the unique gamy flavor of wild venison properly prepared for the table. And never, ever, had she tasted any food in such an aura of sensuality, under such an appraisal by a man who clearly found food to be a sexual delicacy to be tasted, savored, enjoyed in the same way as lovemaking itself.

It was intoxicating and frightening at the same time. Never did he do a thing that could, of itself, be called to account—nothing that could be described in words as being improperly seductive or indelicate or offensive. But he was seducing Judith, and they both knew it. He was seducing her with the pleasures of the meal, the heightened aura of his own attitude, his attractiveness to her—her attractiveness to him! And she was letting him, even helping him.

Because she, too, had always considered the ambience of good food, good wine, and good company to have distinct sexual overtones. It was just that she had never before found all three together under exactly the right circumstances. Until now.

There was none of the blatancy she'd exhibited by accidentally groping him at that earlier dinner together, but the memory was nonetheless tied into his entire attitude, the aura of this experience he was creating with her, for her.

The entire experience became a sort of fantasy. It was like actually being in a silent movie alive with colors and textures and music—until finally the spell ended, broken by the sound of real words when Bevan finished the last morsel on his plate, then leaned back in his chair and spoke.

"Well, Judith Theresa. What did you think of that?"

11

It wasn't the sound of his voice that brought Judith back to reality with a snap, nor was it the hint of smug satisfaction in his voice. It was the use of her whole name, the inclusion of the *Theresa* in a strangely comfortable, complete way, giving the usage a wholeness that somehow seemed just . . . *right.*

Except that he shouldn't even have *known* her middle name. She didn't use it, it had never appeared on her bylines, nobody else ever used it except family members. Like Vanessa!

"Quite, quite splendid," she replied honestly, and patted at her lips with a napkin to cover the confusion she suddenly felt at the sense of intimacy he had prolonged and now enhanced by using her own name against her while she was trapped by his eyes.

Judith Theresa. Nobody had ever put quite that sound to the name before, nor spoken it with quite that sense of intimacy. Her parents had both used *Judith Theresa* when she was in trouble, other family members like Vanessa to indicate some element of the unusual, the serious, in a conversation. But Bevan Keene, who shouldn't even have known it, had added an entirely new dimension to her own name.

It was as if he was able to know her just by looking at her, able to reach out and touch her without actual physical contact. Once again, his use of the word "dossier" flooded into her mind, but now she didn't feel quite so much investigated as she felt exposed, as if this unusual man could actually read her mind, see past whatever human facades she might present, and find the real Judith Theresa behind them all. His gaze reached out to touch her, to probe at her awareness, enlarging it, giving it new substance, new meaning. And she couldn't stop him, not that she really wanted to. What she really wanted was . . .

Judith shook her head suddenly, violently, forcing herself out of this dreamlike, hypnotic state. But even with the return to reality, she felt her entire body still somehow reacting to Bevan Keene's spell. Her nipples were thrusting against the fine fabric of her bra, and she could feel herself wriggling in her chair, responding to a fluttery, airy feeling in the very core of her being.

And he knew it! From those pale gray eyes, the devil laughed, and Judith knew her own inner devils were chuckling in response. That wide, mobile mouth smiled as he reached out to refill her wine glass, and she couldn't for the life of her move to halt his gesture, couldn't speak to say that she'd had enough, more than enough. And wanted more, but not of wine.

Although the wine, dark red, blood red, held its own mystique. She had taken enough and she knew it, but she wanted more, somehow needed more, just as she needed more of this strange magic Bevan Keene was creating without so much as touching her. But she feared it, as she feared his apparent ability to reach out and know her, to somehow strip away her defenses as he might, soon, strip away her clothing.

Around them, the room seemed to have dissolved and reshaped itself. The huge country kitchen, a curious mix of historic and modern in daylight, now seemed almost Gothic, with shadows that lived, and an overall sense of . . . foreboding?

Judith felt herself shiver, and knew it was not only the atmosphere, not only the strength of Bevan's presence, but her own instinctive reaction to him that caused this frisson of alarm. She seemed to watch it all as a sort of separate, detached observer, seeing her hand reach out to take the newly filled glass, seeing it drawn to her lips while Bevan held that *other* Judith with his eyes, smoky eyes that looked over his own glass as he licked the rim of it, then tilted it to let the warm red wine flow over his sensual lips.

His eyes were magnetic, drawing that *other* Judith closer, forcing her to lean toward him as her mouth tasted the wine, her free hand drifting slowly across the table to meet his own. There was an instant—fleeting and then more obvious—when his fingers touched hers, then slid past them to touch at the sensitive skin of her inner wrist, stroking and caressing and somehow serving to calm her, mesmerize her, and seduce her.

In this strange omniscience, it seemed perfectly natural—having taken her fingers, her wrist, having begun to sensitize her to his touch—that he should then rise, still holding her, and move around the table toward her. Even more natural that she should move up out of her chair to meet him, that when his free hand flowed around her waist she should curl into its grasp, her entire body vibrating, now, to the magic of his touch.

Her nostrils filled with the scent of him, a unique blend of the man himself and the pungent but subtle aftershave he used. As his mouth moved down to claim her own, she was vaguely conscious of the taste of him, of the bristly touch of his mustache beneath her nose, but more conscious of the way she seemed to fit just right against him, her breasts against his chest, her height perfect to fit her to his kiss, her body ready for his embrace.

Somewhere in the back recesses of her mind, a tiny, fragile voice cried out in objection, a voice of reason, of sanity, a voice not befuddled by wine, not tormented by the needs of the body that now threatened to melt under the touch of his fingers, the strength of his embrace. But Judith watched herself ignore that voice, watched herself flow against him, her bones like jelly, her common sense dissipated like smoke.

No, no, no. The weak, fragile inner voice was but a whisper. *Not him, not here, not now!* But it was overridden by the roaring of her own heartbeat in her ears, the soaring thunder he created, then orchestrated as his fingers ran the scales up and down her spine as if it were a keyboard.

Judith met his kiss, her lips parted to accept his mouth, to feed on his kisses. Dessert! Her fingers moved into the shaggy, curly hair at the nape of his neck, seeking to draw him closer, to assist in melding their bodies together. Deep below the pit of her stomach, an airy hollowness was filling with fluttering sensations. Lower still she felt herself flooding with moisture, her fickle body preparing for him, yearning for the rigid, throbbing erection she could feel warm against her.

As his hands, butterfly light in their touch and yet crackling with sensation like static, roamed up and down her back, cupping and exploring the terrain of her hips, her lower back, and beyond, Judith could feel herself writhing in response. The warning voice was drowned out entirely now, as was all other sound, all other sensation. She existed only for whatever was developing between them, a riot of feeling and touch and smell and taste. His tongue was exploring in her mouth, fighting with her as she sought to taste him, to experience the very essence of him.

Subliminally, a part of her was aware of the sound of an arriving vehicle, the faint, distant sound of dogs voicing warning. Perhaps Bevan was also, yet in her confusion when the kitchen door was suddenly flung open and his name was called in urgent tones, Judith found no evidence of it. They clung together, unable to break the spell he had created, then turned as one to look with astonishment at the intruder.

"Bevan!"

Again the voice called his name, but now there was a different sense of urgency that cut through the atmosphere of the room like a siren. The speaker was a tall, slender woman, dark-haired, vibrant and elegant in every aspect. She wore designer jeans as if she had been poured into them, and the expensive silk blouse above them, the classic silk scarf at her throat, all shouted compliments to her taste.

Bevan released her, but even that gesture he somehow turned into a sensuous movement, a promise of . . . something. There was no sense of panic, no feeling of being discarded, no sense that he felt he'd somehow been caught out. Judith, on the other hand, felt distinctly that way, and she could feel herself cringing inside.

"Roberta! You're a surprise," he said, once he'd turned to face the woman but still, surprisingly, maintained a hand around Judith's waist, his fingers only lightly in contact but sticking as if sewn to her belt.

"Obviously," replied the dark-haired woman with a quirk of one high-arched brow and a twist of her lips that could have been a measure of anger or amusement or both.

"I was on my way home," she said, "and I happened to notice a spotlight flashing up on that ridge on the Honeymoon Run, so I thought I'd best stop and let you know immediately."

"Too right," Bevan replied, and now he did release Judith, although not before she felt the change in his entire demeanor. It was as if he'd been jolted by some cosmic force. He was suddenly totally alert, his muscles tensed as if for battle.

"Well," the woman said, "I didn't know if you had somebody shooting up there, but you so seldom do, except on weekends, and—"

"And it'll be that little redheaded bastard again. You can count on it," Bevan snarled. "Maybe this time I'll be able to catch him in the act for once."

Striding from the room, he returned a moment later carrying

a high-powered rifle and stuffing a handful of ammunition into his pocket. "If I do nothing else, I might cost somebody a new set of tires," he growled with a savage smile. "Do us a favor, Roberta, and give the coppers a ring. Maybe between us we can nail this joker right and proper for a change."

And without so much as an explanatory word to Judith, he was out the door. The dark-haired woman turned to the telephone, leaving Judith to stand in silence, wondering what she ought to say or do.

Judith listened to one half of a conversation that made only partial sense—a cryptic description of roads and gates and paddocks with names she couldn't understand, then watched as the woman put down the telephone and turned to focus dark, speculative eyes on her.

"I'm Roberta Jardine, if you're wondering," the woman said, offering a strong handshake from a hand clearly accustomed to hard work. "You'll be this journalist person, I presume. Judith . . . something?"

"Judith Bryan. Yes, I am. And a slightly confused journalist person, too. Is . . . was . . . Bevan going out to . . . to actually shoot at somebody?"

It seemed a ridiculous question, even in her own ears, given what she'd just seen, but the image of Bevan Keene going off to a gunfight like some character from a western movie just didn't—couldn't—seem real. Except she knew it had just happened, but somehow her mind couldn't quite connect such activity with the Bevan Keene whose arms had, only moments earlier, held her with such exquisite tenderness.

"Poachers." Roberta Jardine spat out the word as if it tasted bad. "And likely he'd only shoot at their tires, unless of course they shoot at him first. Which has been known to happen."

Her entire attitude suggested that Bevan's action was the most normal thing in the world. And in her dark eyes, something else, but Judith couldn't interpret it. Amusement? Contempt? Whatever it was, there was no doubt that Judith, herself, was the target.

"They're common round here, poachers," Roberta Jardine said, and this time the fire in her eyes was more obvious. Judith couldn't help but get the message—Bevan Keene wasn't the only one with poacher problems. Roberta Jardine also had them—and Judith had just been cast in the role.

"I . . ." Judith paused, uncertain of what she should say, of what she *could* say. The Jardine woman had seen them embracing and nothing Judith or anyone else might say would deny the facts of it. Roberta Jardine didn't need telling where things might have gone had she not interrupted. Judith didn't need telling either; she knew only too well!

Judith suddenly had a mental flash of Roberta Jardine and Bevan locked in passion, their hands moving across each other's body with the knowledge of long experience, their bodies merging with none of the awkwardness new lovers must endure.

Then the woman shrugged, the gesture self-explanatory, saying without words that poachers didn't bother her that much, telling Judith that she was irrelevant in the long term, that Roberta Jardine simply wasn't concerned.

"I won't stay," she said then. "Lord only knows how long Bevan will be, and I've work to do." *Unlike you,* said her eyes, but her voice was different. "I presume we're still planning to get underway next week."

"I guess so. We haven't really discussed it in detail, but most of the equipment has arrived, I believe, and I know Derek Innes is expected sometime next week."

"That's good. We wouldn't want to start this jolly little circus without him, would we?" Roberta's eyes said the rest—*she* wouldn't be involved at all if not for Bevan Keene. And her opinion of their chances for success, it seemed, about matched

Judith's own.

"You don't sound especially enthusiastic," Judith replied, finally having recovered some semblance of balance. If she was going to work with this woman for the next few months, it would be politic to at least try and find some common ground, some understanding of why Roberta Jardine was involved—excluding the obvious—and what she expected from the project.

Again that haughty shrug.

"I suppose I'm not enthusiastic. In fact, I'm definitely not, which isn't anything you have to make a point of telling Bevan, because he already knows. It's damned foolishness, and I've said so, to be importing greenies like this Innes bloke. We've got plenty of radical types of our own, without going to the trouble of bringing in more."

"I can certainly see your point," Judith said. "Tasmania's environmental issues have a history of demonstrators being brought in from the mainland, I understand."

"Hired guns. Oh my, yes. We've had our share of those," was the reply. Bitter. Angry. "Thugs and layabouts and airy-fairy intellectuals who've never done a day's work in their lives and never will. And," Roberta added in a slightly more conciliatory tone, "a lot of well-meaning, honest, well-intentioned people who are simply ignorant. All they think about is pretty, furry little animals and majestic trees, and they forget that the issues are just not that simple!"

Now she looked squarely at Judith, but her anger was directed elsewhere.

"The problem is that everything these days revolves around politics," she said with cold determination. "So what we have is politicians who are too busy playing politics to settle down and run the country, or the state, or whatever, and environmentalists who are more interested in politics than actual conservation, and the poor bloody farmers and timber workers get caught in the middle."

"And it isn't going to get any better," Judith said, caught by the other woman's genuine concerns because they so clearly mirrored her own.

"No," said Roberta Jardine. "It isn't going to get any better. And roaming round the countryside looking for an extinct Thylacine isn't going to make anything better either."

So you think they truly are extinct. But you're still letting yourself be dragged into this.

"But . . . but why are you involved in this, then? I mean . . . surely you have other priorities, other work."

"I have. I've a property to run, just for starters. Twenty-three thousand acres, twenty-three thousand sheep, about fifty million 'roo and wallaby—or so it sometimes seems—and whatever deer the poachers don't get. And Bevan has even more of all that."

"Which doesn't exactly answer my question," Judith insisted, her journalistic instincts surging to the fore. There was more to this than she'd originally thought, and Roberta Jardine might just provide her with the key.

"You're awfully thick for somebody who's supposed to be a hot-shot journalist. We're in it, both Bevan and I, to keep the bastards honest."

The bleakness of the statement put the entire issue in a nutshell. It was an element Judith had, of course, thought of herself. Knowing the desire of some conservationists to lock up every possible bit of land as wilderness, wanting either to keep any future development under strict control or eliminate it altogether, she had instinctively recognized the potential of this tiger expedition to be grossly exploited.

All that would be required, she knew, would be for a tiger to be discovered in the right place—unlikely and/or impossible as that might be—and the howls for a protected environment would give the conservation-movement radicals ammunition for a world-scale campaign.

And wouldn't Derek love that? He's probably on his knees right now, praying for exactly such an outcome.

Perhaps it was the accusation of being thick, perhaps just her own professionalism, now slightly fragile in light of her betrayal by Derek and her own foolishness in that affair. Whatever, it was sufficient to cause a flare of indignation.

"I am not thick," she replied angrily. "I know exactly what you mean and to a very large degree I agree with you, although I can see you hadn't even considered *that* possibility. Because 'keeping the bastards honest,' as you so delicately put it, is part of *my* involvement in this, too. A very large part!"

If she expected to score any points with that disclosure, she was mightily mistaken. Roberta Jardine didn't so much as flinch. She flicked her short-cut mane of ebony hair in a gesture of total disdain as she moved toward the door, then turned back to glare at Judith through hostile, speculative eyes.

"Before you get too far in your campaign to manipulate Bevan," she said, "just remember that he might be doing the same thing to you."

And before Judith could even think to reply, Roberta Jardine was gone, slamming the kitchen door behind her.

12

Reaction set in even as the sound of the slamming door reverberated through the house. Judith found herself trembling, her body as affected as her mind from the confrontation, but more by the incident which had preceded it.

Absently reaching for the remainder of the good red wine from dinner, she had to use both hands to steady the pouring of a glassful, then to lift that glass to her trembling lips.

"What a fool! What an utter half-wit you are!" she told herself, only to flinch at the sound of her own voice, loud in the emptiness of the room. She was still shaken, both by her reaction to Bevan's caresses and by an unexpected and quite surprising reaction to seeing him go out of the place armed and ready for violence.

Judith was no stranger to violence, at least as an observer. She had seen dramatic examples of it during her career, where confrontation between conservationists and forestry workers had become increasingly common. She had seen idiots lie down in front of bulldozers, chain themselves high in trees and fling themselves down as barriers to the chainsaws of working foresters. She had seen allegedly peaceful demonstrations turn into violent mob scenes with pushing and shoving and people with cracked heads and bloodied noses and the aftereffects of mace and pepper spray. She'd seen the results of car bombings and what happened when a sawmill blade struck a piece of steel deliberately inserted into a sawlog.

And in her younger years, when she'd done her mandatory stint on police rounds, she'd seen violence of a different, but no less bloody sort.

But never had she been faced with somebody she knew going out with a gun to do what she reasonably considered to be a policeman's job. She kept seeing in her mind the expression on Bevan Keene's face, a combination of bleak determination and a quite obvious readiness, almost a joy, at the prospect of doing battle.

And this from a man who only moments before had been equally, infinitely gentle, loving her, touching her with caresses of thistle-down softness, kissing her with . . .

"Or putting on a damned good act," she said, suddenly savage with the more likely reality. "And of course that's what he was doing. Even Roberta Jardine could see it. It's only you, naïve soul that you are, who couldn't see the bastard's performance for what it was."

Sipping the wine, she paced the kitchen, wondering now what she ought to do. She didn't particularly want to see Bevan again tonight, and she wasn't even sure about seeing him tomorrow. Roberta's allegation about his motives, however catty, made too much sense to be ignored. She finished the wine, poured herself another glass without bothering to think about it, then found herself staring at the goblet and wondering, for an instant, how it had suddenly gotten full again.

"Enough of this," she muttered, and set it aside while she devoted time to clearing the table and washing up the dirty dishes. That, at least, made some sense, she thought. The problem was that it didn't take long enough. She was finished, had prowled through the cupboards and managed to put everything away where it seemed to belong, and Bevan still hadn't returned.

"Well, to hell with you, then," she told the empty room, and marched upstairs to the bedroom designated for her use. She stripped and stood for an instant, nightgown in hand, then shook her head in exasperation and got dressed again and returned to the kitchen. Whatever the logic, she simply couldn't just go to bed and sleep while her host was out chasing armed poachers.

But what else could she do? She didn't know the situation, would be more of a nuisance than anything if she took her rental car and started driving around the back roads looking for him.

"Stupid . . . stupid . . . stupid," she told herself, then stared at the half-empty wine glass that had magically appeared in her hand. "And this is stupid too," she said, then drained the glass.

Around her, the huge old house creaked and groaned and mumbled to itself in its own language, reinforcing her feeling of being an outsider, perhaps an intruder. A poacher? Judith smiled to herself, whimsically reviewing Roberta Jardine's attitude on that score.

"I suppose from her point of view I might be," she mused aloud. "If only she knew what a ridiculous suggestion that really is." *Stop kidding yourself, Judith Theresa. If she hadn't interrupted, he'd have finished seducing you without any argument at all—and you'd have been loving it.*

Judith moved out to the back verandah and idly scanned the night sky, her ears cocked in a futile attempt to interpret the sounds around her. From the kennels, one dog ventured a tentative challenge to the sound of the kitchen door opening and closing, then quieted. In the distance, a cow rumbled some message, spawning a host of replies, and somewhere nearer in the night a mob of frogs played a monotonous game of *rock, rivet, rock, rivet* over and over and over again.

On some distant road, she could hear the muted rumble of a vehicle, but she listened in vain for the sound she wanted to hear, that of Bevan's vehicle returning. At least, she thought, she hadn't heard the sound of gunfire. Or would she? She had no idea of the distances or directions involved. Perhaps at this very moment Bevan was playing a deadly game somewhere out in the scrub.

Finally, the coolness drove her back inside, and she turned to the extensive library for comfort. There were countless books there she'd never even heard of, and it didn't take long to lose herself in the rare collection of works about the elusive Tasmanian tiger.

Fascinated, she took some of the material over to where she could lie down on the big leather couch with its excellent reading light. The minutes disappeared as she became increasingly engrossed in the book, then faster still as she drifted into slumber, waking only at the touch of something soft at her throat.

Judith opened her eyes to see Bevan's departing figure, and she lifted her hands against the mohair coverlet he'd apparently spread over her.

"Bevan?" Her cry caught him in the doorway, and he turned to smile at her.

"Ssssh. There's a lady sleeping in here," he replied softly.

"You're . . . you're all right?" Judith ignored his low-key jest. "I was worried." And she paused, unable to put into words exactly what she felt, because she was no longer certain herself, now that she'd seen him again.

"Bit tired is all," he said, and walked over to seat himself on the edge of the couch and look down at her. He reached out one hand as if to stroke her cheek, then hurriedly checked the motion and put the hand down by his side. But not before Judith's attention was drawn to it.

"Let me see," she insisted, and grabbed at the hand, only to jerk her own away again as he winced in pain. "What have you done to yourself?"

"It's nothing," he said, but too late. Judith had already turned her gaze to his other hand, which was in full view. Two of the knuckles were lacerated and oozing blood.

"Nothing? Let me see your other hand," she demanded, slithering to sit upright, reaching out again to grasp—this time—at his right wrist. The right hand was more severely damaged. All four knuckles were cut, one almost to the bone, and already the hand was starting to swell badly. It was covered in dirt and blood.

Judith gasped at the sight, then pressed against Bevan's bulk, trying to move him so she could get herself off the couch. "We have to get that cleaned up," she said, angry now because of her worry. It was all too obvious how he'd injured his hands, and she wondered at the condition of the other person, or persons involved.

"I was about to do exactly that," he said calmly, rising with lithe, fluid grace to let her bounce to her feet, where she stood glaring at him.

"I'll just bet." Then she paused, eyes wide and mouth open, as she finally noticed the slight cut to his chin as he bent his head to stare ruefully at his damaged hand.

"Well, I'd hardly leave it like this, would I?" he muttered.

"How should I know?" she countered. "You walk out of here without a word, carrying a gun like some sort of idiot cowboy or something, and then you come back all covered in blood. How do you expect me to know anything?"

Grabbing him by his shirt-front, she began to drag him toward the kitchen, muttering under her breath as she did so. Once at the sink, she started cold water running and ordered him to put both hands under it.

"What have you got to put on the cuts?" she demanded, and was already walking away toward the bathroom and the medicine cabinet she expected to find there.

"No, in that cabinet right there," he said, waving a dripping hand toward the far end of the room.

Judith changed tack and yanked open a cupboard door to find a veritable wilderness of jars and tins, salves and ointments and powders. She was fumbling around, furiously reading one label after another, unsure which was for humans and which for dogs or horses or sheep, when Bevan's calm voice finally got through to her.

"I know you'll find this quite hard to believe, Judith, but there was a semblance of order to that cabinet before you got messing round in there. Can I suggest you just look for iodine, and if you can't find that, there's a bottle of Watkins liniment on the bottom shelf. That'll do just as well."

He'd finished washing his hands by this time, and stood calmly drying them on some paper towel, watching Judith and shaking his head in apparent amazement.

Iodine? Not that she could find. The liniment, however was plainly visible, so she grabbed it up along with a packet of cotton buds, then returned to the sink, trying to read the liniment label as she went.

"Are you sure this is what you want?" she asked. "It doesn't say anything about being a disinfectant or anything."

"That stuff," he replied, "cures anything! And be sparing with it, please, because I have to have a friend bring it in from Canada for me whenever he makes a trip, and I don't want to waste it."

"I will use as much as I think I need," she snapped, scowling when she saw that his hands now looked worse clean than they had dirty. "And I hope it stings even worse than iodine!"

"It will, but don't let that stop you," he replied, grinning hugely now. "Not that I expect it would. You may be lovely, but I doubt you're overendowed with nursing-variety empathy."

"No kidding," she muttered, then busied herself dabbing the foul-smelling liquid onto his abraded knuckles. Whether it stung or not, she couldn't tell. Bevan obviously wasn't about to reveal himself by letting her know. He seemed oblivious to any pain he might be feeling, and when she looked up, it was to find him observing her with a slight grin and an expression of wry amusement in his pale gray eyes.

"Right! And if you're done with your tortures, Ms. Bryan, then I suggest we both go and get some sleep. I know you've had a bit, but I'm fairly whacked."

Earlier in the evening, they'd been within an inch of going to bed together, but now he made no such suggestion, didn't even seem aware of it. Not that she really cared, since it wasn't going to happen, no matter what. But still . . .

You're a slut, Judith Theresa. At least wait until you're asked. Angry-making thoughts from a neglected conscience.

"Aren't you going to clean your rifle first?" Judith asked, the words popping out without her even thinking. "Isn't that one of the rules? Weapons have to be kept spotless at all times?"

"My dear Judith Theresa, whatever are you on about?"

And there was something in his voice, some slight, off-key tone that made Judith's hackles rise in suspicion. And sure enough—this time, when she met his eyes, they projected such a total expression of appealing innocence she nearly laughed out loud. She pondered only an instant, then threw caution to the winds and let fly!

"I was on about the poacher you went storming out of here to confront, but then you didn't have to shoot him, did you? You just beat him up instead."

Her tone was scathing, deliberately so, but her anger was directed at Bevan for reasons that had nothing to do with guns or poachers or fistfights, and she had the uncomfortable feeling he knew it.

"I'd ask whose side you're on, but of course I know you journalistic types are always scrupulously neutral," he replied, and there was a hard edge to his voice, the sarcasm of the last few words undisguised. "But just in case you're overwhelmed with sympathy for this poor poacher, let me assure he's not out there poaching the king's deer like some modern-day Robin Hood because he's got a mob of starving kids and nothing to feed them on. This bloke's got a mob of kids all right, but they're far from starving and probably wouldn't eat good venison if they were offered it.

"This charming fellow is home at night so seldom I don't how he *made* the kids, because he is forever out shooting stags for their heads, my dear journalist. He leaves the meat to rot or feed the Tasmanian devils and native cats. He just walks away, the same as he just walks away if he happens to shoot a doe by mistake, or after he's cut one of my fences to get on or off the property. He does all this not because he's hungry, but because he likes to kill things and he likes to flout authority . . . any authority. And he'll go to court in the morning, where the magistrate will slap him on the wrist and tell him he's a naughty boy and let him go so he can poach another deer. But not until he buys some new tires for his ute!"

There was a savage satisfaction in the last remark, but it was tinged with sadness too, the bitterness Judith had all too often heard from people hamstrung by a legal system that seemed to favor offenders' rights over those of the victims.

She wasn't about to argue. No matter what she said, it would be wrong. But still . . . the question leapt to her lips before she could turn off her mind.

"You shot out his tires?"

Bevan laughed, a huge, bellowing, gargantuan laugh of what appeared to be genuine pleasure.

"You really have a thing about guns, don't you? No, my dear, bloodthirsty Ms. Bryan, I most emphatically did not shoot out his tires. I did not fire a shot, neither in anger nor with malice aforethought, nor even as a warning."

Then he grinned, and it was a wicked grin, a grin seething with smug satisfaction. "I will admit, however, that while he was busy hacking the head off the stag he shot—a trophy now being held in evidence against him, along with the carcass he'd intended to abandon—*somebody* appears to have stuck a knife into all four of his tires and the spare, to boot. It wasn't me of course. I didn't even get there until it was all over."

Liar! That much was obvious. Judith thought it but didn't say it.

"And I suppose there wasn't a fistfight, either?" she asked with deliberate innocence. "You injured your hands by hitting a tree in frustration?"

"I injured them protecting myself. No more than that." His voice was calm, but his eyes danced with delighted, unrepentant laughter. "The rotter had the effrontery to accuse me of slicing his tires, he did. Even took a poke at me, right there in front of police witnesses." And again that mischievous grin, followed by an overly broad shrug of innocence. "So I defended myself. Can't fault a man for that, surely?"

"Surely not," she said, pushing the words out as if they tasted bad, which they did. "And now if you'll excuse me, it's been rather a long night and I'd like to get some sleep."

"That's one of your better ideas," he said. "Want me to come along and tuck you in and kiss you goodnight, or good morning, as it is now? Although," he added, and she couldn't tell if his grin was rueful or playful, or both, "I've probably had about all the excitement I can handle for one night."

His eyes laughed, their smoky depths gleaming.

Judith ignored the temptation, although she didn't attempt to deny its attraction—to herself. To him, however, she denied it emphatically. *Liar, liar, pants on fire.*

"Please don't be ridiculous," she said and turned on her heel and walked away, her back ramrod straight, her entire attitude one, she hoped, of rejection. But the sound of Bevan's delighted laughter followed her up the stairs and echoed in her appointed bedroom long after he'd called a cheerful good night from the hall outside her room.

13

It was that same laughter she heard first upon awakening, though in her mildly befuddled state she took a few moments to realize he was downstairs talking on the telephone.

More than likely talking to Roberta Jardine, she thought as she made her way to the shower. The few words she could distinguish sounded very much like "poacher" and "tires." When she eventually made her way down to the kitchen, it was to find Bevan finishing the conversation and a cup of fresh-perked coffee awaiting her.

But Bevan's good mood—if indeed it had been that—seemed to have evaporated, fled down the telephone lines. He greeted her politely enough, but there was a chill in the air that was almost tangible.

And so it stayed throughout the day, a day spent unpacking, sorting, and repacking all the paraphernalia that related to the months of work ahead. Tents, sleeping bags, all manner of cooking and camping gear had arrived, but it was swamped by the huge amount of specialized equipment for the search itself.

Judith on her own wouldn't have recognized most of it. She had no idea how it should actually work. But Bevan clearly understood and lost no time in enlisting her aid to sort and list the highly specialized motion detectors, the solar collectors that would power them, the cameras, the portable hides, and the complicated lists of instruction for everything.

"I'm told this Jan Smythe woman is a miracle worker with

this stuff," Bevan said in one of his few comments beyond what was absolutely necessary. Judith had already given up any attempt to converse. She now felt herself in a holding pattern, a nonverbal, nonresponsive condition, and since she couldn't understand his icy attitude, she'd decided to accept it.

When they stopped for lunch, it was quickly made sandwiches and coffee, which Bevan carried away with him, muttering something about having "my own work, while there's time." He was back in half an hour but offered no explanations.

The tension just seemed to grow and grow. By tea time, they were like two stray dogs, circling and eyeing each other with suspicion, ready to snarl and growl at the first hint of excuse. Bevan had asked Judith if she'd mind preparing the meal, then left with an open brief, saying he'd be back in "a couple of hours" that turned out to be three and a half, during which she tried four times to phone Vanessa, who seemed to have camped on the phone at her end.

By which time her carefully prepared roast chicken was overcooked, dry as an outback evening, and—at least to her—totally unappetizing. Bevan ate like a starving man and even apologized for being late.

"My fault," he said. "I'm used to living by my own time, never even thought about the time until it was well and truly too late."

After the otherwise silent meal, she was banished to the library while he tended to the dishes and was interrupted only when he peered in to say, "I'm off for a bit of a prowl around. Don't wait up or get worried. I don't know how long I'll be."

Judith didn't wait up, but when midnight arrived and there was no sign of him returning, she did begin to worry despite telling herself not to be silly. But when she finally roused after a fitful night's attempt to sleep, somehow knowing he still hadn't come in, she began to worry in earnest. And to get angry.

Part of her was tempted to just peek into his room to be sure he hadn't sneaked in while she slept. But a wiser, stronger, more stubborn instinct told her to stay as far away from Bevan's bedroom as possible. That inner advice came as she stood outside his bedroom door, curiosity sprouting antennae like some demented pincushion. The pealing of the telephone saved her, and she fled down the stairs to answer it, one ear cocked behind her in a half certainty he'd have caught it on an extension before she could manage the stairs.

He didn't, but his answering machine did, and Judith opted for the easy way out, listening through some neighbor's message that it wasn't important and he'd call back later. She did the same when the phone rang again half an hour later, and again a few minutes after that. But the fourth call brought her to a frantic fumbling to turn off the machine so she could reply to her cousin's husband, whose agitated voice had begun to leave a message for Judith.

"Vanessa's just gone into labor," Charles explained when she finally managed to force the machine to let her speak to him in person. "She's at Calvary Hospital, everything's going according to schedule, and you've plenty of time to get here, so don't rush it. Drive carefully and remember which side of the road you're supposed to be on."

"I'm on my way," Judith replied, and it wasn't until she'd hung up the phone that she realized the crazy predicament she was placed in by Bevan's absence. His unfamiliar answering machine had probably been given terminal hiccups by her attempt to reply to Charles, and she felt uncomfortable leaving without seeing Bevan.

Now she was forced to check his room. She could hardly leave without a word if he did happen to be asleep. But he wasn't, nor was he there, and somehow she wasn't surprised.

"Well, Mr. Keene, I'll just have to leave you a note," she muttered, trying to ignore the visions that plagued her conscience. Bevan Keene lying somewhere on the property with a broken leg or a sprained ankle or—and this was the worst—wounded by a poacher's bullet.

When she'd checked all the various sheds and the carport where she remembered seeing his vehicle, now gone, it was easier to imagine him stuck in the mud somewhere, until that thought was replaced by one in which his truck had tipped over and he was pinned inside.

"Damn you!" she cried, having packed her bags and gotten her own small rental car mobile and ready for the trip south to Hobart. She sat there in the driveway, pondering her options and liking none of them. Of course, he'd known she would be returning to Hobart for Vanessa's birthing, and of course he'd told her—hadn't he?—not to wait up and not to worry. So why was she worrying? And why wasn't he back?

"The note will have to do," she mumbled as she steered the rental car westward toward the Midlands Highway and her route south to Hobart. But still she kept an eye out for Bevan's truck, even speculating that if she encountered anyone who seemed an obvious neighbor, she could at least pass on the message that he was apparently missing and that she had been forced to return to Hobart without seeing him.

It seemed a good enough idea until she saw not a neighbor, but Bevan himself. Then it fell apart in a screaming heap of emotional turmoil she only just conquered in time.

Rounding a curve in the road, she suddenly found herself approaching a gateway, and in the gateway were two vehicles standing side by side and nose to rump like two friendly old horses. But friendlier yet, it seemed, were the figures who disengaged from an embrace as Judith's rental scooted into view.

Bevan and, of course, Roberta Jardine. Judith had no choice

but to pull up. Both of them were standing there looking at her, and it was clear enough that both she and her car had been recognized. She gulped quickly, fighting for composure as she coasted to a halt on the verge. So this was how Bevan *prowled,* she thought, and fought back the bitter taste of spiteful anger that threatened to gag her.

"I'm glad I caught you," she managed to say, avoiding the hypocritical "Good Morning" with which she might have begun. As she raced to inform Bevan of the circumstances and her need to hurry, she could feel herself getting more and more tense, more and more agitated. Her nerves were taut as a bowstring. She could hear it in her own voice and could only hope Bevan didn't pick up on it as well.

He and Roberta listened to her spiel, but Bevan didn't even have the decency to look embarrassed. The bastard! Instead, they both sent along good wishes to Vanessa—Judith hadn't even known Roberta and Vanessa were acquainted—and then Bevan suggested he'd keep in touch by telephone if he didn't get into Hobart himself during the postnatal confinement.

"And thanks for your help up here," he ended up by saying. "It's given us a good start on things, so when the rest of this mob shows up, it'll be all ready for a shakedown expedition. But don't worry about that just now. Don't even think about it. You just get yourself back to Hobart and keep our Vanessa under some semblance of control. You'll have to, because Charles bloody well can't."

He grinned after he said that, and there was something, some not-quite-comprehensible expression in his eyes and voice. It was almost as if he were going to lean in through the car window and kiss her goodbye. Judith, totally unsure if she'd have reacted by spitting in his eye or accepting the kiss just to see the expression on Roberta's face as she did so, did neither. She merely drove off, angry and confused.

Her anger and confusion intensified during the long drive to Hobart, and no quantity of redneck music could salve it. She found herself, at one point, shaking so badly she had to pull over and stop because she was becoming a danger on the highway.

The whole thing was quite ridiculous from the get-go, she decided. She had no claim on Bevan Keene, didn't want to have. And yet, as she drove, the thought of him spending the night with Roberta Jardine after telling *Judith* he was going on what she assumed was a venture to inspect his fences or patrol for poachers—well, it simply made her wild.

Prowling, all right. Like a tomcat. You give the word a whole new meaning. Not that I'm surprised, I know what a tomcat looks like. They have them in America, too. But I should have seen it.

I should have seen it.

How often had she said the exact same words after being so thoroughly used and betrayed by Derek? Who would soon be arriving in Tasmania with every intention of doing it all over again.

And of course she ought to have recognized Bevan's game. Roberta had gotten it right the first time. He was only using her to ensure some advantage for his faction in this ridiculous project. No matter how it turned out, the conservationists would be trying to make the result appear to their advantage, and Bevan was doing nothing different. Except he was obviously intent on using Judith to aid him.

Just like Derek!

She found it all spinning repetitively through her thoughts as she drove. Only occasionally was it countered by thoughts of simple confusion. How could anyone so blatantly leave a houseguest to her own devices so he could go off tomcatting?

Especially when said houseguest would have been more than willing to let you play tomcat right there at home. AND you knew it, too, you bastard!

No matter how she looked at that question, no matter how objective she tried to be, no matter how much she allowed her hurt feelings to provide the answer, it still didn't make sense.

"It's just plain bad manners and rudeness," she said in a savage voice, knowing even as she did so that it was for exactly that reason she found it hard to believe, despite all the evidence he'd done exactly that. He had wanted her, had gone so far as to virtually seduce her right there in his own kitchen. And then he'd abandoned the pursuit, just like that.

But why? Why, after what he'd clearly shown her of his true character, did she find it impossible to believe he was that type of person? He had done nothing to convince her that he was inherently a gentleman, that he wouldn't display such bad manners. And yet . . . somehow he *had* convinced her.

Or else she'd convinced herself, which was even more worrying.

"You are a fool, Judith Theresa. A fool to have come to Tasmania, a worse fool for taking this damned job, and a worse fool yet for letting Bevan Keene get under your skin," she told herself, repeating the words like a mantra, a litany. Until she believed it—almost.

The problem was that, as the kilometers passed, her mental picture of Bevan was not one of him snuggling with Roberta Jardine. It was far more complicated than that, a picture clouded by anger and admittedly hurt feelings, but also one clouded by the tactile memory of his fingers at her wrist, of his lips meeting hers, not Roberta's, and the sooty, smoky color of those incredible gray eyes.

It would be all too easy, this morning's revelation notwithstanding, to imagine herself emotionally involved with Bevan, even though all her common sense dictated otherwise. *And easier yet to imagine yourself physically involved with him, no sense lying about it.*

Her arrival at the hospital, managed only after considerable consultations with a street atlas and even longer efforts to find a place to park, thankfully cleared her mind. The twins hadn't bothered to wait for her. They must have been born, she realized with baffling clear hindsight, almost exactly at the moment she'd been speaking to Bevan alongside the road, the instant she'd been wondering if he would kiss her and if she'd allow him to kiss her.

The twins were beautiful. Identical as two wrinkled prunes, which to Judith's eyes they resembled, although she did not put it that way to their delighted new mother.

"One of each. Isn't that wonderful?" Vanessa had come through the experience with minimal problems, and now, several hours later, she was chafing at the bit to gather her brood and go home.

"Wonderful indeed," Judith replied. "Although I do think you might have spared them the carrot tops." She had eventually grown used to her own copper-orange tresses, but as a child had never been much impressed by the color of her hair. Plus, she'd been teased mercilessly, the epithet "carrot-top" the mildest of her playmates' torments.

"It runs in the family. You're proof of that," Vanessa replied. "And how are you getting along with Bevan?"

Judith blinked at the abrupt change of subject, then said, "Not—if you want me to be honest."

"Oh, what a pity." Vanessa was her usual optimistic self. "You're still speaking, I hope. I'd hate for my children's godparents not to be on speaking terms."

"Oh, Nessie! You . . . you wouldn't!"

"I certainly would. Although only with your approval, of course. I've named the children after you, though, so you'd best think a bit before refusing . . . Judith Theresa, what's so damn funny?"

Judith had collapsed into uncontrollable laughter, her only defense against the tears that otherwise would have erupted.

"Oh, Nessie, you have absolutely made my day," she finally managed to gasp, not sure whether to laugh or cry, shaking her coppery locks at the sheer insanity of it all.

14

The voice on the telephone only added to the confusion of a Monday morning in which everything that could go wrong had, and everything to come seemed headed that way.

"You about over being clucky yet?" Bevan asked without even bothering with the social niceties of "Hello" or "How are you?" His voice brought an instant vision to Judith's mind, and even as she answered, she was making comparisons between Bevan and the man who sat across from her in Vanessa's kitchen.

Derek Innes hadn't changed. How could she expect him to change in only a matter of months? He'd stepped out of a taxi, totally unexpected and unannounced, only moments before, obviously expecting Judith to just drop everything and cater to his every immediate need. That, she thought, was typical.

And yet, somehow, he had changed. She couldn't exactly say how, but even without the nebulous and indescribable changes, he simply didn't stand up to comparison with Bevan Keene.

How could she ever have thought those beady eyes, blatant in their cunning and deceptiveness, to be even remotely forthright or truthful? Indeed, Derek's entire attitude now seemed smug and self-serving, rather than bold and adventurous as she had once thought.

Ignoring the word "clucky," which she assumed had something to do with . . . well, with hens clucking, she said, "Not having started, I'm hardly likely to be over it." As she replied to Bevan, she watched Derek's eyes narrow in speculation. Obviously, he was trying to monitor the conversation. For an instant, she considered asking him to leave the room, but it seemed hardly worth the effort, all things considered. Moments later, she was glad of that decision.

"I don't suppose you've had any word from your little mate in Queensland?" Bevan asked. "The one who was supposed to be here last week? Everyone else is raring to go, and if he'd deign to make an appearance we could set out tomorrow for a few days shakedown to see how all this hi-tech equipment is going to work."

Judith paused before answering, actually found herself savoring the moment. Then she poured mental quicksilver along her tongue and said, "As a matter of fact, he's sitting here right now. Why don't I put him on the phone and you two men can discuss all this?"

"Not for just a minute," was the brusque reply. Which in one sense rather disappointed her, because Derek had definitely pricked up his ears. She had hoped for some recognizable reaction from Bevan, without knowing exactly what it should be. Still, in another sense she was flattered he wanted to speak with her rather than Derek.

"I hope you're able to tell me he isn't a full-boogie vegetarian, like two of his local compatriots claim to be," Bevan said then. "My oath! The way they go on about any sort of decent tucker, you and I will have to go off by ourselves in a corner someplace just so we can enjoy a decent bite of steak."

She couldn't help but laugh, then laugh even more at the petulant look on Derek's face because he didn't know why she laughed. Derek didn't enjoy being left out of a joke. Perhaps he feared it meant he could be the butt of it.

"No, not that bad," she said, carefully choosing her words. "There might be problems if there are any dragons in the party though."

Derek's objection to anyone smoking was almost legend. Given the opportunity, he'd have lobbied for tobacco to be placed on the same blacklist as heroin and cocaine.

Now it was Bevan's turn to chuckle, and Judith realized she had just played right into his hands by revealing she was attempting to keep Derek from easily following their conversation.

"So he's listening in, eh? Reckoned so. And he doesn't smoke and doesn't think anyone else should, either. Just as well you gave him away, Judith Theresa. A man with no vices isn't worth the trouble. Downright boring, if nothing else."

No vices? Judith shivered as she struggled to find a proper reply. By comparison to the vices she now realized Derek did have, smoking was very minor league indeed. But damned if she'd succumb to telling that to Bevan.

"Hardly the way I'd describe it," she eventually said. "Now, is there anything else before I put him on the phone?"

"Oh, I could ask you how you feel about sharing this godparenting business," Bevan said, and she could hear a mischievous lilt to his voice now, for sure.

"Don't!"

"Ah. I rather thought it might be like that. I don't know why you should feel that way, though, my girl. I'm told both the rug rats have your hair. If anybody should be complaining, it ought to be me."

"As you wish," she replied calmly. And stopped right there. This was not a subject she wanted to discuss at all over the telephone, much less in front of Derek.

"I'm inclined to be a bit cranky with Vanessa about the naming business, myself," Bevan continued, ignoring her demand. "I mean, what's going to happen when we get married and have kiddies of our own? If we pass our names on to them, the future will be amazingly complicated with a Judith, and a Mummy Judith and a Cousin Judith and an Aunty Judith—"

Judith's irrepressible spluttering cut him off in mid-sentence. Something inside her boiled over at his suggestion, let alone the implications involved. She felt herself going all breathless, her tummy roiling with a sensation she'd never encountered before.

Even worse was how quickly her fertile imagination created a magical montage of erotically specific images, revealing precisely how such a situation might be accomplished.

Dangerous ground, this. Get out. Get out now!

"I'm going to put Mr. Innes on the phone," she managed to say after she'd caught her breath. *It's either that or hang up on you, and wouldn't Derek love being a witness to that?*

She gestured to Derek, handed him the phone, and told him who was on the other end and why. Then she said, rather pointedly, "I'll just go out on the porch and give you some privacy."

If Derek noticed the implied criticism, he didn't reveal it. Even before Judith was out of the room, he was sliding into his oily, insincere, and yet so horribly plausible role, one she now found distasteful to the point of nausea.

"Phony as a politician's promise," she muttered to herself as she left the room, then immediately regretted not having stayed, just to hear what approach Derek would attempt to take with Bevan Keene.

15

Reality struck at Judith about halfway along the journey from Hobart to Bevan's property, and reality's arrival was so surprising it nearly caused her to veer off the highway.

Listening to Derek's unceasing prattle, she suddenly became aware that he didn't even realize that she knew his role in the incident that had caused her to lose her job, had, indeed, threatened her very career. If anything, he seemed to think her withdrawal to her cousin's side in Tasmania was solely because of her embarrassment at having been sacked, not in any way because of his personal involvement and betrayal.

And as they traveled farther and he talked on and on and on, boasting of his accomplishments and of having landed this plum of an opportunity, she also came to realize that he hadn't—in his own mind—betrayed her at all. He'd merely used her, and he seemed to accept quite happily that she'd been placed on earth exactly for that purpose.

By the time they stopped for coffee at Ross, Judith didn't know whether to laugh or cry or up and shoot the bastard, whether to be outraged or indignant or simply explode with amusement at how ridiculous the whole thing now seemed.

Hindsight, she decided, was a marvelous leveler. Looking back, she could see so easily how she'd been deceived, how she had, indeed, deceived herself, mistaking the rhetoric for the man, the apparent idealism and high standards Derek had built into his own façade. How downright egotistical and small-minded he really was. Derek lived in a world with only one agenda—his own. He was the center of his own universe, a power-hungry little man who would, she suddenly realized, stop at nothing, stoop to any extreme to gain and maintain power.

Now, sitting across the restaurant table from him, Judith was hard put to keep from crying at the ease with which she'd allowed herself to be manipulated by Derek, at how easily she'd let her emotions be twisted and her normal common sense be diverted by those emotions.

For shame, Judith Theresa. Are you really so insecure that you'd let a little weasel like this one lead you astray? Or is it because you're that desperate for masculine attention? Shame . . . shame . . . shame . . .

And Derek was somehow oblivious to it all.

"You must tell me about this Bevan Keene," he said. "I know, of course, that he's some kind of local identity, whatever that might be worth. But is he going to be important in forming the overall intellectual framework of this expedition?"

"You'll have to decide for yourself when you meet him," Judith replied evasively, wondering in her own mind at the seemingly blinkered attitude Derek was revealing. Bevan, she knew, was of vastly superior intellect to this pompous little bureaucrat, but Derek seemed convinced he could be dismissed as irrelevant just because he was a native Tasmanian.

"Well, of course," he said. "But I had hoped for a bit of input from you, Judith. I realize that Jeremiah thinks highly of Keene, and I expect he will have some local contacts that might be useful, but . . ."

The carefully stage-managed shrug said the rest.

"I believe this is your first visit to Tasmania, isn't it, Derek? Don't you think Mr. Keene's local knowledge might be of value, considering that fact?"

"Perhaps. Although of course the others on my team are also

locals. They're veterans of virtually every significant conservation campaign in Tasmania. The Franklin blockade, Lake Pedder, the Lemonthyme, Farmhouse Creek . . ." He continued through a litany of protest events, most of them highly confrontational, in which his new team had played significant roles. Then he changed the subject abruptly.

"Which brings me to the publicity aspects of this whole thing, and I must say, Judith, that we are not off to a very good start. For instance, I more than half expected to be met at the airport with photographers and requests for interviews. I did ensure that the media at home knew I was coming here to Tasmania, and I would have expected the local media to follow through."

"Tiger searches aren't exactly big news here in Tasmania," she said, hiding an amused grin. "Unless they're successful, which of course none of them have been."

Judith had already had any notions of her publicist role dramatically reconstructed by the Tasmanian media. They'd hardly heard of Derek and weren't particularly interested, and even the authority of Bevan Keene's name hadn't been enough to get her more than token coverage of the expedition thus far.

"It might have helped if I'd known when you were arriving," she continued. "Perhaps I could have arranged something. But I didn't know, Derek, until I found you on the doorstep this morning."

"I expect they were more on their toes when David Bellamy was here," he said, not in reply but merely continuing his original train of thought.

Judith bit her tongue, forgoing the urge to mention that whether you agreed with his views or not, the noted English conservationist David Bellamy had a vastly higher profile than Derek.

She waited until they were on the road again before casually prompting her companion for the information that she personally thought most relevant.

"I'm rather surprised at your personal involvement in this venture, Derek," she said, careful to keep her voice from revealing just how surprised. "Surely there's nothing to a tiger hunt for somebody of your stature? I mean, it's a billion to one chance at best."

"Odds have a way of changing," Derek replied obliquely, and Judith kept her eyes on the road, suddenly conscious of the exploratory look he was sending her way.

There was a short silence before he embarked on a convoluted explanation about the importance of having the conservation movement involved in any such expedition, of how important it was to ensure the strictest guidelines, the purest of motives.

They were almost at Bevan's gate before Derek finished what Judith had earlier recognized as the well-rehearsed spiel he'd prepared for the media who hadn't arrived. *And I'll bet you spent the entire flight from Brisbane rehearsing it, too!* There was savage satisfaction in the thought.

But she said nothing, lost in the sobering realization that her private prejudices had already colored her own role in the proceedings, and that she must now strive to find professional balance, strict neutrality, or risk severe problems for herself over the next few months.

And it wouldn't be easy, she thought, realizing that she was no longer uninvolved, no longer as professionally neutral as she wanted to be, as she had to be. The worst part wasn't facing up to her prejudice against Derek and her personal feelings there. She'd already done that, and her reaction to him now, while slightly surprising because she could see more clearly, was not a problem. What she now had to consider was her attraction to Bevan Keene, not least because she had to face up to the fact that she'd been denying her feelings for the Tasmanian grazier even as they had been forming.

Except for the physical attraction. No sense trying to deny that, especially to yourself.

These two men, she thought, would be fortunate indeed to agree on anything much past the time of day, while she would be stuck firmly in the middle, between a rock and a hard place no matter what she said or did or felt. It wasn't Jeremiah Cottrell's fault, but her own, which didn't keep her from blaming him for luring her into this insanity, then damning herself for agreeing to it.

And when they arrived at Bevan's kitchen door, she damned him too, double-damned him for the look he gave her, a look so filled with smoldering promise, or threat, that she could almost taste the flavor. Then he had the audacity to reach out and, before she could imagine his intent, much less thwart it, he lifted her hand to his lips in a gesture that would have seemed totally ludicrous except for the spasms of reaction it sent shooting up her arm.

"Welcome back, Number One Godmother," he said with a slow grin, obviously delighted with himself for his ability to upset her, to stir her emotions to the point of total distraction.

Judith was reduced to a stammering introduction of Derek, and only by seeing the expression in his eyes did she realize the full impact of Bevan's performance.

Branded, just like one of his cows or sheep. And it wasn't even meant for me, just the first blow in his campaign of one-upmanship with Derek.

It was a telling blow, if all the more unnerving for that. Derek's chilly courtesy was evidence he'd gotten the message, while Bevan's casual air of patronization suggested even more strongly that he didn't care much one way or the other. He'd staked his claim, stamped his brand, advertised the fact and dismissed Derek as any sort of competition—all in that single gesture.

And all without giving a damn what I think about any of it! Worse, Judith wasn't herself sure whether to be furious or flattered. The look on Derek's face had been almost worth it.

"Roberta's stopping at home, and everybody else is bunking in at the shearers' quarters," Bevan said, his gray-eyed gaze on her face. "Do you want to bunk in with them, or would you prefer your old room back?"

No hint of anything untoward in his voice, and he asked the question as if it were the most logical thing in the world, but once again Judith sensed that aura of gamesmanship. Or maybe it was simply a furthering of his claim. Either way, it served to fuel her concerns at her role in what was to come. It seemed too logical that she would become a pawn in what could only be described as a fiercely competitive macho contest.

"Where everyone else is, of course," Judith said, knowing it was really not her first choice and half afraid Bevan knew it too. But she couldn't compromise herself any further, and staying in the house with Bevan while the rest of the team bunked in together would be the height of folly.

"Well, let's get at it then," was his simply reply, and he strode to her rental car and began hefting out the various items of her gear and Derek's. "I expect we'll want a full-scale strategy session now that everybody's finally here," he said. "So I've laid on tea a bit early."

It fell to Bevan to make the group introductions, since he alone had now met everyone to be involved in the expedition. And he kept the occasion light and informal despite visible signs that an undercurrent of tension already existed.

Judith was not surprised. *This is like trying to mix oil and water. Or worse, sparks and gasoline. Talk about volatility!*

On the conservation side, Jan Smythe was a springy, nervy blonde whose only interest seemed to lie in her role as chief technician for the myriad cameras and motion sensors. Reg

Hudson was tall, lanky, slow-moving and quiet, but his placid pale-blue eyes held the intensity Judith had so often seen in committed conservation zealots. Ron Peters was exactly what she might have expected—bearded, militant, and aggressive. He looked and sounded exactly the type to be dumping sand in logging equipment fuel tanks or spiking sawlogs in a bid to make things difficult and dangerous for forest workers.

I'm surprised this one and Bevan haven't already come to blows, she found herself thinking, and then found herself even more surprised at how diplomatic and at ease Bevan seemed to be with all his visitors, including the truculent Mr. Peters.

Roberta Jardine, who was expected for tea with a promise of fresh-baked scones and bread, apparently had already met everyone but Derek, and the final member of the "establishment" team, Ted Norton, was a tall, emaciated, very quiet, very old man who said almost nothing, but whose washed-out blue eyes missed nothing either. He would have to be, Judith thought, in his late eighties or even older, and he looked as if he'd been put together from old leather and fencing wire.

"I've said this before, but it bears repeating," Bevan quietly emphasized after finishing the introductions. "When it comes to the bushcraft end of things, or if anybody gets into any kind of situation where survival skills are required, Ted's your man. He's forgotten more about getting about in the scrub than most of us will ever learn."

Bevan grinned at them all then, devils dancing in his eyes.

"He's also, by the way, the only one here who's actually had his hands on a real live tiger—several, in fact—which is worth bearing in mind."

The statement drew the expected reaction from his audience. There was a tangible heightening of interest all round, and a glare from Ron Peters, who looked at Ted as if he were the devil incarnate. Peters appeared about to speak when the old man's quiet voice slid round the gathering as if on ice.

"Just for the record," he said softly. "I've never killed a tiger, nor tried to, nor wanted to."

His rheumy eyes swept from one newcomer to the other, meeting each in turn as if daring them to challenge the statement. Nobody spoke, whereupon the old man nodded sagely and somehow faded into the background. Judith didn't hear another word from him the rest of the evening.

Bevan merely continued grinning mischievously, then announced he had work to do and would see them all later. Derek took this as his cue to collect the greenies together—was it coincidence or a deliberate decision, Judith wondered after not being included—and led them outside, presumably for a more private setting in which to prepare for the evening's strategy meeting.

Old Ted Norton picked up some leather he'd obviously been plaiting and followed them outside, although Judith noticed he turned away in a different direction. Judith was left on her own to find a vacant bunk, stow her gear, and then wander out and sit beneath one of the huge pine trees in the house yard, where she pondered the day's events and wondered about those to come with the evening.

To think much beyond that, she decided, was tantamount to folly, and wondered if Jeremiah Cottrell had any conception of the explosive forces he'd schemed to bring together with such a disparate group on such a mission.

"There is no way this group can get along for six days, much less six months," she muttered. And silently wondered how Bevan Keene expected to keep the two factions—so clearly at loggerheads before the expedition had even begun—from erupting into open warfare.

She was sitting, eyes closed and mind busy composing possible openings for the stories yet to be written, when some silent, inner warning system roused her and caused her to stare wildly about her with alarm.

16

"Don't tell me they've turfed you out of the inner circle already," said Bevan Keene. "And by the way, you'll get a crick in your neck if you take naps in a position like that."

"I haven't been—." Then she stopped, suddenly unsure. *Had* she been napping?

Bevan's expression said she had. His grin widened, a sure sign he'd caught her out and was going to enjoy rubbing salt in the wounds.

"You've been asleep about twenty minutes, by my reckoning," he said, and she saw the devils come into his eyes as she flinched at the realization he'd been watching her so long. "Although I'm sure you'll say you were just resting your eyes and pondering the wide range of disparities in our little band of happy wanderers. Fair bit of room for thought there, eh?"

"It is certainly going to be an interesting mix of attitudes and personalities. I don't envy you the job of keeping the peace."

Now the devils in his eyes laughed with him. "Keeping the peace isn't part of my contract, Judith Theresa. It would have to be in yours, if anyone's, since you're allegedly the only truly neutral figure in the drama. Presuming, of course, that you're really as neutral as you say you are."

"Meaning, I presume, that you don't believe I am?"

Judith was fully awake now, although becoming so had only served to heighten her defensiveness and the curious feeling of vulnerability at the knowledge that Bevan had been able to observe her for so long without her being aware of it. As he could have, and likely did, from his hunkered-down position against a nearby tree trunk.

"Meaning I hope you're not fooling yourself about this entire performance," he said, one eyebrow arched in skepticism. "It isn't going to be any tea party, and I just hope you realize that."

"I realize I'm already getting a bit sick of you setting me up to be the meat in the sandwich," she replied hotly. "Not that it will do you any good," she continued, lying now, but convinced of her ability to hide it. "However, I will say this once, for the record. I have no intention of being used, not by you, not by anyone! And I will not be some sort of weapon, or victim, in whatever hostilities eventuate between you and Derek, or anyone else for that matter!"

"Hostilities?" His voice trilled with false innocence, and his eyes laughed in accompaniment. "Whatever do you mean, Judith Theresa? Hostilities?" He shook his head in apparent amusement.

"You know very well what I mean," Judith said, but had to admit privately, in her mind, that even she didn't really know exactly what she meant, only that all logic suggested Derek and Bevan could never, ever, be what she would term compatible. And, she reasoned, Bevan knew that as well as she did, whether he chose to admit it or not.

"I know what you think you mean," he said after what seemed a year of silence, a year in which his eyes seemed to darken into pools she could willingly have drowned in. "But I have to say this, Judith Theresa, just so that we understand each other. Your little mate Derek isn't going to cause any hostilities and neither am I, for that matter. He isn't worth the effort."

Judith didn't know what to say. Bevan's assessment fit too closely with her own newly discovered knowledge of Derek and how Derek operated, now that she'd seen him afresh, with the clear vision of distance and time. He wasn't really that important. He was—

"Nothing more than a politician, after all," Bevan said, and she couldn't stop the strangled outburst of laughter those seven words provoked, because he'd used her own terminology. Bevan watched quietly as she huffed and howled until the tears poured down her cheeks, and when the spasms had subsided enough so that he could be heard, he said, "I wouldn't have thought it was all *that* funny."

"Because," Judith gasped, "you don't know *why* it was so funny."

And never will, she thought. How could he? She would never dare to admit she'd been thinking of Derek in exactly that word—politician—when she'd been so quiet and distracted at her cousin's dinner party, much less how striking she had found the difference between Derek and Bevan himself.

"You might try explaining," Bevan said, fishing.

"I could, but I won't. Except to say there's an even more descriptive word for him. 'Wolverine.' "

Bevan lapsed into concentration, obviously comfortable in the situation, not at all threatened by having to sit and think about what she'd just said. It was this quiet self-confidence, Judith thought, that was among his major charms. He was secure in himself, not afraid to admit that he wasn't perfect, and he didn't have to put himself forward as a know-it-all. The silence lengthened, flowing between them now like a broad ribbon, almost visible. Bevan's eyes were on her, but his focus was not. It gave Judith time to observe him without seeming overly curious. And she took it, letting her gaze roam across his face, letting her gaze touch the flaring mustache, the strong, thrusting chin, the sensuous mouth. In his neat khaki work clothes, he seemed a curious combination of rural and urban. His hands were work roughened but his face revealed a complex sensitivity. She allowed herself the luxury of stroking him with her eyes, touching the crisp hair in the hollow of his throat, the muscular chest and flat stomach. Then she dropped her gaze to his strong thighs before moving upward again, always with half an eye to ensure he was still in that thoughtful trance and didn't catch her at it.

By the time she reached his eyes, he was still lost in thought. And then, abruptly, he wasn't. She actually saw the focus of his eyes change, realizing as she did so that he had just caught her staring at him.

"Wolverine," he said, mouthing the words as if he was reading from a blackboard in his mind. "Nasty little North American beastie, cousin to the weasel. Famous for destroying what it doesn't eat itself, usually in a manner most foul. *Carcajou,* in French."

Then he looked at her, looked into her, and nodded his head sagely. And he understood. Judith knew without another word being spoken that he knew exactly why she'd used the term wolverine as a synonym for Derek.

"Yes, I can see how the description would fit most politicians," Bevan added.

No mention of Derek specifically, and Judith knew there wouldn't be. Bevan had achieved his understanding. He knew it and he knew that she knew it too, but he wouldn't beat her over the head with that knowledge, didn't have to. To do so would serve only to boost his own ego, and Bevan didn't have that type of ego, that type of destructive need. Not like Derek.

The sound of an arriving vehicle shattered the moment, and Bevan heaved himself upright, then crossed the small distance between them and held down a hand to Judith.

"That'll be Roberta with the best home-baked bread in Christendom," he said. "Let's help her with the rest of the tucker, and once we've got this mob fed, we can get the show on the road."

Lifting Judith easily to her feet, he kept her small hand enclosed in his own as they walked round to the shearing quarters, where Roberta was already unloading what appeared to be food enough for an army. She swung around at their approach, a greeting for Bevan on her lips. But Judith saw it falter, then divide to include them both, and noticed also that it ended nowhere as effusively as it had begun.

It was only when they paused directly in front of Roberta, Bevan exclaiming at the splendid aroma of the fresh-baked bread and scones, that Judith realized he was still holding her hand, that he had been doing so ever since helping her to her feet.

She flushed at the realization, but her attempts to dislodge his grip were wasted. Despite Roberta's scowl, he kept Judith's palm in his grasp long after it had become obvious to everyone that she was trying to free herself.

And when she finally did manage, he grinned down at her with those damned devils laughing from his eyes, clearly enjoying the exercise of making her uncomfortable, putting her off balance.

And, she wondered, did he also enjoy making Roberta Jardine feel the same? It seemed that he did, but to what possible purpose?

17

Dinner that evening was, Judith thought, one of the strangest, most astonishingly weird experiences she'd ever had involving food.

It was like something from an off-beat movie, both real and unreal, familiar and yet totally strange. Again, as she had since the beginning, she was struck by the sheer incongruity of the people and the situation into which they were heading.

The enticing aroma of Roberta's fresh bread must have permeated the entire farmstead because moments after her arrival the various members of the party began to straggle in from all directions, sniffing appreciatively.

Derek and his crew were, as expected, together, and Judith assumed there had been some fairly intensive discussions since the Queenslander's arrival. The group entered the dining room together with the Tasmanian contingent almost protectively behind Derek, a subtle but significant move that indicated they had already accepted his leadership. And he knew it!

Judith knew him well enough to read that extra hint of authority in his stride and bearing. Gazing round the room, she realized too that nothing was quite as subtle as she had originally thought. Old Ted Norton was glancing round with a look on his face that suggested he, too, was aware of the tension in the air, and once Judith caught Roberta sending an anxious glance to where Bevan presided over the cooking of steaks and chops for those who fancied such food.

For the vegetarians, who turned out to be Jan Smythe and the ever-scowling Ron Peters, Bevan turned out a very impressive rice dish, and with it a quiche that would have done credit to any restaurant. But when complimented on it, he retorted, "Don't let this go to your heads. Once we get out in the bush, it'll be share and share alike when it comes to cooking duties, and I'll expect as good in return."

Then he winked at Judith and added, "Except that those who don't or won't eat meat won't be expected to cook it. Or allowed to. I don't mind the occasional feed of rabbit tucker, but I'm damned if I'll have my carnivorous tastes upset at the hands of infidels."

He grinned hugely to show he meant no real hostility, but it was a gesture largely wasted. Jan Smythe ignored the jibe entirely, and Ron Peters's scowl was largely unchanged. The others in the room merely smiled politely.

Conversation during the meal remained fairly mundane as everyone present strove to avoid friction. It would, Judith couldn't help thinking, have made an exceedingly boring dinner party. But once they'd reached the coffee stage—herbal tea for the truculent Ron Peters—things livened up considerably.

Bevan kicked things off by reading various e-mail correspondence from Jeremiah Cottrell, as if to remind everyone specifically of the chain of command and their various roles in what was to come.

"That's the official version," he said. "But in the field, I suspect we'll find things working out a bit more flexibly." Which was the opener to a round-table discussion that ranged from the esoteric to the blatantly ridiculous, provoking howls of outrage at some moments and howls of laughter at others. Even the laconic Ted Norton was seen to smile.

They thrashed things out from every possible viewpoint, it seemed to Judith, then turned everything upside down and started again. Voices were raised, invectives hurled, insults exchanged. Why there weren't fist fights, Judith didn't know. At one point she was certain there would be when her own neutrality was called into question by, of all people, Derek!

The comment drew an angry glare from Bevan, apparently on her behalf, but before anything else could happen the conversation had veered ninety-five degrees and was off to somewhere else.

At one point, Bevan produced several cardboard casks of wine and some glasses. At another, Roberta slid between potential antagonists bearing a platter of assorted biscuits and cheeses. And finally, well into the small hours of the next morning, there was a semblance of agreement: they would spend the next day—today, actually—packing and sorting out, then move out the following day for a trial run of the equipment and their proposed program for the tiger search.

Which was how it went, although it had to be admitted that the day of packing and sorting and organizing was of questionable success. Almost everyone suffered from too little sleep, too much wine and/or arguing, and far too much confusion.

"This is all your fault." Judith found herself complaining to Bevan later in the day, when it seemed everything that could go wrong had, and what hadn't yet was on the verge of doing so.

"My planning, not my fault." He smiled at her through remarkably healthy-looking eyes. Although he and Ted had done their share of damage to the long-deceased wine casks, neither had shown the slightest effect since rising before dawn. The same could not be said of Derek and his crew, all of whom spent the day nursing headaches and suffering from lack of sleep.

"The logic of it totally escapes me," Judith insisted. "I would have thought things were volatile enough last night, and then you had to go and start them on the vino. What were you trying to promote? A full-blown riot?"

"Just a mob of happy little vegemites, which I got. Just look at them. Not a harsh word among them, quite splendid co-operation, no hostilities at all."

"No energy, no get-up-and-go, either," she replied hotly. "They're too damned tired and hung over to fight, that's all."

"Whatever works. They got most of their hostilities out of their systems last night, and that's the main thing. Better that than spend the next week with it all stewing and burbling away inside everybody. We'll have enough problems when we go bush as it is, including pent-up hostilities."

The two of them had paused for a quick coffee and now rested in the shade of the huge pine trees. It was a much-needed rest since they'd been on the go since dawn with only the briefest halts for meals. Breakfast had been very much a catch-as-catch-can situation, with everybody expected to help themselves. Few had seemed able to summon up the energy.

"I don't think most of them realized you were orchestrating much of that performance last night," Judith said, suddenly forced from silence by the realization of how Bevan was looking at her. His eyes seemed like deep, gray pools, but their increasingly strange habit of luring her to stare into them was disconcerting.

"I'm not surprised," he said. "After all, you didn't realize it until just a minute ago." And he laughed aloud at her expression.

"I . . ." She had to let it go. He was right, and to argue would only make it worse. She was tempted to just keep quiet, knowing he had the upper hand for the moment and wouldn't hesitate to use it. Except . . . he kept *looking* at her.

"I was afraid at one point that you'd gone too far," she ventured. "There was a moment when I half expected you and Derek to . . . uhm . . ."

"Come to blows? As in fisticuffs? Over you?"

Bevan's expression was so bland, so totally innocent, that for a moment she wondered if he even remembered the incident. She was not long confused.

"Ah, you mean when he started in on you and your questionable neutrality. Hell, Judith Theresa, I wasn't going to hit him for that." And his grin broadened. "I was actually more afraid of having to jump in and protect *him* from *you.*"

Bevan was clearly enjoying her discomfort. "After all," he said, "I could hardly go about hitting him for thinking almost exactly the same thing I was, could I?"

Judith could only sit and stare at him. Her mouth was capable of moving—in fact she was certain her jaw had dropped and she was sitting open-mouthed—but she couldn't find or form the words of any sensible reply. In her mind, however, the words flowed easily enough for her to think. How dare he question her neutrality? And what was this rubbish about protecting Derek from her? Nonsense.

"Actually, it was quite an informative evening all round," Bevan continued. "I learned that your boyfriend is hard to provoke, but he can be led into indiscretion, no doubt about that. And I'm fairly sure now that I know where the biggest problems are going to come from during the next several months, or, more correctly, who they're going to come from. And then, of course, there is what I learned about you . . ."

He let that sentence slide into completion like the end of a disappearing act, obviously savoring the malice in the gesture. Judith wasn't even tempted to bite. She was still seething about what he'd said earlier.

The problem was knowing the truth of it and having to deny it at the same time. Of course she was biased, in the sense that she felt certain Derek would attempt to manipulate this project to his own advantage no matter how it turned out. But that, she determined, at least to her own satisfaction, was distinctly different from being biased in the way Bevan had implied.

"I am inclined to think—using one of your unique Australianisms—that you've both got kangaroos loose in the top paddock," she finally said. "Or maybe it's your own biased view of all journalists that's showing. I am strictly neutral in this. I intend to record things exactly as I see them, exactly as they happen."

"I hope you can stick to that," he replied with a wry grin. "But just remember, Judith Theresa, what happens to people who sit on the fence too long. You have far too lovely a rump to have it all scarred up by barbed wire."

And before she could think of a reply he was gone, on his feet and moving like a great predatory cat, walking away without a backward glance.

18

There was no partying that night. Everybody was quite obviously pooped by the time all preparations were completed and the sun long past setting. Bevan's announcement of a pre-dawn start was greeted by sighs of dismay, but no obvious dissent, and everyone was abed as early as they could manage.

With all the gear already loaded, they were able to be on the move in accordance with his deadline, and by sun-up the ill-assorted fleet of vehicles was deep in the scrub, fighting their way along apparently little-used tracks to some vague destination known only to Bevan and old Ted Norton.

Bevan and Derek led the convoy in Bevan's battered old four-wheel-drive, followed by the greens in an equally battered Land Rover. Judith and Roberta were jammed in with Ted in a vehicle of uncertain pedigree and vintage that was clearly designed to provide anything but comfort. Dust both inside and outside the machine obscured much of their vision as the truck lurched and groaned at the tail of the procession, giving Judith the impression it might expire from exhaustion or old age at any moment.

Ted, taciturn as ever, made no attempt at conversation. He grunted every once in awhile at some maneuver by the vehicle ahead of them, but whether in approval or contempt was impossible to determine. Roberta seemed equally happy to make the journey without trying to talk over the noise of the engine and the creaking, groaning, rattling bodywork. Judith, jammed between them on what remained of the front seat, was too busy hanging on to care.

The journey seemed endless, not least because Judith was more than half convinced she could have walked almost as fast and in a great deal more comfort. When they descended a steep cutting to cross a rock-strewn and almost-dry stream bed, she could only sigh with relief to find the first two vehicles halted and preparations underway for morning coffee.

It was no surprise, somehow, to find the track got worse from that point, and worse still after the short break Bevan allowed for lunch. Much of the time, Judith wasn't sure there still was a track, though of course Ted had only to follow those ahead of them.

On and on they went, the vehicles rolling and pitching like ships on a stormy sea, more dust inside than out and the questionable coil beneath Judith's "lovely rump" becoming increasingly intrusive as the day wore on.

I think that barbed-wire fence would be an improvement over this, she thought to herself at one point, and by day's end she was very nearly certain of it. But not so sure that she would admit to it when asked almost that exact question by the man himself when he strode over to meet their vehicle on arrival at the chosen campsite.

"You have a warped and evil sense of humor," she said hotly, accepting the hand he offered to help her down from the truck, then trying to ignore the easy familiarity with which he had offered the same assistance to Roberta. And the familiarity with which Roberta had accepted it.

Jealous? Stop this, Judith. Stop it now!

It was insane, she realized, to even think about being jealous, which didn't explain why it was happening. Whatever was between Bevan and Roberta was clearly of long standing and none of her business. All of which would have been easier to accept if her fingers hadn't tingled at his very touch and gone on tingling even after he'd released them.

Ridiculous, she thought, to thrill so easily to any man's touch. Worse, to be so sensitive to Bevan that he could stir her insides to jelly with a simple, direct look. As he was doing right this instant, having held onto her fingers much longer than necessary as he helped her down from the vehicle, having asked, with laughter in his eyes, if maybe fence sitting mightn't be preferable after all.

"You sound about as frazzled as you look, Judith Theresa," he said with a grin, reaching out to wipe at a smudge of dust from her cheek. "You should see yourself. You look like something the cat dragged in. Freckles upon freckles."

Judith flinched angrily from his touch. She had seen the layer of dust on Roberta and everyone else, knew her own face would look equally grimy, perhaps worse because of the freckles.

"It's nothing to laugh at," she growled, only to find herself positioned so she could see herself in the big side mirror of the truck. Her sunglasses removed, she looked all googly-eyed, like a demented raccoon. And, objections or not, decidedly laughable.

"Oh, all right," she grudgingly admitted. And broke into a grin of her own, shaking her head at the weird image in the mirror. "It is something to laugh at and I admit it."

"Nice to see you've kept your sense of humor," he said, now moving his gaze along a distinctly unlaughable tour of her equally dusty figure. It suddenly seemed to Judith that he was capable of dusting her off, especially in strategic places that actually cried out for it, with his eyes alone. They touched, caressed, appreciated. And infuriated.

"I really do wish you'd stop looking at me like that," she heard herself say, knowing it was silly to bother, a dangerous admission of his growing power over her.

"Like what?"

Like you want to eat me for dinner. And like you know I want you to.

And his eyes twinkled, revealing all too well his amusement at her dilemma, his total awareness of that ability to influence her emotions.

"You know very well like what," she snapped. "And I don't know why you persist in doing it. It isn't accomplishing anything, and it isn't going to."

Bevan just laughed, white teeth gleaming from a face almost as dusty as her own. "Must be accomplishing something, or you wouldn't be getting so frothy about it," he said. And then, softly, insidiously, "And why on earth shouldn't I look at you, Judith Theresa? You're eminently worth the effort."

"And you're so full of it your eyes are brown," she snapped, turning away, knowing it was a form of retreat but unable to be sure that she wouldn't say or do something even more foolish if she stayed. She stalked away, feeling his gaze tracking her every step, his eyes touching like a caress along her flanks. Even his quiet laughter, which she could hear, was a subtle form of caress.

That laughter continued to bother her throughout the rest of the late afternoon as Bevan seemed to be everywhere at once, organizing the setting up of their camp. It seemed that everywhere Judith became involved, whether in helping to pitch a tent or store the various scientific equipment under proper cover, he was always nearby, always laughing, always watching her. At one point, finding him the only man in camp because everyone else was out getting firewood—at his instigation—she angrily muttered that he ought to be doing his share of the wood gathering. A wasted gesture.

"Organizers organize," he said, once again using his eyes to laugh at her, showing that he knew he was getting to her. "No sense having a dog and barking yourself."

To which she had, as he had obviously expected, no reply that wouldn't merely serve to make things worse. Judith had also noticed the curious glances sent her way from Roberta, who seemed to be enjoying the byplay. That was sufficient to make Judith determined to put an end to it if she could!

The layout of the camp was simple enough, having been determined before they'd left the property. The three women shared one tent, Bevan and Ted another, and Derek and the two local conservationists the third. A fourth had been brought to house equipment, and a fifth to serve as communal kitchen. Their first bush dinner was a haphazard but cheerful affair, enhanced by the anticipation of the next day's activities—their first real test of the equipment and the procedures that would see them through the coming months of the tiger hunt.

Jan Smythe was most visibly affected. Her photographic and technical specialties would be significant now, and she was obviously looking forward to it. Her bubbling enthusiasm permeated the camp. Jan was teamed with Ted Norton, whose local bush skills and experience, according to Bevan, would be sorely tested before the expedition was over.

"I'm not overly worried about whether Ted can find us a tiger or not," Bevan said during dinner. "The main thing is whether he'll be able to find whichever of you is the first to get lost, once we've gone bush for real."

The comment drew howls of protest from the entire conservation element. Even Derek, who'd never been to Tasmania before, was moved to an eloquent defense of his bush-craft skills and those of his companions.

"Nobody's questioning your competence," was Bevan's blunt reply. "I'm just reminding everyone of the simple fact that people do get lost, or have accidents. It can happen to you, me, or anybody else. Even the getting lost part. I suspect that although Ted would never admit it, he's been lost too, on occasion."

"Not true," was the denial in the firmest voice Judith had ever heard Ted use. "I've never been lost in the bush in my life. I've had a fair few camps get lost, and my truck's been lost so often it should carry one of those satellite gadgets. It got lost for an entire week, one time. But I've never been lost. I've always known exactly where I was."

It took a minute to sink in, but everyone eventually got the point and laughed. Judith did think, however, that at least some members of the group had to force their laughter just a tad. For her own part, she had no false confidence. She would not only be taking the warnings to heart, but would be extra careful to ensure she wasn't the object of any embarrassing rescue missions.

After dinner they sorted out the next day's agenda, which would involve splitting the party into two. Ted and Jan, with the cameras and sensor gear, would do a broad swing to the north and east of camp, with Reg and Ron serving as bearers, while Bevan, Roberta, and Derek made a somewhat less expansive expedition to the south and east. Judith was free to join whichever party she chose, although Bevan somehow managed to imply that he'd prefer it if she went with the others.

"We'll be taking some cameras and equipment," he said, "but mostly we'll just be out for a sticky-beak and a wander. Jan's the real expert here, and I'd prefer she and Ted combine their talents as much as possible."

"There is no way we can set out all the cameras in one day anyway," Jan said. "I expect there will be a lot of fine-tuning before we start to get any proper results at all."

The rest of the discussion was brief. Everyone was bone weary from the rough drive and the work of setting up camp, and they were all in their sleeping bags by nine o'clock. Five minutes later, or so it seemed to Judith—and she was not alone in her thinking—it was morning, or at least that dim, silent, almost unreal time of mists and half-seen shadows.

19

"It can't be morning already. I only just got to sleep," muttered Derek as he nearly trod on Judith emerging from her tent.

"It's an insane time to be getting up," grumbled the ever-surly Ron Peters, leaving Judith to wonder what sort of conservationists these people were, that they seemed happiest spending half the day sleeping.

Only Roberta seemed totally comfortable with the early rising. She was already halfway through getting a hearty breakfast together when Judith entered the cook tent. "At least we've got half decent weather for the beginning of it all," she remarked, her smile broad and genuine, her elegant beauty obvious even in the bush shirt and jeans she wore.

"Uhm," Judith replied. Such cheerfulness was frightening. She knew herself to be barely able to communicate without several cups of coffee inside her, and her glance strayed immediately to where a huge pot of that vital brew was steaming.

Roberta was busily laying out the tables and preparing the various ingredients for what seemed an enormous breakfast, and Judith, once fueled by a few sips of coffee, offered to assist.

"Nothing much left to do. I've got everything just about ready, and if Bevan and Ted would hurry up and get back with the trout they promised me, I could start cooking. Which do you fancy? Steak and eggs or eggs and trout?"

Judith shuddered at the thought.

"I'll stick to coffee for now, thanks, and ask my stomach

when it finally wakes up. A bit of toast when it's ready might be good, though."

"You'll waste away to a mere shadow," said an all-too-familiar voice from behind her, and she turned to face an annoyingly bright-looking Bevan Keene, one hand occupied waving half a dozen pan-sized trout in front of her nose.

"Ugh. Take them away. It's too early in the morning to even think about food," she said.

"Might be the last chance you have until lunch," he said calmly, turning to hand the fish over to a much more responsive Roberta, who enthused over the offering. "I would have thought you'd be a proper breakfast person," Bevan added, "given your taste for rare steaks."

"There is a time and a place for everything."

"And everything in its place. Yes, I know."

He was totally unflappable, Judith thought, which was doubly annoying at this hour.

"And the time for eating is now because Bevan's right," said Roberta, a huge frying pan in her hands. "We might none of us even get back for lunch, and I'm certainly not packing any cut lunches, so you'd best forget your squeamishness and get around some of this. It could be a long time to the next proper meal."

Jan Smythe entered the tent—and the discussion—with a totally disinterested glance at the fish and the thawing steak all ready to be cooked. "If you all had the sense to be vegetarians, we could be finished breakfast and on our way by now," she said, pouring herself a cup of tea and throwing muesli into a bowl.

Judith's own folly in ignoring a hearty breakfast was screaming insults at her even before their brief stop for morning tea. At first, finding herself less and less able to keep up with Jan's party despite their heavy loads, she thought it was simply her lack of recent exercise, but when she staggered into the rest break with sweat pouring from her and her legs like string, old Ted was the first to comment.

"Tomorrow, you'll eat," he said. "Your body isn't used to this, and you put yourself at a disadvantage before you even started by not eating."

Jan was more practical, offering a grateful Judith substantial helpings of the trail-mix she'd packed to serve as lunch and snacks for herself through the day.

Being hungry was only one part of Judith's problem. More important was trying to figure out what, on a day-to-day basis, her role as official recorder might actually mean. There was little enough to record, except a lot of tramping around in the scrub, and since she couldn't be with both parties at once, she could only do half a job at best. She was also finding it difficult to determine her status amongst the other members of the two groups, since both "leaders" clearly distrusted her neutrality. Derek seemed sure she was on his side but didn't trust her, and Bevan was equally sure she stood with the conservationists and didn't trust her either. That rankled.

Derek, she knew in her soul, was going to do his best to manipulate the project, but she couldn't figure out how. It would be first for his own benefit, but beyond that everything made little sense because she couldn't figure out what he could possibly do.

And Bevan was also scheming. He wasn't as obvious about it, holding to his group's stated intention of keeping the expedition honest and above board. But he was scheming just as much as Derek, and this was his turf, after all.

And neither of them trusts me. I suppose it's no more than I should expect, to be fair—except who wants to be fair?

But even that degree of self-honesty didn't override the fact she felt somehow soiled by Bevan's assumption she was part of the enemy camp.

"I am not biased. I'm not," she muttered aloud as she panted along behind Ted and Jan, and it wasn't until Ted dropped back to ask if she was all right that Judith realized to her horror she'd been chanting the declaration in time to her plodding footsteps. Ted didn't comment, but the look in his eyes told her he had both heard and somehow understood exactly what she was on about.

They were back in camp by late afternoon, footsore and weary but also flushed with enthusiasm at the success of the day's work. A full dozen cameras, both still and video types, had been set out using the latest in solar technology to provide power for the cameras and sensor equipment.

Judith found everyone's enthusiasm a bit overwhelming, and Ted Norton was even less amused. "This is only a shake-down cruise," he was heard to mutter. "We'll be lucky to get anything but pictures of devils and wallabies, and all that'll prove is that the equipment is working."

"You never know your luck," was Bevan's reply, and Judith noticed that when he said the words, he was looking across the evening campfire at her, and his eyes were putting a quite different meaning to his words.

20

Bevan had been watching her ever since their return to camp, almost as if he was expecting something, but what? During dinner, it became so unnerving Judith almost stood up and walked out. She had the feeling she had somehow become the butt of some terrible, malicious joke, only no one was laughing.

Now, the entire atmosphere altered by the eerie flickering of the fire and the night shadows and noises, she decided Bevan was trying to rattle her, and she was equally determined not to let him get away with it.

She got a sort of chance when she caught him deliberately leading the conversation round to where he gently but firmly pointed out that the area directly west of camp was, as of now and until further notice, totally off limits to everyone.

"We stay this side of the creek and out of that west gully entirely," he said, looking from face to face, making firm, direct eye contact until he seemed satisfied with the level of acceptance.

"But why?" Judith protested, making the objection for the sake of doing so, and certain he knew it.

"Because I say so," was his blunt reply. "All will be revealed at the proper time, but for the moment I must have total cooperation from everybody. You'll just have to take it on trust that this is important."

Yeah, sure. And pigs do fly.

"I have a great deal of trouble taking things on trust," she insisted, still deliberately stirring the pot despite having no idea of the contents.

"So I've been led to understand," Bevan said, and his eyes flashed a warning of some sort before flitting to Derek and back again.

Alarm rose to choke off Judith's retort. Something was very, very wrong here, she decided, and her first reaction was to wonder what Derek had been telling Bevan. What lies? And—perhaps worse yet—what truths? Derek was, she knew, more than capable of twisting any truth to suit his own needs.

Suddenly she shivered uncontrollably at the brutal mental picture of Derek bragging to Bevan about his own involvement with Judith. It was no satisfaction to have that thought followed immediately by the certainty that Bevan wasn't the type to indulge in locker-room gossip. *How do I know that?* Still, the mere thought of such a ploy by Derek made her skin crawl.

"On second thought, I guess I might allow you to be the exception to the rule, considering your official capacity as recorder of the truth," Bevan suddenly said, bringing her to suspicious attention. He rose lithely to his feet and loomed specterlike across the fire, looking down at her. "Let's you and I take a moonlight stroll, Ms. Bryan, and I shall attempt to explain to you the logic of it all."

Not on your life, she thought, the idea of walking off with Bevan Keene into the darkness of the night suddenly terrifying. But even as she thought it, she was rising and moving around the fire to join him. Just as he'd known she would! His eyes laughed at her, devil's eyes in the red glow of the flames.

But he waited—thank goodness!—until they were out of sight and hearing from the others before taking her hand, the gesture provoking a curious mixture of emotions in Judith. It was both completely natural and innocent, considering the darkness and the circumstances, and also somehow threatening. Her first reaction was to accept his hand, but her second was to flinch at her own reaction to his touch. Her third was to pull back in trepidation.

"You're going out of your way to be difficult about this, Judith Theresa." Bevan's voice was whisper-soft but clear in the sudden silence of the night that cloaked them. "I wonder why."

"It isn't a matter of being difficult," she said. "I just don't want to take anything on trust. That's not what my job is about."

"Are you talking about me, or the concept in general?"

"From anybody!" She was firm in her reply, but cautious. She would trust Bevan with her very life, if it came to that, but she wasn't about to trust him when it came to any discussion involving her past relationship with Derek. Not even to assert the now total distrust she had of anything the conservationist leader might say.

"Your boy speaks very highly of your journalistic integrity," Bevan said, and Judith paused, tugging against his grip on her fingers as they moved along the narrow, ill-lit, forbidden track leading west from the camp. His simple remark was pregnant with unspoken possibilities, hidden messages. He was leading up to something, and Judith was dead-set certain she wasn't going to like it.

"He is NOT 'my boy,' " she snapped, angry at herself for letting him get to her, angry with him for trying, and the more so because of his success. "He is not *my* anything!"

"Uh huh."

Which to Judith's confused mind translated as, "That's not the way *he* tells it."

"Not that it's any of your business," she continued, half her mind wanting her willful mouth to shut itself and the other half wanting to scream out at him, to deny whatever Derek had said, to deny anything and everything.

"It isn't my business, I agree," Bevan said, voice infuriatingly calm. "But only as long as your personal situation doesn't start influencing our objectivity. There's a lot riding on this little junket, or at least there could be, and your objectivity might be the key to everything before all's said and done."

"Damn you! You're off on that hobby-horse again, questioning my professional integrity without any basis for doing so." The fierceness of her reaction wasn't only the result of injured dignity. She had suddenly become far too aware of the way his fingers gripped her own, and of the way his thumb seemed to stroke at the throbbing pulse at her wrist. And how ridiculously intimate it all was, and how she wanted him to stop and didn't want him *ever* to stop.

Whereupon he did stop. At least he stopped walking, only to turn Judith toward him and stare down into her eyes, his own features shadowed against the starlit sky above.

"No basis?"

His words seemed muffled, sounded as if they came from a great distance, like a vagrant wind. Perhaps because even as the words escaped his lips, those same lips swooped down to capture her mouth.

His kiss was forceful, demanding, but Judith knew instinctively that the demand had little if anything to do with the question that had preceded the kiss. This wasn't a question, it was a claim, a deliberately provocative gesture that was only confirmed when he eventually released her mouth so he could speak to her.

"I've been wanting to do that all the damn day," he said, his voice as soft as the black velvet sky above. Whereupon he proceeded, without waiting for any reply, to repeat the kiss, this time adding to its potency by the touch of his fingers along her spine, the warmth of his loins against her as he pulled her close.

His readiness was unmistakable. As was her immediate and instinctive response to feeling him swollen, hard, thrusting against her tummy, his agile tongue thrusting its way to a tryst with her own all-too-willing one.

Judith didn't try to fight her body's responses. Even as her mind questioned the logic of it, she was fitting herself into the embrace, thigh against thigh, her breasts crushed against the furnace heat of his chest, her hands moving to reach the muscular column of his neck, the sturdy bulk of his shoulders.

This is wrong, wrong, wrong! He's only manipulating me, using me. He's as bad as Derek. Worse! Because . . .

Because I'm damned well falling into lust with him, and I'm afraid he knows it. Because he's right, my objectivity is open to question, although not in any way he needs to be worried about.

Because . . .

The inner questioning slid away like smoke as her body took over, tingling and stirring to his every touch, flinging off any semblance of control as strong fingers stroked her breasts with infinite gentleness and other fingers played a tune along her spine and drew patterns of fire along the softness of her waist, tugging her shirt free so as to reach the skin beneath.

Madness!

And worse than madness. She could feel the growing maleness of him against her belly, throbbing in tune to the melody his fingers drummed along her spine. When those same fingers reached to unsnap her bra, she twisted not in opposition, but to ease his task, and when he reached to unbutton her shirt, to lift the bra so her breasts could thrill to the touch of sensitive, *knowing* fingers, the sigh that escaped her came straight from the core of her desire.

Bevan's head dipped so that he could take each breast in turn between his lips, his tongue rousing each nipple to a rigid, almost painful reaction that caught at her breath and made the velvet sky and white-hot stars swim in her blurred vision.

Judith threw back her head and closed her eyes against the

instability of the night above, but one treacherous hand slid down between them to clutch at the strength of him, marveling at the firm, tangible evidence of his desire. Now it was Bevan's turn to sigh, and his sigh was a groan of need, of wanting. He throbbed beneath her fingers, and his tongue against her nipple seemed to flutter in tune.

Madness . . . but delightful madness.

His knuckles brushed her own as his fingers traced a slow, deliberate, tantalizing track along the swelling of her tummy, then hesitated before loosing the waist of her jeans and running paths of fire along the smoothness of her panties, circling ever lower until they reached the moistness his lovemaking had created.

One finger slid inside her, its tip gliding up and back against her, creating a rhythm that throbbed through her entire body, vibrating, thundering in her head, trembling in her legs.

"Madness!" His whispered voice echoed her thoughts as he slowly, agonizingly, drew his fingers away, brushing aside her grip on him as he stepped back, away from her, no longer touching her, head tilted to stare into the night sky as he repeated the single word like a mantra. "Madness!"

Madness it was, but she didn't care.

"Not now. Not here," he said. "Our time will come, but this isn't it."

He didn't speak again until Judith had time to zip her jeans, to replace her swollen, over-tender breasts into confinement, to button her shirt, but when he did speak, there was no hint of apology in his voice, nor—thankfully—any hint of self-satisfaction, either.

"This isn't exactly what I brought you out here for," he said, finally looking down to meet her eyes, reaching out to take her hand again into his own.

"I'm glad you finally remembered that," she lied in a voice

still shaky, a voice that trembled along with her insides. Even as she spoke, she was thinking she must have lost her mind to have let this sort of thing happen. Especially now, with both Bevan and Derek obviously plotting and scheming at things which could only end up with her being the bunny!

"I'm not sure I am. Glad, I mean," Bevan said, then turned away along the track, his grip on her hand ensuring she would follow him.

They walked in silence then, Judith lost in a whirlwind of totally irrational thoughts and Bevan thinking . . . whatever he was thinking. She didn't want to know.

They moved quickly, considering the darkness, Bevan obviously confident of his orientation, surefooted as a night predator. Not surprising, Judith found herself thinking. Virtually every native animal in Australia was nocturnal. Why not him?

Suddenly the track ended in a broad, level clearing that was so specific it might have been deliberately carved from the surrounding scrub. And as they moved a few steps farther, it became evident to Judith that her impression was correct. The clearing was definitely man-made, and actually formed the turnaround at the end of a quite proper road.

Even in the starlight, it was obvious this road was far superior to the rough bush tracks they'd been lurching and bouncing and jouncing on for a full day just to reach this point, but the significance wasn't entirely clear, and her first thought was to ask why.

"It's a road," she said. "But . . . so what?"

"Well, for starters, it means we won't have to bush-bash another full day when it's time to head home," Bevan replied with a slow grin that was almost apologetic. Or downright sinister. "There's a passable track between here and camp, a bit rough but we can make it usable. Only it's obscured at that end. For now." And this time the grin was decidedly sinister.

Judith could only stare. What sort of convoluted mind did this man have?

"Are you telling me that we drove all day to get here, over those horrid, so-called tracks, eating all that dust, and we could have gotten here in less time and on a decent road? But why?"

"The best of reasons," he said. "Simple psychology. Because of the rough trip in, everybody who doesn't know better reckons they're now in something approaching proper, pristine wilderness, so they're acting accordingly. If they'd got here too readily, they'd be complaining that we might as well have done the testing in the scrub right behind the back paddock."

"Which we probably could have. I wondered before why we had to go to all this trouble, just to test a bit of equipment."

"Which we are!" And now the grin threatened to overflow. "If you and I set out to walk it, we could be watching the late evening news on the telly at home before that mob"—with a gesture behind them—"had barely got their swags warmed up. A swag is a bedroll, but you know that."

His laugh, now, was infectious. But scary. Bevan Keene was enjoying this far, far too much for Judith's taste.

"Actually, that's not such a bad idea," he said. "We could snuggle up on the sofa and—"

"You're . . . you're . . . impossible," Judith stammered. "You're as crazy as a . . . a—"

"Fox," he said, not bothering to hide his amusement. "And not really crazy; just sneaky is all."

"But why? What is the point of it all?"

"One point is to show you that I trust you, and that I want you to trust me in return," he said with a wry grin. "And it does clarify all those greenie claims about how great they are at bushcraft, doesn't it? Although maybe it's just that, being bushwalkers, they don't bother to consider directions when they're being driven." And he laughed again, softly.

"So we're not, as everybody was told, just on the southern edge of Ben Lomond National Park? We're—"

"Maybe half an hour from home as the kookaburra flies. Ben Lomond is that way," he said, gesturing with an expansive wave of one hand. "But because we're down in this little valley, you'd have to be part mountain goat to get to it, or get a sight of it."

Judith simply couldn't help it. The absurdity of what he'd done finally reached through the fog and found her funny bone. The laughter started deep down in her belly and rumbled up with ever-increasing, undeniable force. She could only just make out his next words as the almost-hysterical laughter took control of her.

"Of course it helped tremendously that the day was so cloudy," he said. "Even a good bushman could be excused for getting turned around a bit when it's cloudy."

And he said it with a totally straight face, the bastard! Judith finally gained a measure of control, but it took effort. "They might shoot you when they find out," she said, struggling for breath. "And you'll deserve it, too."

"It might be a small test of their collective sense of humor," he admitted. "But not the real test. That's still to come."

"Surely you don't mean there's more?" Judith gasped out the question, unsure if she dared believe what she was hearing. Did Bevan think this was all just some sort of game? She was suddenly struck with the thought of how she would be forced to try and explain all this in the written reports of the expedition. Not a welcoming thought.

"Fred," he replied enigmatically. "But Fred is something you really *will* have to take on trust. Even Roberta and Ted don't know about Fred—yet."

"Which means, I presume, that they both knew about *this* . . . this deliberate deception?"

Bevan's grin gleamed sharklike in the starlight. "I expect Ted might have twigged to it about halfway here. Maybe sooner. Roberta mightn't have been as certain until we actually got here. She's never been on the route we took, but she knew where she was when she arrived."

"So it's all been just one gigantic charade?" Judith found herself even more appreciative of the cunning involved, especially in light of Ted Norton's discourse during the day's long journey about tiger sightings and his early bush experiences.

"Ted even showed us a place where he said he'd actually seen a tiger trapped," she added with a chuckle.

"Don't make more of a meal of it than it deserves." Bevan's voice now serious. "Ted did see a tiger trapped there. He showed me that very place when I was just a little tacker. And tomorrow maybe I'll show you a place where I saw a tiger myself, or what I thought was a tiger, anyhow. I still think it was, or maybe I just fancy the delusion."

And he smiled gently down at her, reaching out to take her fingers in his large, strong hands.

"Make no mistake, Judith Theresa, this *is* Tasmanian tiger country. If such a thing still exists, we've as good a chance of seeing one here as anywhere in the state. Probably better, really, than where your little mate's planning for his 'proper' search. Nobody's being cheated by us coming here."

They made the return journey without talking, although Bevan held her hand the entire way and Judith made no attempt to forestall him. But her mind was no longer in tune with the situation. She found her thoughts awhirl at how strangely complicated everything was becoming.

It wasn't until they were in sight of the fire that the obvious question flashed into her mind, and by then it was too late to ask it. But even as she snuggled into her sleeping bag, already halfway to slumber, she found herself thinking it.

Fred?

21

Breakfast the next day was a slightly uncomfortable affair for Judith. She kept feeling that everybody was watching her, but she wasn't sure if it was because of her nocturnal stroll with Bevan, her inner guilt at the illicit pleasures now imprinted on her entire sensory system, or that other guilt—risen sure as the sun—at knowing something the rest didn't.

The crew spent the day following where Bevan, Roberta, and Derek had traveled the day before, locating cameras, sensors, and batteries, discussing the future plans for the expedition and toying with the myriad interrelationships that would be involved in turning such a disparate group into something approaching a real, proper team.

Which, Judith thought, was all laid on the shakiest of possible foundations. Bevan's game playing was hardly conducive to any sort of team spirit. Once his deception about their location was known, he'd be more likely to be strung up by the ears than accepted as any sort of team leader.

And for herself? She was beginning to wish she'd never come to Tasmania, had never—ever—encountered Bevan Keene, and especially never gotten herself involved in this ridiculous, ill-fated expedition to search for an extinct animal species that was more myth than anything else.

Her own role in the affair was becoming increasingly complicated. She felt compromised now by Bevan's disclosure, felt it had somehow forced her totally onto his side in the confrontation she knew must eventually happen.

When everybody made much of getting a photographic record of where Bevan had "maybe" seen a tiger when he was a boy, Judith was positive he was laughing at the lot of them, certain he was laughing especially at her, enjoying the way he'd involved her in his devious schemes.

I'm going to end up in the soup no matter how this all turns out. It's as if everything that happens is part of some grand design just to get me. And it's your damned fault, Bevan Keene, and don't think I don't know it, too!

Throughout the day, her mind kept returning to Bevan's deceptiveness and the elusive, mysterious "Fred." She was certain her gaze strayed to that taboo west gully so often when they returned to camp for lunch that everyone simply couldn't help noticing. Bevan noticed—that much she was sure of.

As well he should! Judith had no doubt his memories of their nocturnal ramble were as vivid as her own and was almost brought undone when she discovered that she could rekindle those memories in Bevan merely by pointedly staring at his crotch and letting him catch her at it.

The first time was by accident. She was lost in her own pleasant thoughts of the night before and scarcely realized her gaze was focused there until she saw the movement, could almost feel the growth of his sex beneath the moleskin slacks. Then she'd looked up to see his eyes fairly glowing with an unholy light of anticipation that matched her own.

By noon, she was reveling in this newfound power to excite Bevan Keene, this blatant control she had discovered. By mid-afternoon, the whole thing was starting to backfire. She began to feel the moistness between her thighs, could feel her tummy going all fluttery, was having too many daydreams about being alone with Bevan, of what they might and could and should and almost certainly would do, if only they could find the privacy.

The entire group walked the original line of cameras and sensors that afternoon, collecting and replacing film but making short work of the journey without having to carry all the equipment. It would be different on Monday, when it all had to be gathered up again.

The fact that each and every camera had been triggered brought an air of anticipation to the evening ahead. Everyone rushed through dinner and the requisite chores while waiting for Jan Smythe to disclose what was on the various videotapes. The cameras with digital film, for this test expedition, at any rate, would await downloading later. Full computer facilities would accompany them on their main search expedition once a location had been decided upon.

Judith personally thought the still-unresolved disputes about where to concentrate the main search were typical of the way the entire project was shaping up. The greens wanted to dedicate their energies to the so-called Tarkine Wilderness, a vast area of Tasmania's far northwest proposed for World Heritage status by the Wilderness Society. The historical aboriginal name for the area had only come into usage in late 1992—some said solely as an invention of the conservation movement—and the entire region was the subject of highly controversial disputes between the various conservation, forestry, and mining interest groups and lobbyists.

It was also, according to her own research, far from the most likely region to center a search for tigers, being mostly dense, wet sclerophyll forest or even more dense proper rainforest. Only in the buttongrass plains of the coastal region and a few fringe areas bordering on agricultural areas was there even possible Tasmanian tiger country. That was her view, and it was one shared by Ted Norton and Bevan himself.

"We're sitting right on the edge of the finest tiger country in the state right now," Ted remarked as they sat over a final coffee while awaiting Jan's readiness to begin the video show. "You've only to talk to those in the parks service who really know, and they'll tell you the most likely areas are between Goulds Country and Fingal, which is closer to here than you'd think, along with one area east of Cradle Mountain and another a bit inland from Burnie."

Judith looked around to be sure nobody was in close earshot, then leaned close to hiss her question at Bevan.

"Then why are we here? I thought you swore black and blue that no sane grazier would ever admit to seeing a tiger on his own property, much less take a search expedition out to look for one right in his own back yard. Aren't you taking a huge risk? I mean, what if we find one?"

"Life is full of risks," he replied with a cocky, disarming grin. But the look he gave her held messages that spoke of far different risks than elusive, extinct animals. His gaze was a bold, sensuous caress that touched like fire on her lips, her cheeks, her throat, then moved lower to pluck at her nipples, which thrust themselves hard against the material of her bra in an involuntary response she couldn't halt, couldn't even begin to control.

"But both you and Ted have said you'd seen tigers here, *right* here, right where you've got these people looking for them. You said yourself that if a tiger was found, unarguably, provably found, anywhere in Tasmania, they'd lock up the area and throw away the key."

"Which they would, or at least I'd hope they would," he replied calmly. "If they didn't, we'd have every ratbag poacher in the entire country down here trying to find and shoot the damned thing."

"And you out trying to shoot *them,*" Judith retorted, shivering inwardly at the memory of how she'd worried so much about him that night. Was it only weeks ago, when it felt like forever?

"Not the point," he said. "Okay, there's a margin of risk. I'll grant you that. But think about it, Judith Teresa. I've been wandering round this country for most of my life, and Ted's been doing it practically forever. Judging from our collective experience, the odds aren't much of this mob sighting a tiger in mere days. They're lucky to be able to find each other, by my reckoning."

"You make no sense," she insisted. "You should, by that logic, be arguing against us moving to the Tarkine Wilderness, but you're not. And you know as well as I do that on existing information we could be wasting our time if we continue the search there. Surely you can't expect me to believe you really want this expedition to succeed?"

"Well, of course I do." The vehemence of his reply smashed at her like a physical blow. "Bloody oath, woman, don't you think I've got better things to do than bugger about in the scrub with a bunch of conservationist wankers like this mob? You think I'm doing this just for my health? Of course I want us to find real, living proof that tigers have miraculously escaped extinction. It could be the saving of Tasmania, an end to the wanton resource mismanagement, maybe the one big chance that's left to return to sane land management policies in this state."

Bevan was breathing heavily, almost snorting through his mustache, and Judith had an irreverent vision of him head down, charging at a gate like some modern Minotaur. She had to stifle the giggle it threatened to provoke, then fought for something—anything—to say before she actually did laugh.

"What's a wanker?" she asked, keeping as straight a face as she could manage, averting her eyes so he wouldn't see the laughter in them. It was a fair enough question, although she'd heard the expression often enough that she knew very well it could mean anything from masturbator to lazy layabout.

"Not a word to be used in your dispatches from the front," Bevan replied. "Or even in polite company, truth be told. It means . . . well, let's just say 'idle time-waster,' shall we? That's close enough."

But his eyes said he lied, or at least was stretching the truth a great deal. Judith made a mental note to try the question on him again, sometime when he'd least expect it.

"Or better yet, some day when the time is right, I'll show you," he said, and the devils pranced in his eyes. "But this is definitely not the time," he added, with a sidelong glance to where Ted Norton was studiously ignoring them.

"Tell me again why you aren't arguing against us going to the Tarkine Wilderness," she said in a skilful change of subject that Bevan, cunning devil that he was, fielded with equal skill.

"The quickest way to force that issue to the wrong conclusion is to start arguing against it," he said, one dark eyebrow raised in a sardonic expression that could have implied almost anything. "In fact, I'm seriously debating whether or not to start insisting we do go there, just because it would be the quickest way I can imagine to make our happy little band of greenies change their collective mind. They're so damned convinced that we're the enemy—your good self excluded, I hope—that they're bound and bloody determined to do exactly the opposite of whatever they think I want, on the assumption I'm trying to steer them away from any real chance of success."

"And your little mate Innes has big plans to link his name with the Tarkine if he can find a way to make it a national issue like the Franklin," interjected Ted Norton, shooting a particularly venomous glance toward where Derek was holding court.

Judith bit like a ravenous trout. "He is *not* my little mate," she snapped before she had the chance and good sense to think better of such a response.

The retort brought a bark of laughter from Bevan.

"Careful, Judith Theresa, your journalistic integrity is playing up again," he warned. "And I'm not sure we've got enough antacid tablets in the camp to keep it under control."

"Journalistic integrity? I saw one of those in a zoo once," Ted Norton said, his eyes twinkling. "But I think it died without breeding. Just like the last tiger."

"The journalistic integrity I heard about got all emotionally involved with a journalistic neutrality and ended up with a bad case of fence sitter's disease," Bevan added somberly.

Judith fought for control and against the urge to stand up and run away, not to hide her anger, but to ensure that if she fell about laughing, it wouldn't be where either of these two potstirrers could get the satisfaction of seeing her do it! She was saved by the throaty roar of the portable generator. Jan Smythe was ready for action.

22

An hour later, Judith was half inclined to think she'd have done better to run away—it might have been more productive than looking at fuzzy images of what almost everyone agreed was the same Tasmanian devil caught by each of eleven different cameras! She knew for a fact that every individual Tassie devil had unique patterning within the mostly black-and-white fur, and this was clearly the same one.

"He's proper curious, that one." Old Ted laughed when the stocky little black-and-white animal peered nearsightedly into the lens of the last camera, then scuttled away into the shadows.

"It proves the cameras work," said Derek. A trifle too defensively, Judith thought. "And there's some quite good footage of native cats and wallabies, too."

"And that feral cat was a prize," Jan said, bubbling with delight at how well the equipment had worked, the failure to capture a tiger seemingly irrelevant to her.

"I reckon we ought to knock off a couple of wallabies in the morning and bait one or two of the camera areas." Ted directed his remark to Bevan, as if the rest of the crew would automatically accept the suggestion.

Bevan didn't even bother to look around. He didn't have to—the first squeak of outrage shot from Ron's lips with predictable venom.

"I protest!" he cried. "We're here on a scientific expedition, not a hunting trip. We just can't go around slaughtering native wildlife. It's . . . it's . . . it's absolutely disgraceful!"

Peters looked to Derek and Jan and the ever-quiet Reg Hudson for support. And got it, which didn't surprise Judith in the slightest. Nor did it seem to surprise Bevan and Ted, logically enough.

"Ron is right, of course," said Derek. "How would it look in the reports if we had to admit to slaughtering one sort of wildlife just to lure another?"

"Unthinkable!" Jan said it with an emphasis apparently shared by Reg, who'd been nodding vigorously if silently throughout the tirade.

Judith, positive now that Bevan had put Ted up to asking the question as much for the stir it would cause as for any real purpose, didn't bother to join the row. Anything she said would be misconstrued by one side or the other—then she wondered if that, too, wasn't part of Bevan's purpose.

Ted acquiesced—too easily. "You're probably right," he said. "Although my reasoning was that by baiting, we could keep that cheeky little devil and his mates in one place for a bit, if nothing else. And maybe keep him from following Jan around like a lost puppy dog. Let's have another think about it when we collect the videos tomorrow if all we get is repeat performances from our curious little mate."

"I am against the needless slaughter of native wildlife for any excuse," Derek insisted, totally ignoring Ted's comment now that he was on one of his hobbyhorses and about to set the spurs. "It simply cannot be justified!"

"Not even, I suppose, when the wallabies are eating you out of house and home?" Roberta had been silent, but now she spoke through clenched teeth, clearly struggling to keep her temper.

Remembering Roberta's comments about having so many acres, so many sheep, and so many *more* kangaroos and wallabies, Judith glanced around apprehensively, suddenly concerned this would develop into a full-scale shouting match. Or, as Ted would call it, a raging blue.

In her research and from discussions with various authorities, she knew there were numerous times and circumstances throughout Australia when kangaroo numbers reached plague proportions that caused immense damage to crops and grazing potential. Indeed, it was said the country had far more kangaroos now than had ever existed before white settlement had provided better grazing and improved water sources for the native animals.

In Tasmania, where the "Forester," a local subspecies of the Eastern Grey Kangaroo, were totally protected except under special permit, such damage was common, and the wallabies were so common throughout the island state as to be considered almost vermin by most graziers. There was a regular season during which wallabies were shot for pet meat, and many Tasmanians considered them equally good "people tucker."

"Don't you realize this is the only country in the entire world where people actually eat their national wildlife symbol? It's disgusting, absolutely disgusting!" Derek scowled.

He was getting into high gear now, and Judith braced herself for a proper slanging match. It was this sort of fanatical cant, she knew, which often brought conservationists and graziers to physical confrontation.

In which I'd bet on Roberta. She'd have you for breakfast, Derek.

She was surprised, although not disappointed, when Bevan, Ted, and Roberta didn't snap at the bait. They all looked at each other, eyes passing some silent message between them, but kept silent, whereupon the argument quickly died away from a sheer lack of fuel. And, Judith suspected, because everyone was physically exhausted from the day's activities. Certainly, the aura of antagonism around the camp faded as quickly as the echoes of the thumping generator, which Ted had insisted from the very start could be used only in emergencies and to run the video equipment.

"Anybody who wants to spend time in the bush watching bloody television can do it without me," he'd stated emphatically during the very first planning session, with an attitude that brooked no argument. "And the same goes for the wireless."

His truculent attitude was explained by Bevan's relating the tale of how Ted had once been weathered in during a prospecting trip with a much younger man and a transistor radio. "The boy survived because Ted kept him fed," Bevan had said. "The wireless starved to death in a matter of half an hour."

That night, everybody seemed glad enough to hear the end of the generator. They all headed for bed within minutes. Judith's tent companions were asleep in moments, but she slid into a series of erotic nightmares that were so vivid that she thought, in the cold light of dawn, she'd have done better to have stayed awake.

The worst part was not being able to remember them except as mingled images that were wildly erotic, exotic, and probably psychotic. Images of Bevan and her finally alone together, naked together, laughing and crying together. And mingled with that, images of wolves and Tasmanian tigers and even real tigers, all jumbled together in an orgy of sexuality that made no sense whatever when she awoke.

The next day, Saturday, was the first proper full day of monitoring. Everyone but Roberta trekked round the entire run of cameras and sensors, exchanging film and discussing the possible results with enthusiasm that seemed to expand visibly as each camera was found to have been tripped into use. But it was a long day made longer by the need to spend time sifting through each new video, only to find the same cheeky Tasmanian devil still intent on becoming a movie star.

Ted's cackling *I-told-you-so* laughter did nothing to improve the situation.

"The little bugger's got your number, Jan," the old bushman said during dinner. "I reckon we'll have to lay a bait or two just to keep him in one place. Otherwise, it'll be just more of the same. I think he's in love with you, myself."

Jan didn't seem enamored of the idea, and to Judith's discomfort, Bevan not only laughed, but seemed to take the comment as an excuse to resume his watching of Judith. Fair enough for him to be bored by the video show. He'd certainly seen as many wombats, Tasmanian devils, wallabies, and native cats in his life not to need more, but he spent the entire show looking at her, touching her lips, her cheeks, her breasts with his saucy glances. His smile tormented her, his occasional twisted, quirky grin promised things she'd rather not have thought about.

The issue of laying baits was raised again with breakfast the next morning, Ted insisting that if they didn't do something to occupy the curious Tassie devil's attention, they would only end up with more videos of the cheeky little devil at the expense of anything better.

"Nothing much else is going to travel around that area with our scent and his all over the place," Ted insisted. "And sure as damn it you won't have any hope of drawing in a tiger; I can guarantee you that."

"I am totally against it," insisted Derek. Not unexpectedly. "All the research is quite clear that tigers never return to a kill and will not take baits, but you want to go off and slaughter innocent wildlife anyway."

"Tigers don't usually return to a kill, and no, they aren't noted for taking baits, either," Ted said. "But they are known to investigate them. I can personally assure you of that. As for the innocent wildlife, if we don't give this devil something to occupy himself, he'll just keep on following Jan around disrupting everything. I'm sure the state can spare a wallaby or two in the interests of science and my poor old geriatric belly. Or didn't you know that wallaby is about the best meat a person can eat in terms of low fat and low cholesterol?"

"I do not *have* a cholesterol problem," Derek replied almost haughtily, "and even if I did, I certainly wouldn't use it as an excuse to go around destroying native animals."

After that, the argument began to escalate. Judith stayed out of it, and so—surprisingly—did Bevan, but Roberta and Ted both seemed to have awakened in a particularly frothy mood, and both were spoiling for a fight. They laced into the conservationists in a combined assault, Roberta citing documentary evidence about how many kangaroos ate how much grass compared to how many sheep, Derek responding with the argument that kangaroos did less damage to the environment than sheep, and Ted chiming in, occasionally, about the quality of 'roo and wallaby meat and its ultimate potential both for the restaurant trade and export markets.

When he tried to turn to Judith for support, she found Bevan watching her closely but making no attempt to interfere as she was forced—against her better judgment—to confirm much of what both sides were shouting.

I'm the meat in the sandwich here. And she decided moments later it was a particularly apt cliché, considering the way Bevan kept watching her and licking his lips.

As the participants grew more and more vocal in their argument, pans were rattled and the table thumped and voices raised to the point where Judith thought they might as well forget about seeing any wildlife at all that day because everything would have been alerted for miles around. The day before they had spent a half hour watching a mob of Foresters lounging in a warm, sunny clearing, and later an echidna rollicking his way along the track in front of them, safe in his armor of hedgehog-like spines.

But now, over breakfast, it was Roberta's unexpectedly vehement attacks on the issue that surprised Judith the most. Bevan's attractive neighbor, who truly deserved the cliché about being beautiful when angry, seemed to be deliberately fomenting the situation, her dark eyes flashing like black opal and her entire aura alive with energy.

At the same time, she continued her cooking and serving duties without missing a beat. While Derek was spouting off about protecting wildlife and the like, Roberta was snarling her rebukes and thrusting a plate of steak-and-eggs under his nose at the same time.

Ted Norton, Judith suspected, was just stirring for the sake of stirring. Or so she thought until he glanced her way with a particular mischievous twinkle in his eyes. Then she caught him exchanging glances with Bevan, who returned that mischievous look. Suspicion no sooner flared than it was confirmed. Ted returned to his now-hoary cholesterol argument. Derek, in the process of eating the second large chunk of steak to hit his plate, responded as expected, with nods of approval from his conservationist companions, and Roberta pounced.

"Right," she declared. "I've had just about enough of this rubbish. You have got cholesterol problems, Mister high-and-mighty Derek Innes, right between your ears! But if you don't want to eat wallaby, you shouldn't have to, and I'd be the last one to force it upon you—SO GIVE IT BACK!"

Judith nearly fell off her chair as the verbal missile found its mark. And she was not alone. Everyone sat mesmerized, their gazes switching from Derek to Roberta and back again as the conservationist leader absorbed the message.

At first he registered surprise, then his expression ran the gamut from utter astonishment to outrage as Roberta reached her hand toward his plate and its half-eaten steak.

"You . . . you . . ." he spluttered, his gaze flickering from Roberta to the plate and back again. "You mean this . . . this . . . this . . . I . . . I . . ." He couldn't manage to complete any statement. Words formed and reformed as his Adam's apple pulsated in tune to his obvious distress. Around the table, his companions stared at the offending wallaby steak as if it might suddenly bound off the plate before their very eyes.

Jan Smythe, the most confirmed of the vegetarians, swallowed a gulp that didn't want to stay swallowed, and with an anguished, apologetic glance at her chosen leader, fled the tent with one hand over her mouth.

Now that's an overreaction if ever I saw one. You haven't touched a bite of meat since puberty, by your own words, but you get sick because somebody else does? Judith, already having problems keeping from laughing aloud at Derek's dilemma, found Jan's reaction only added to the humor of it all.

"You had it for dinner last night, too," Roberta said with a sneer at the dumfounded Derek. "And you thought it was bloody wonderful, then! Flaming hypocrite!" Roberta's dark eyes flared with frank delight at his stammering confusion.

"But I . . . I . . . wouldn't have if I . . . I'd known!" His despair was almost childish, but he got no slack from Roberta.

"You wouldn't know if your ass was on fire," she snapped, snatching up the plate and dumping its contents into the rubbish bin.

Judith, who'd actually thought she was eating venison and was enjoying it thoroughly, looked down at her own plate and shook her head, more in wonderment at Roberta's outburst than anything else. Certainly not, she accepted blithely, with any feeling of concern about whether the steak was wallaby, venison, or spring lamb. It wasn't quite rare enough for her taste, but that was all.

Damned good steak, wherever it came from. I'll never be a proper conservationist, I guess. She speared another morsel and chewed it thoughtfully, holding back the urge to laugh at the horrified looks her actions gained from the remaining greenies.

A pall of silence hung over the large cook tent, tangible in its aura of discord and anger. The inhabitants seemed willed to stillness, sitting and staring at each other with something, Judith thought, approaching total disbelief. This time, when Roberta spoke out, it was to Bevan.

"I'm sorry, Bevan. I guess I've stuffed the whole thing up rather thoroughly, but I just couldn't take any more," she said, contrite now that the explosion was over. "I'm just not devious enough, I guess."

23

"I've never seen anything like it," Judith told her cousin Vanessa two days later, days in which preparations for the great tiger hunt took a ninety-degree turn that gave all participants a week off to regroup and replan.

"For a moment there, I thought Bevan would pick Derek up and shake him like the mangy dog he is," she continued. "But he just kept agreeing with Derek, and asking more and more questions, and adding more and more suggestions, and the next thing you know, Derek was agreeing with *Bevan* and everything had miraculously changed."

"It's called 'agreeing until you get what you want.' It's a feminine ploy you should know well enough, Judith. I expect Bevan learned it from his sister, and you'd have recognized it if you weren't so emotionally involved. And speaking of changing . . ."

Judith's no-longer rotund cousin had only been half listening, keeping one ear tuned to the nursery where the infant Judith and Bevan had been napping between feedings and now were making sounds of wanting to be changed—or fed some more.

A moment later, Judith was holding her namesake while the baby Bevan—"demanding to be first—typical male," according to Vanessa—was enjoying his first meal of the day before the subject of the other Bevan was raised again.

"So, have you slept with him yet?" Vanessa asked.

The question was so unexpected, not least coming from a

woman with a babe at her breast, that Judith nearly dropped the twin she was holding.

"Certainly not!" Judith managed to get the words out in what she hoped was a suitable denial, but she'd dropped her head to hide the blush provoked by the question, and had to repeat herself after Vanessa failed to hear her. Or pretended she hadn't heard. Judith's cousin was nothing if not devious.

Worse than devious. Vanessa had an uncanny talent for luring even total strangers into admitting the most intimate personal details. Judith knew she had to change the subject quickly or she might find herself admitting—*boasting, Judith Theresa. You'd be boasting!*—that she mightn't have slept with Bevan, but she'd come dangerously close and loved every inch of the experience.

The real problem was that thinking about sleeping with Bevan had never been far from Judith's mind since they'd left the bush camp in an exodus so cunningly orchestrated that everyone was back at Bevan's and deep in the planning for next week's return to the tiger hunt before most of them even realized what was happening. Bevan's revelation of the trick he'd played drew only polite laughter and insincere complaints about the unnecessary long trek they'd made to end up only a few minutes' drive from where they'd started.

And Judith had been the most confused of all. Still was. From the moment it had been stated openly that Judith was considered manageable, Bevan's attitude toward her had become steadily cooler. He designated her a seat in a different vehicle for the brief trip back to his property, had pretty much ignored her once they'd gotten there, and without actually saying one word on the subject, seemed to have shunted her squarely into the conservationist ranks.

So much for trust.

She'd thought, and uttered, far more colorful comments on his abrupt change in attitude during her long drive alone back to Hobart, knowing she was venting, suspecting she might be overreacting, but unsure. The sole saving grace of the journey was not having to share her vehicle with Derek or any of the other conservationists.

Vanessa's curiosity, however, made it difficult not to think of Bevan, and the blatant question brought forth a flood of repressed feelings Judith would have been happier to have kept repressed.

She was utterly, totally confused by his rapid change in attitude. She was hardly less specific in replying to Vanessa's next question, a question about trust.

"He's told me he trusts me, and he obviously expects me to trust him," Judith said, letting her anger spill into her voice. "But then he goes along with his plans, refusing to tell me anything! That's not trust, Nessie. That's blatant manipulation."

"You have so much to learn about men, Judith," was the calm reply.

Vanessa didn't divert her attention from the feeding frenzy, and the infant Judith held was writhing and fussing, clearly overdue for her own feeding.

"When a man says he trusts you," Vanessa continued, "he expects absolute, unwavering, blind faith on the subject in return. He doesn't expect to have to repeat himself constantly just to be sure you've gotten the message."

"There's damned little sense in me being the information hub of the expedition if nobody is going to give me any information," Judith said. "I'm telling you, something's going on that I should know about, and I don't, and it's driving me crazy, and your Mr. Bevan Keene knows that and doesn't care one whit so long as his planning isn't disrupted by it."

"He's not *my* Mr. Bevan Keene. He's all yours, and you're welcome to him," Vanessa replied. "I've got enough trouble with his godchild, here. The original would be too much to expect a new mum to deal with. And too much for you, too, obviously," she added as she adroitly disengaged her male infant—now finished with his noisy suckling—and swapped him for the girl-child Judith had been holding. "Here. Do something really useful and burp this monster."

Then, once baby Bevan was suitably burped and his sister happily attached, Vanessa said, "Maybe you *should* sleep with him. At least you'd be sure about getting his attention for a little while."

Judith gasped, more in pique than surprise. She'd already recognized that her cousin's sense of humor was typically Tasmanian in its directness and shouldn't be taken seriously.

"I'm not even talking to him until next week, and maybe not even then, unless he gets his act together and starts treating me like a professional instead of some sort of yellow-dog lackey for the green movement," Judith replied huffily. "And I have no intention of sleeping with any man I'm not even talking to."

"You Americans are very strange people," Vanessa said, amazingly oblivious to the fact that she was, at least by birth, one of them. Judith had already found herself astonished at times at just how thoroughly Vanessa had taken on the speech patterns and attitudes of her adopted country. "You take everything literally, and far, far too seriously. Be fair, Judith, at least to yourself. You have every intention of sleeping with Bevan, talking or not. You're in love with the man, which is hardly surprising. Why can't you just admit it and get on with things?"

"Once bitten, twice shy, that's why. And before you even ask, Nessie, I did *not* sleep with Derek Innes either, although it wasn't for lack of trying on his part. But at least when Derek was being devious, he was properly devious about doing it, not right up front and in-your-face like Bevan."

Vanessa's laugh tinkled through the room, nearly drowning the lighter sound of the doorbell. "I wish you could hear yourself," she said. "And you the professional communicator. You've got it bad, my girl, and unless I miss my guess, it's about to suddenly get much, much worse. Go answer the door, would you? I'm sort of busy here."

Judith crossed the room, cautious of the squirming bundle of baby Bevan in her arms, then nearly dropped the infant when she opened the door to find an adult, full-sized Bevan smiling down at her.

What are you doing here? Go away. I'm not talking to you. I don't even want to see you.

But she said, "This is a surprise," and stepped back to allow him into the house, drinking in the sight of him, reveling in the sight of him, even as she called out to alert Vanessa to their visitor.

Bevan was dressed for the city. An expensive Harris Tweed jacket over a ribbed, camel-colored turtleneck over chocolate brown slacks and the inevitable—if highly polished—elastic-sided riding boots favored by so many graziers. Good enough to eat, Judith thought, and had to shake the thought from her mind. *I don't care how pretty you are. I'm not talking to you!*

A huge, work-roughened hand reached out to gently touch the cheek of the sleeping baby she held, and the baby Bevan stirred slightly at the rumble of the older one's voice.

"Suits you," he said to Judith. "Is that one yours or mine?"

"*He,*" Judith said through gritted teeth, "is Vanessa's."

As well grit her teeth at the wind. Bevan didn't even blink, although he allowed himself the flicker of a wry grin.

"Ah," he said. "So that's the way of it." And marched calmly past her into the house, and towards the kitchen, his boot heels clicking on the tiled floor.

"What've you done to upset Judith, Nessie?" he called out. "She's gone all cranky, and it can't be just from carrying that ugly rug rat around."

"That rug rat is far more attractive than the man he's named after," came a reply from the kitchen, and Judith could only marvel at how Vanessa could remain so calm while trying to readjust her clothing and get the baby settled at the same time. Judith followed Bevan into the kitchen, his namesake slumbering now on her shoulder, and stopped dead at the sight of her cousin still calmly feeding the other twin and smiling up at Bevan.

"Now *this* Judith, you'll notice, is happy as a clam," Vanessa said, twisting so Bevan could see the part of the baby's face that wasn't clamped to Vanessa's breast "As for your Judith . . . well, maybe a change of formula would help."

Vanessa turned her attention to Judith, who wasn't sure if she was blushing because of Vanessa's remark or the situation in general.

"Goodness, Judith Theresa," Vanessa said with a grin. "Stop looking so shocked and horrified or you'll go all strange and drop my child. This man is a grazier, dear cousin. Do you think he's never seen an infant suckle before? Besides, Bevan is an old and *very* dear friend."

Judith couldn't find real words to reply. All she could do was stand there, stunned into silence, and try—as Vanessa had demanded—not to drop the baby. She knew the two adults were both laughing at her, knew she was supposed to fall in with the joke and laugh with them, but being in the same room as Bevan and all this intimacy had completely unnerved her. Even a lovestruck fool could see that Bevan's attention was on the baby, not the breast, and even a lovestruck fool couldn't fail to notice how gentle he was when he turned and plucked his namesake from Judith's shoulder, holding the baby aloft so he could compare the faces.

"Well, I guess they're twins," he said, handing back the baby to Judith but speaking to Vanessa. "But this one's better looking, more masculine, somehow. Although the filly's got Judith Theresa's hair. I just hope she has your temperament."

Which got him the laugh he was after, although Judith had to force it through clenched teeth.

"So, Bevan, what brings you all the way to Hobart at this hour of morning?" Vanessa asked, and Judith thought she could finally breathe again, dared to hope they were finished toying with her.

"I have business," Bevan said. "Some of it with your good husband, and some with my solicitor, just to be sure he isn't planning to abscond with my investments and run off to Cuba or someplace with his secretary. And I had thought I might take your ravishing cousin here to lunch, assuming she's agreeable."

"My ravishing cousin, in case you hadn't noticed, isn't speaking to you," Vanessa replied with studied innocence. "I am not game to ask why."

"Just as well, too," said Bevan. "Because it would probably force her into lies, damned lies, and obfuscations, and it's too early in the morning for that. Okay, I'll take you both to lunch. That way you and I can converse like adults and Judith Theresa can play mother hen to the rug rats and talk baby talk."

And that was that. Without Judith actually being consulted, it was somehow agreed that Bevan would return to take the lot of them to lunch. He was out the door and had the engine of his vehicle turned on before Judith could even think of anything she could have, would have, should have said!

Even worse, Bevan was a man of his word. Once they'd managed to get mother and babes installed properly at the family-run seafood restaurant where both he and Vanessa were obviously well known and highly valued as customers, Judith was indeed relegated to the role of babysitter while her cousin and Bevan discussed all manner of things she could hardly understand. And on the rare occasion the conversation did touch upon her, it was in the form of questions—very pointed questions—to Vanessa, inquiring about the history of twins in their family, and the predilection for red hair and questionable temperament. With Vanessa's seemingly innocent but blatant collusion, he played Judith like a piano all through the luncheon.

If she'd been cranky with him before, she was three times more so by the time they returned home and got the babies settled down in their cribs. By which time it was too late. Bevan didn't stay long enough to confront, and Vanessa pleaded a sudden headache and a need to go and lie down. Judith was left to stew in the juices of her own frustration, secure—for whatever that was worth—that she'd just been led down the proverbial garden path, yet again, by a man who seemed to take abnormal delight in rattling her chain!

She spent the evening trying to watch television, but her mind did the seeing, and it kept showing her images of Bevan Keene with Vanessa's babies, images of a man who clearly loved children, was comfortable with them, wasn't afraid to let the world know that. She was reminded of the old tale about the famous bullfighter surprised in his kitchen while doing dishes and wearing a frilly, quite distinctly feminine apron. When chastised for risking his macho image, the bullfighter was reputed to have replied, quite calmly, "*Anything* I do is macho."

And Bevan, too, was totally, undeniably macho, so secure in his masculinity that he did exactly as he pleased without regard for how it might appear to critics. He'd shown a similar strength of character throughout their days in the camp, a man rock solid in who he was.

Which would be wonderful if he wasn't so damned elusive about showing his trust, and if he'd quit playing me like a damned fiddle.

The thought brought Judith onto treacherous ground, mingling her intellect with her emotions, but doing nothing to resolve the way she felt. And to have Vanessa come right out and suggest she should sleep with Bevan as a way of sorting herself out! Judith could only shake her head in wonder at the temerity of the suggestion.

There wouldn't be much sleeping done, just for starters, dear cousin. If any!

Whereupon her imagination took over, and she found her entire body reacting as she recalled her earlier encounters with Bevan, his kiss, his touch, the way their bodies seemed to mesh.

There was no denying that. He had only to look at her that certain way and she *needed* him, wanted him, and could feel that need sending waves of desire through her entire body. The flimsiness and slithering touch of her housecoat only served to enhance the feelings, and she was aware with every movement of the touch of the material against her breasts, the smooth skin of her thighs.

Then she heard a soft *tap-tap*, a noise so tiny it nearly escaped her notice. Once—*tap-tap*. Then, as she listened intently, it came again.

Judith was already on her feet, the television clicked off, her feet pointed toward her appointed guest room, the first time she heard it. She turned, at first uncertain about what she'd heard, then heard it again, this time more distinctly.

A *tap-tap* on the front door. Not the doorbell, which might have made some sense, even at this late hour with everyone else in the house long abed, but just that tiny, almost audibly invisible sound. *Tap-tap*.

Barefoot, she tiptoed cautiously to where she could peer through the spy hole in the front door. She wasn't afraid, not even overly cautious. This was Hobart, Tasmania, not the wilds of New York City. But still . . .

And, quiet as she was, she must have made some sound, because what she heard next was her own name, whispered seductively in a voice even quieter than the taps had been.

"Judith? Judith Theresa?"

She peered through the spy hole, already wondering why she need bother. She knew who this was, knew it from the first whisper, confirmed by the second as her name was breathed in a caress only one person could create. A glance confirmed it, and she opened the door to confront the late-night visitor.

24

"Damn it, Bevan Keene, what are you doing?" The words were out of her mouth before the door was fully open, and Bevan stepped back, briefly, before pausing to shrug aside the force of her verbal assault.

"I've come to beg a bed for the night, Judith Theresa," he said in a voice much quieter than her own. "Hardly a thing to damn a man for, I wouldn't have thought."

"It's the middle of the night, for God's sake!"

"Which is a logical time to seek a bed, is it not?" His teeth gleamed in a flickering smile and the light danced in his eyes as his glance roved across her scantily clad body. "Looks like you're headed in that direction."

"Yes. And alone," she said, fighting the softness that flowed through her tummy, wanting to clutch at the nightgown so it wouldn't reveal the way her nipples responded to the touch of his gaze.

And he noticed.

Of course he noticed; the man reads me like a book and plays me like a fiddle!

"And besides," she added, "there's no room for you here. I'm in the one guest room and the other, in case you've forgotten, is now a nursery."

"Of course I know that. I've been coming here for years," he replied glibly. "But there's a couch, isn't there? All I want is a place to lay my head for a few hours, then I'll be up and away and out of your hair. Honest. But I'm too damned tired right now to try and make the drive home. It wouldn't be safe for me or whoever else is dumb enough to be out on the roads at this time of night."

And without waiting for her reply, he shouldered past and headed unerringly for the lounge room, leaving Judith to follow in his wake, marginally thankful to be behind him, to have the chance to rearrange her gown and run fingers through her tousled hair. Bevan shed his jacket as he entered the room, then kicked off his boots, loosened his tie, and flopped down on the sofa as if he owned it.

"I just hope you don't give Vanessa a heart attack if she comes out and sees you there," Judith said, wanting to turn away, wanting to retreat to her own room, equally wanting to throw herself beside him on the couch.

"She's found me here before, a time or two," he replied, reaching back to tuck a spare throw cushion behind his head. "Your cousin was quite the party animal before she went into the maternity business. I don't suppose you knew that."

If he *had* owned the sofa, Judith found herself thinking, he might have thought to trade it in on one which fit him better. The cushion supported his neck but left his head sticking out past it, and at the other end, the arm of the sofa tucked neatly in behind his knees.

"I'm beginning to think you two might know each other better than I thought." She made no attempt to disguise the curiosity in her voice, but she did hide the surge of satisfaction at his answer.

"Not as well as you obviously think," he said, and grinned hugely, as if he'd read her mind.

Or was it more a mighty yawn than a grin? Bevan was obviously worn right out, literally asleep on his feet before he'd flopped down on the too-short sofa.

And sleeping like that will cripple you, damn it. I can't . . .

"Get up!" she demanded, the words out of her mouth almost before the thought had solidified in her mind. Then she was reaching down to physically drag him to his feet, sssshing his objections as she steered him out of the room, down the hall and into the guest room—her room, with her bed.

"In," she ordered. "You can't sleep on that sofa. You'll cripple yourself."

"I've slept on it before and I'm still walking," he said, his voice almost petulant, except for the slight tone of mischief she couldn't ignore. But since he was calmly divesting himself of his tie, Judith ignored the tone and turned to leave the room.

"Where the hell do you think you're going?"

"To sleep on the sofa, of course. It isn't too short for me."

"No way! I will not be accused of having driven you from your bed," he said, and was there at the door before she'd walked that far, moving remarkably quickly for a man half-asleep.

"Nobody's accusing you of anything, damn it. It's just that—"

"What? You're afraid to sleep in the same bed with me? Bloody oath, woman, I'm too fagged out to be much of a threat, not that I would be anyway. And it's a double bed, after all. Plenty of room for us both."

"Do you honestly think I'm going to—"

"If you want me in that bed, you'll be on the other side. That's what I think. I can't be expected to sleep with a bad conscience, and mine would be terrible if I turned you out of a nice warm bed to sleep on a sofa that's not fit for anybody to sleep on."

"But you said—"

"That I'd slept on it before? Well, I have, several times. But I didn't say it was comfortable, Judith Theresa, and those other times I didn't have the option of sharing this bed with you."

"And you don't have it now," she said, her mouth working but her gaze locked with his, trying to ignore her peripheral vision of his fingers tugging the tie loose and starting to unbutton his shirt.

Only now it was Bevan's turn to be authoritative. "Just get into bed, Judith," he said with a huge sigh that was half a yawn. "I promise I won't touch you, or molest you, or torment you, or even ravish you. All I want is to go to sleep lying down before I do it standing up. Now stop being obstreperous and just get in. I'll be good. I promise. I won't even kiss you good night if you don't want me to."

Nor did he. Not ten seconds, it seemed, after Judith had gingerly slid under the covers with her back to his side of the far-too-narrow double bed, she felt the springs move as Bevan's tall, muscular frame flopped down beside her.

" 'Night, Judith Theresa," he whispered, and was apparently asleep before she could even reply.

You might at least have tried to kiss me goodnight. Because I did want you to, and still do, and you know it, too, you arrogant, rotten man.

But she said nothing, nor did she move. Instead, she lay curled hard against the edge of the bed, her back to Bevan, her toes and fingers hanging out from beneath the eiderdown spread, and she thought about how uncomfortable it was trying to sleep in a nightgown and how dangerous it was—or should be, could be, would be—to be sleeping without even that flimsy protection under these insane circumstances.

She had, she was certain, heard his slacks being removed. But what else? Was he lying there now, inches away, stark naked? Or wearing only shorts and socks? She had to stifle a giggle at that thought. She simply couldn't imagine him not removing his socks. But imagining him removing his shorts was all too easy to imagine, and so was the frisson of sensation she felt at the mere idea of being only inches away from his totally naked body.

I promise I won't touch you, or molest you, or torment you, or even ravish you. He hadn't added "which is probably what you really want," but he didn't have to, and his words echoed in the silence of the room, thundering above the soft sound of his breathing, clouding her mind, disrupting her thoughts—no, dominating her thoughts.

She huddled like a terrified animal, afraid to get up and flee the bed, afraid to stay, certain he was already asleep and wouldn't notice anyway, equally certain he would catch her if she tried.

The confusion made sleep impossible, and she wriggled restlessly, afraid to turn over, afraid to just straighten out her huddled body and relax, afraid . . . afraid . . . afraid . . .

Her fear lasted minutes that seemed like hours, days, years, but eventually she slept, and woke with no confusion about one thing. Bevan hadn't come naked into her bed!

25

It seemed so natural, waking up snuggled in against Bevan Keene's back, her body stretched along the length of his, her arm flung carelessly across his waist, her own knees tucked into the curve of his. Spoon-fashion, her mother would have called it.

Judith, luxuriating in the warmth of his body against her own, swimming slowly upward from the soft, silent depths of slumber, sighed with contentment as she let her fingers slide across the warm flesh of Bevan's hip and stomach. Then they touched the fabric of his boxer shorts—and what was beneath them—and she woke up sufficiently to realize where she was and what she was doing. And with whom.

Which was sufficient to bring the still-slumbering, all-too-masculine figure in her embrace fully awake, and before she could disengage, rearing backward in astonishment, a strong male hand had captured her straying wrist, and she was held fast as he rolled beneath her.

"Why, Judith Theresa," he said, meeting her gaze with laughing, gray velvet eyes. His mustache quivered as mobile lips parted in an equally amused grin. "If I'd known you were this frisky in the mornings, I'd have tried to join you in bed long ago. So you're a morning person, eh?"

Bevan wriggled just sufficiently so that Judith ended up lying squarely on top of him, the warmth of his muscular body flowing easily through the flimsy fabric of her sleep-twisted nightgown, the blatant solidness of his erection hard against her pelvis and his strong arms now wrapped around her, holding her in place with not even wiggle-room. Not that she'd dare to wiggle. Things were quite provocative enough without adding to her problems.

"Let me go," she said, her voice half pleading, half breathless with a desire that suddenly terrified her. Against the warmth of his chest, she could feel her breasts reacting to her needs, knew her nipples were firming, thrusting against him just as he was thrusting against her body, lower down.

"Make me." And it was a blatant challenge that he followed up by reaching one large hand up to draw her face down to meet his own, the words barely past those gleaming white teeth before his lips captured her mouth, teasing, tormenting, absorbing her gasps of objection and turning them to sighs of delight.

The kiss went on, and on, and on, Bevan's tongue urging her lips open, teasing her with its touch against her teeth, flirting with her own tongue. His fingers played an erotic tune on her spine, moving from the nape of her neck down to where her buttocks swelled and throbbed to the heat of his body beneath her. He wrapped both his long legs around hers, effectively imprisoning her against him while he plundered her mouth. And when the kiss ended, it was only so that he could run his warm lips along her cheek, down the long, pulsing column of her neck, touching, caressing, arousing.

One hand moved between them. Strong fingers plucked at a nipple as he shifted subtly to bring her higher along his body so that he could take her breast into his mouth, could let his tongue flicker like lightning against the rigidity of her nipple, sending spasms of delight and desire all through her body.

Judith was lost now and knew it. If her body had betrayed her even in sleep, it was all the more treacherous when wide awake, alert to every touch from this man, responding to his lips, to the fingers that flicked along her rump, then teased their way between his body and her own, searching and being aided by her instinctive response as she moved to ease his way.

She lifted a hip, searching his throat with her own lips even as his gentle fingers searched between their bodies, gliding down the flatness of her belly, pausing only for an instant as they reached the softness of her pubic hair, parting that to reach deeper, flicking through the dampness, becoming slippery with her own sexual juices.

When he first touched the center of her sex, Judith had to stifle a gasp of sensation, having very nearly climaxed just from that first gentle, almost tentative touch. Then Bevan paused his fingers as he chose instead to hold her there—in readiness—while he searched her breasts with his lips and tongue, laving kisses from nipple to throat and back again.

She was aware of Bevan's sigh, heard the growl of his passion from lips that swept along her throat. His fingers inside her moved with the skill of an artist, flicking here, touching there, forcing a crescendo of sensation that seemed to spread from her loins right up through her body, turning her legs to mush, her tummy to jelly, her mind to a thoughtless abandonment of any and all logic.

When he spoke, his words a harsh but gentle whisper in her ear, she didn't understand him at first, too caught up in the roller-coaster ride of sensation he was creating with lips and hands that played her body like some finely tuned, exotic musical instrument.

"I didn't come prepared for this." He whispered the words into the softness of her belly as his lips strayed downward from her throbbing, aching breasts.

Judith, body arched like a bow to ease his passage, didn't reply. Couldn't. Words were beyond her by this point. She could only gasp and sigh as he took her to the brink of climax, balanced her there with delicate touches of fingers and tongue, then tipped her into a vortex of sensation that whirled away all reality except that experienced by her body.

Bevan held her while she plunged, and was still holding her when she returned to what should have been reality but seemed, somehow, totally unreal. She opened her eyes to see his gray eyes watching her, a slow grin quirking his lips before he bent to kiss her forehead. It was a tender smile, a lover's smile, filled with satisfaction. But a sort of shared satisfaction, she thought.

Shared? It was all for me. He didn't even give me a chance to—

"That'll have to do," Bevan whispered. "For now, anyway." He looked round the room, almost as if he suddenly felt himself a stranger, then glanced back at Judith, fondness in his eyes, softness in his voice. "I'd best be away or your sweet cousin will have my guts for garters," he said, then rolled lithely from the warm bed and into the complex procedure of getting himself dressed.

"But . . . but . . ." She floundered, searching for words that stuck in her throat and threatened to gag her.

Bevan was already out of the bed before her befuddled mind could fully comprehend what he'd said, what he'd done. He hadn't come prepared, which meant he didn't carry a wallet stuffed with condoms? Or that he hadn't expected her to succumb? Or . . . ?

This is not the time to tell him there's one lone, very geriatric condom in my handbag, there on the dresser. No. Not the time for that. Too late for that, maybe too late for anything even remotely sensible. Damn you, Bevan Keene. Was this all just to prove that you COULD?

Now totally unsure of herself, of him—*especially* unsure of him—she retreated into sarcasm, hating every word that emerged from her kiss-swollen lips, hating herself, hating Bevan, hating . . .

"Very well, then. Just leave the money on the dresser," she

snapped, then rolled over and hid her flaming face beneath a pillow that smelled of them, of their sex, of their togetherness, of their apartness. It wasn't hiding place enough. Bevan's laugh sliced through it like a razor, and there was no satisfaction that it sounded a genuine laugh, a laugh suggesting that he understood her confusion, perhaps even shared it just a bit.

"Damn it, woman. I don't know what you're being cranky about. Can I do nothing right with you?"

Then she heard the muted snick of the bedroom door closing behind him, a signal that she could give vent to her feelings by beating up the pillow and staining it with tears as she berated herself for being a fool, and worse than a fool.

And when she eventually left the bedroom herself, eyes puffy, temperament on the ragged edge between rapture and despair, the smug, knowing glance thrown by cousin Vanessa, infant at breast, was all it took to bring on a fresh spate of angst.

"Not one word, cousin," she snarled. "Not even carrying my namesake would be enough to save you."

"This one's not your namesake. It's his. And I was only wondering why *he* didn't stay for breakfast," Vanessa replied. "Here, take this." The infant Bevan was thrust unceremoniously into Judith's startled grasp, then Vanessa flounced off to collect her daughter, her entire attitude suggesting that she, too, thought Judith was a fool.

Judith looked down into the curious, innocent eyes of her godchild and found an instant reality check. By the time Vanessa returned, she was able to relate the less salacious details of Bevan's nocturnal visit and share her cousin's laughter.

But she didn't see or hear from Bevan Keene again until it was time for the *real* tiger hunt to begin.

26

Mother Nature seemed to smile on the party as the convoy invaded the Tarkine, moving at a leisurely pace down through the Wedge Plains, across the Arthur River, through the Milkshake Hills, then across Rapid River, moving steadily south by west through the Dempster Plains to the crossing of the Horton River on the track toward Balfour. The sun shone, the tracks were in good shape, and the weather was as perfect as it could be for the season.

Less might be said for the party itself, Judith thought, constantly amazed by how disparate the members of the group were. Something had changed. She knew it, could recognize that much, but couldn't figure out just what had changed. Or why. Part of the problem was that the leadership issue had somehow disappeared, and that made little sense.

Bevan seemed to have withdrawn from any show of actually leading the expedition, although he showed typical enthusiasm for the processes of organization and preparation. Derek, by comparison, had taken over the reins with a veritable vengeance, and it was under his direction that they wended their way farther and farther into the Tarkine Wilderness, going from rough but passable tracks to rougher ones, to even worse ones, always heading south by west, always seeking to do as little environmental damage as possible in the process. The caravan of vehicles moved slowly but steadily up and down ridges, through forests of tall eucalypts, across creeks, through narrow and wide buttongrass plains, pausing only when Derek said so, and then only long enough for him to consult his global positioning gizmo and the sheaf of maps he guarded like the crown jewels.

When they finally reached his chosen destination, Judith could see no difference between that site and twenty others they'd passed en route, no obvious, logical reason for Derek to have chosen this particular area as the center of their search for the supposedly extinct tiger. Yes, there was a small, twisty, crystal-clear creek with sandy verges and bars that seemed ideally suited to revealing tiger tracks if such existed. But they'd crossed a dozen such creeks getting to this place. Yes, there was a nearby buttongrass plain, and the surrounding scrub was typically temperate forest, rather than the wetter, heavily canopied rain forest she might have expected. But there was nothing unique, nothing that stood out to make this chosen site significant.

Bevan appeared contented with Derek's choice. He made no comment except to nod as he set about directing the offloading of gear and the laying out of their campsite. Old Ted Norton was equally satisfied, it seemed. He looked around, grunted, then stepped in to help with the work ahead. And there was plenty of work to be done, with evening not far off and the always-possible risk of a serious change in the weather in this far western region of the island state.

In the end, everyone helped, and well before dark, with Roberta's fresh bread sending out aromas of promised delight, they had a camp in place, everything ready for the days ahead, and there was still time for Ted to take a brief wander up the creek before it became too dark to see anything.

"Good country," he said upon his return. "I've found a logical route for the first run of gear, and if the terrain is similar downstream, setting out another one in that direction shouldn't be too hard, either." The remark was aimed primarily at Bevan and was followed by a scathing glance to the camp's outskirts, where Derek and his cohorts were huddled over the global positioning device. "Isn't modern science wonderful?" the aging bushman said with a sneer in his voice. "Just push a button and you know exactly where you are."

"It's a logical piece of equipment for a job like this," Bevan replied calmly. "And don't tell me you wouldn't have liked something similar back when you were a serious prospector."

Judith, openly eavesdropping, expected some disparaging reply, and got it.

"Knowing where you are is one thing," Ted said. "Knowing how to get from there to where you want to be is something no hi-tech gizmo can provide."

Then his voice lowered, becoming inaudible most of the time as he continued, so that what Judith heard was only, ". . . track over . . . east side . . ."

And that one single word that exemplified the mystery of it all—"Fred."

Bevan's reply was more audible, but made no more sense. "It'll be another week or so, I reckon. Maybe two. Plenty of time."

The return of the conservation crowd, chattering like magpies, drowned out whatever reply Ted made to that, and Judith could only spend the evening wondering what crucial information she'd missed.

The days that followed were no more enlightening, except in providing the expedition with a thorough and detailed exploration of the region around their camp. It was agreed—albeit, with masses of often loud and contradictory discussion—that they would set their cameras and sensors both upstream and down from the camp, but that they'd keep to their own side of the rivulet Ted said was a minor tributary to the Horton.

They worked from dawn to dusk, every day, regardless of

weather, laying and expanding a network of cameras and sensors and baits in a huge semicircle around their camp. There was a good deal more work involved than had been needed for the test run, and by evening each day, everyone was exhausted. The evenings consisted of a brief recap of the day's efforts while everyone helped Roberta clean up, a quick viewing of what film they'd collected, then off to bed. Dawn came earlier each day, it seemed.

Judith wasn't surprised to see teams formed that balanced membership between what she was thinking of as "The Greenies" and "The Others," but it was less easy to determine which side was actually in charge. Bevan seemed content to let Derek take charge, but in point of fact, everyone was working too hard to have much energy for bickering.

Or for romance! It wasn't that Bevan was avoiding her, or so she hoped, but he certainly made no attempt to find opportunities for them to be alone. It was as if there was a mental wall in place, as if he was deliberately trying to keep from compromising her, as if he wanted to keep her alone in a no-man's land between the two sides of the expedition.

All quite understandable, or so she kept telling herself. But it hurt. As the days passed, she found herself becoming more and more sensitive to the situation, even to the point where she began to avoid him, as much as that could be done within the confines of the unique situation. Because really, almost nobody was ever much alone. They all shared sleeping quarters, dined communally, and worked from dawn to dusk in teams of two and three. Only Ted Norton and Derek himself ever seemed to find time to wander off. Ted prowled the creek banks every morning in the half-light of dawn, while Derek had adopted a habit of going off somewhere by himself each day about noon.

Within four days, they had it all down to a well-rehearsed routine. Within a week it had become almost boring, not least because all Jan's film ever produced was the same types of animals doing exactly what was expected of them in expected ways. There was even a suggestion—not totally in jest—that Jan's star-struck Tassie devil had managed to find his way all the way across the state to continue his movie career. Either that or he had a double. It was amusing, for a day or so, annoying as hell after that.

By the end of the second week, it had become a curious game akin to musical chairs, with each dawn bringing a change usually orchestrated by Bevan. He had them alternate partners, alternate collection routes and times, anything to try and reduce the inevitable boredom of walking the same trails, with the same people, listening to the same arguments and ideas.

Only the weather really changed, and that happened almost daily. One day brilliant sunshine, the next torrential rain that made travel a nightmare. Then would come a day where the moisture-laden air hung in streaming curtains of mist so thick, Judith thought the cameras couldn't have penetrated them had an elephant triggered the shutter.

Just their luck, she would later think, that it was on such a day that everything changed!

27

The entire crew was in the mess tent watching Roberta prepare breakfast, most of them only half awake and the rest engaged in what seemed—to Judith—to be the hundredth inane discussion about the relative values of eating vegetables as opposed to red meat. Jan Smythe, for some reason crankier than usual about this, her favorite argument, threw her hands in the air and flung herself out of the tent, declaring herself bored and disgusted by the attitudes of the carnivores amongst them.

But only seconds later, it seemed—Roberta and Ted were still exchanging glances of surprise at Jan's attitude—and Jan was back, eyes wide, lips moving in a vain attempt to get the words out.

"Nnnnnobody move," she finally managed to stammer. "Ddddon't move, don't say anything, don't do anything."

She scrambled past them, reached the rear of the tent where her camera bag lay, and her hands shook in her excitement as she fumbled to get out the smallest of the video recorders, discarding the lens cap and letting it fall ignored to the floor of the tent as she scurried back to the exit. Her eyes were wide with mute pleading that was followed by the actual words.

"Please, oh, please," she whimpered, waving both hands at them all in a gesture of unmistakable clarity. Then she was sliding through the doorway, her movement sinuous, cautious in the extreme. Behind her, the final word—"tiger"—hung almost visible in the silence.

Bevan was the first to move, and before anyone else could even think of it, he was there to halt the rush, his arms outstretched to block the exit of the conservationists as they plunged in a body to follow Jan.

"Give her a chance, for God's sake," Bevan hissed, his voice in a low whisper but firm in its demand.

He and Derek stood eye to eye, but there was no question in Judith's mind of who would win the encounter. And she was right. Derek's eyes flared in anger and frustration, but he backed down almost immediately. The other two greenies never even made a show of challenging Bevan.

Who held them back by what seemed sheer willpower for what seemed an awfully long time. But finally, as if satisfied with his control, he turned and eased open the tent flap just enough to peer out. An instant later, his free hand beckoned as he whispered to them to seek positions that would allow them to see out without actually going out, and everyone stretched, stooped or knelt to take a vantage point.

Everyone but Ted and Roberta, Judith noticed in passing, then ignored the fact as she, too, moved to peer through the narrow tent slit, controlled by Bevan's hands and body.

If he'd let them explode through the tent flap, as they'd wanted to, Jan Smythe would have been trampled. She was just outside the tent, sprawled flat on the ground, her attention locked on something up along the narrow track which linked their camp to the outside world. One eye was covered by the viewfinder of the video camera and then, even as they watched, she slithered across the ground to crouch behind one of the vehicles, where she glanced quickly down at the camera, then brought it up to her eye again.

All gazes followed the line of the camera, then the tent was filled with a communal hiss of amazement as they saw, seemingly in unison, what Jan was trying to film.

Tiger!

Judith's reaction was disbelief, but how could she not believe *this?* Even as she doubted, she was ticking off mental notes: the size, the outline, the reddish-brown color, the dark stripes that ranged from shoulder to flanks like spur marks moving to the curiously rigid tail, the shape of the head—everything! And it all seemed right, even though her common sense cried out that it simply could not be!

The beast was well over a hundred and fifty meters away, standing in a mottle of light and fog and shadow. It was a ghost figure in the mist that seemed to swirl about it like living sorcery. But even so, it was unmistakably, clearly, and *definitely* a tiger!

Except that it couldn't be. It simply couldn't. All Judith's logic, all her knowledge and beliefs about coincidence, all her skepticism screamed that it could not be. Not here, not so conveniently within sight of their camp, in what was no longer the deceptive partial-light of dawn but was closer—the mist notwithstanding—to proper daylight. Not just where everybody could see it, where Jan could capture it with the magic of the video camera. *No,* Judith thought. *No. There's something fishy about this!*

And she remembered how Bevan had rushed to hold back everyone at the door, and how Ted and Roberta hadn't joined the rush in the first place. Suspicion grew, and she was almost turning to see where Ted and Roberta were now, when the animal turned its head toward them, opened a cavernous mouth and yawned! Judith felt her heart lurch, knew she was holding her breath, knew they all were, wasn't sure if she would ever breathe again.

This was the final, definitive clue—that enormous gape so peculiarly specific to the tiger. Jaws that could stretch far beyond the capacity of any dog, seeming almost to unhinge. Her mind was photographing the image, burning it into memory forever, when the animal turned and strode away, moving only a few steps before it disappeared into the surrounding scrub, flowing into the mist as if already just a memory.

But it all fit. Memory served to superimpose over the vanishing figure the few bits of film clips she'd seen, film taken of real, living tigers. Even the movement was right.

Jan was running full-tilt down the track after the animal, and now, somehow, everyone else was outside the tent, some staring after Jan, the rest staring at each other, mouths moving in a cacophony of questions, everyone—or so it seemed—talking at once.

They were still milling about like a mob of hysterical, clucking chooks when Jan returned, walking now, scuffing her feet and beating one fist against her thigh in some sort of ritual suffering. "Waste of time," she sighed as she reached the group of suddenly silent onlookers, all looking to her as if for some explanation, some confirmation that they'd actually seen what they thought they'd seen.

All except Bevan, Roberta, and Ted, Judith noticed, having determined as soon as the animal had gone from sight that whatever she had seen, whatever had happened, these three knew more than they were letting on. The old bushman simply hadn't shown enough surprise. And Bevan? Bevan hadn't joined the excitement outside the tent—not really. He'd made a good show of it, but Judith was almost certain it was just a show, although in what cause she couldn't imagine.

Derek, too, seemed to be reacting strangely to the situation. Distracted, somehow, she thought. He kept looking toward where the animal had disappeared, then shaking his head as if bewildered. Only it wasn't quite the same bewilderment everyone else was exhibiting; Derek had something on his mind, something besides what would have to be the most significant, exciting conservation sighting in fifty years.

Judith kept on watching the two apparent leaders of the expedition, her mind racing with speculation. Both of them, she decided, weren't acting quite right about it all. She couldn't put her finger on what wasn't right, but it was something. She looked around to check on Roberta's reaction, then had her attention returned when Bevan's voice, in tones that would have stopped a runaway bullock, snapped out a command, "Hold it right there, you two!"

She turned to see Ron Peters and Reg Hudson twenty yards up the track and looking at Bevan with undisguised surprise.

"We'll just let Ted have a sticky-beak first," Bevan told them, expanding the remark to include everyone else within hearing. "We all get roaming around out there and whatever tracks there are will be messed up beyond any hope of recovery."

He then asked Roberta if perhaps it wasn't a good idea to make fresh coffee and gently herded everyone back toward the cook tent. It was all done very subtly, but quite deliberately, it seemed to Judith, who was now starting to feel the first real frissons of genuine suspicion. Ted Norton began a slow, ambling walk toward where the animal had been seen, but nobody was paying him any attention as Bevan drew the excited expedition members into an animated discussion aimed at easing them into the tent.

Judith held back, deliberately putting herself outside the discussion, rock-solid now in her role as unbiased observer. She was intent on listening, watching, gathering information and opinion, but staying sufficiently aloof that she couldn't be drawn into the center of the situation where she might miss things through simply being too close to them.

And Bevan—damn him!—seemed instantly aware of this alteration to her attitude. He caught her with his gaze and held her like a butterfly pinned up for display while he moved quickly over to join her.

"You okay?" But there was no real concern in his voice, and he didn't give her a chance to even reply before silently mouthing the words, "Trust me!"

Judith could only glare at him, her entire attitude now defensive and cautious. *Trust you? Not on your life, Bevan Keene!* But she didn't say it, nor say that she wanted to trust him, needed to trust him, and couldn't admit it. How could she?

Then his gaze shifted beyond her, over her shoulder, and she suddenly realized what he was doing. In moving to join her, he had used their bodies to effectively block the line of sight from the cook tent entrance to where Ted was meandering around where the tiger had been sighted. The gesture wasn't that obvious to anyone else—they weren't paying much attention in the first place—but once seen, it cried out like a siren to Judith.

Spinning on her heel, she followed Bevan's gaze to where Ted was now shuffling along the track close to where the animal had been seen. Half crouching, shading his eyes with one hand, the bushman was moving with obvious deliberation, quartering back and forth across the narrow track.

Seeking the animal's tracks? No! Judith's eyes widened in shock as she realized the obvious alternative. He could just as easily be wiping them out. She froze in position, rigid against Bevan's light touch on her shoulder, wishing she could be as rigid as his insidious whisper in her ear.

"Trust me, Judith Theresa. There's a helluva lot riding on this."

"Is Ted doing what I think he is?" she said, astonished at the calm in her own voice, at how she made the question so casual, at how she could keep herself from turning to meet Bevan's eyes, at how she could keep herself from screaming out an accusation.

"Trust him, too," was the evasive reply.

And now she felt the warmth of his breath on her neck, and

shivered at the way it made her feel inside. *Insane!* Worse than insane, she thought, to be so conscious of this man and the way he made her feel at a time like this, when her every professional instinct was aroused, alert, cautious. The problem was that her body was equally aroused merely by Bevan's nearness.

"You're asking a lot. Perhaps too much," she whispered in reply. "I don't think I can take that much on trust."

"Of course you can. Whatever happened to your professional judgment?"

And now she had to meet his eyes, expecting to see them dancing with amusement, surprised to see them calm, quiet, serious.

Whatever happened to your professional judgment? Gone! The one-word reply hovered inside her mouth, a mouth suddenly turned desert-dry as shivers of delight scampered up her back from where his fingers now idly stroked her lower spine.

"Why should I trust you?" she asked, half her mind in the agony of memory—after all, she'd trusted Derek once—and the other half floating in the sweeter agony of Bevan's caress.

His reply was half hidden in a chuckle, but the words were clear enough. He might as well have shouted them.

"Because I love you and because I trust *you*. And you know it."

His fingers on her lower back punctuated the reply, and Judith shivered with the delight of it. *Because I love you. Did he really say that?* Her mind said she'd heard it, but her heart was less sure.

"I *know* that you trust *me?*" She *had* to ask it, and did.

"Of course you do."

No uncertainty in that voice. It filled her ear with the ring of calm, total assurance. Which, she thought, could be no more than a trick—a politician's trick, a trickster's ruse. Only it wasn't, and she somehow knew that, even if she still couldn't be sure she'd heard him say, "I love you," and even if she didn't dare admit any of it to herself, much less to him.

"Believe nothing of what you hear and only half of what you see," she chanted in a nonsense reply, wishing he would stop doing that with his fingers, and at the same time, wishing he would never stop.

There was a pause, and Judith realized he was concentrating on the hubbub behind them in the tent. Her own ears had caught the slight lull in the conversation, too, only now the tempo quickened again. Nobody was paying them any attention, it seemed.

Which was just as well, Judith realized. She was backed in so tightly against him she could feel the warmth of his desire, the strength of it, throbbing against her buttocks. She could feel the warmth of his breath against her neck, the whisper of his voice like an insidious melody in her ear.

"Backwards, in this case," he was saying, his voice low and melodious and making no sense at first. "You can believe what you hear because you know it's true, Judith Theresa. But not what you see. What you've seen! Not by half, even. I told you about the Fred factor."

And now, she had to see his eyes, had to watch their expression. Judith spun in his grasp, then almost shied away as she realized how it must appear, how it was. To any onlooker, a distinctly compromising position so close against him she could feel his body heat, feel her tummy tingle at the touch of his erection against it, the curious softness that flowed through her loins. Close enough to kiss, to be kissed, with just the merest movement of either head.

She met Bevan's eyes, then broke off to peer past his shoulder, sighing visibly when she realized the others were so busy with their discussion that he could have kissed her without anyone bothering to notice.

Wishing he had!

And from the look in his eyes when she met them again, he very well might. Against all her instincts she eased herself back to a more conversational, less dangerous distance.

"Fred?" she asked.

"Uh huh." And his eyes were laughing now, the devils dancing in them. Laughing at her, or at the situation?

Judith glared at him, shrugging her shoulders in a demanding gesture. She wanted to scream at him, to somehow make him tell her about Fred, to make him tell her everything. Now! And she wanted him to get back to holding her.

"And that's all you're going to tell me, isn't it?" she demanded, knowing the reply before he gave it.

"I don't want to totally stuff up your reactions if and when things really get dicey," he said. "I want all your skepticism turned on, full bore. It's important."

"All my skepticism, but you expect me to trust you."

"I'm depending on that, more than you know." Bevan glanced away, over her shoulder. "Here comes Ted. Let's grab some coffee and see what sort of hornet's nest he stirs up."

The old bushman's entrance provoked an immediate, anticipatory silence in the cook tent, but it erupted into bedlam after his typically laconic report.

"No tracks," he said. "Not a sausage. The ground's too hard, too rocky. I could barely make out where Jan had been, but nothing else."

The sighs of disappointment were overshadowed by a wail of anguish from the photographer, who closed her eyes and beat her fists on the table in obvious self-disgust. "Damn, damn, damn," she cried. "I never even thought. I was so concerned with trying to get more pictures that I never thought about the tracks. I'll bet I walked over everything. Oh, I could just shoot myself."

"No need," Ted growled. "There's no evidence you messed up anything at all. It's just damned poor tracking ground. And worse in the scrub around. I couldn't figure where the beast came into the open or left it, and that's a fact. Damn it! I reckon it was headed for a drink, and if we'd been a few moments later there might have been proper tracks in the sand along the creek, but there's nothing. Not a skerrick!"

From there, the discussion quickly degenerated into a free-for-all, with almost everyone voicing some opinion about the importance of the missing tracks. Everyone, that is, except Ted, Bevan, and Roberta. Judith wasn't at all surprised when Derek's contributions positively but subtly steered whatever blame might be involved onto Jan, nor was she surprised when the abrasive Ron Peters—with far less finesse—backed him up.

The amazing part was how Bevan allowed the scapegoating to continue without interference. Jan was in tears, Judith was ready to explode, and even the implacable Ted Norton seemed near the end of his patience when Bevan finally did put a halt to it, although at least when he did so, he got in a few licks himself.

"You're a fine lot of ratbags," he snarled, the strength of his voice smacking everyone else's comments into instant silence. "Here's Jan, the only one who's done anything bloody well positive at all, and you lot can't do anything but rubbish and abuse her." His blistering scorn was sufficient to create at least a semblance of contrition, and when he walked over and put one arm around the slender photographer's shoulders, muttering, "Ignore them, love; they're not worth feeding, the lot of them," Jan's look of thanks quickly turned to a glare of contempt thrown in Derek's direction.

"Right! Enough of this rubbish," Bevan declared. "If the tiger were here now, he'd be talked to death, which isn't the point of the exercise. I'm going to go fire up the computer so we can see what Jan did accomplish, and then I suggest it might be time to start talking about what we do next."

He paused briefly to ensure he still had their attention, then shot Judith a warm and gentle look before scowling again and saying, "Because it may not have occurred to any of you, but I don't think there's one damned thing in the planning for all this that lays down any procedure in the event of success."

28

Disappointment filled the tent, hanging in the air like wood smoke, but somewhat more pungent.

"I can't believe there's only ninety-three seconds of film," moaned Jan Smythe, shaking her head in anger and frustration at how little video material she had actually gained. She'd warned her audience before she showed them the video that time might have been distorted by the excitement of the moment, but even she was clearly surprised at how little useful film there was.

"Well, I don't believe the animal was really that far away," said Derek. "What did you do, Jan? Put your telephoto lens on backward?"

The comment was so typical of Derek, Judith thought. He would always try to cast blame on somebody else—anybody but himself. So when Jan responded by flinging a filthy glare in his direction but not bothering to reply, Judith found herself nodding in agreement with the photographer.

She, too, was disappointed in the video, but only half her mind had been occupied in watching it. The rest was far too involved with trying to sort out the things Bevan had said, trying to put what was happening into some sort of perspective.

Had Bevan really said that he loved her, that he trusted her? She could replay the words from memory, even see in her mind's eye the look on his face as he'd spoken, but she found it truly difficult somehow to believe she wasn't making the whole thing up, wasn't just imagining it!

"I paced it out at a hundred and twenty yards," Ted Norton said, and Judith was gently amused at how he so steadfastly refused to modernize his thinking into metric.

"And what's that in real measurement?" somebody else asked.

"Near as dammit a hundred meters," said Derek, who still seemed far too upset by the entire incident for Judith's understanding. Instead of being as excited as everyone else was—with good justification, surely?—he had a sour, distracted air about him that was confusing.

"Easy shot," muttered Ted, obviously talking to himself now, and thankfully oblivious to the astonished and angry looks the comment drew from the conservationist element.

"Let's see it again, Jan," said Roberta, which gathered expressions of disapproval from the greenies, especially Derek.

The jeers as the video began yet again were almost sufficient to drown out the obscene racket of the generator outside, and to make things even worse, the video appeared even more vague on second viewing.

Jan, unlike her audience, watched the entire ninety-three seconds in silence, but as the tiny, ghostly figure on the video stepped into the fog-shrouded obscurity of the surrounding landscape, she uttered a defeated sigh. "I could shoot myself for not trying to get closer when I had the chance," she complained. "I might have spooked it, almost certainly would have, but looking at this . . ."

"It might have put some movement into the picture, at least," said Derek. "The thing might as well have been a statue except for the last few seconds. Nobody would ever believe it was real, I'm afraid."

"There was movement," insisted Reg Hudson, for once right in the thick of the conversation. "I'm positive I saw it flicking its ears, even though that doesn't show up very well on the film."

"Because it's so damned far away," snarled Derek. "It's so far away that I'm not sure the video is worth anything at all." He pounded one fist into his opposite palm in a gesture of apparent frustration, continuing—as he had all along—his attempts to denigrate the significance of the video and the sighting itself.

"Why do I get the impression you're protesting just a bit too much?" Bevan entered the debate for the first time with a voice soft and calm, but authoritative. His voice remained soft, his tone nonaccusing, but the message was there, and nobody—least of all Derek—could fail to understand what he was getting at.

Derek merely tried to bluff his way past the direct question. "Just what's that supposed to mean?" he demanded, the reply uttered in a tone of innocent indignation that Derek somehow, to Judith's ears, didn't quite carry off. He didn't even turn to look at Bevan while replying, as if he knew that doing so would give away his lack of assurance.

And Judith didn't need to look at either man to know the answer. Derek should have been, on past performance, lauding even this miniscule bit of evidence to the very skies. She knew it, Bevan knew it, Derek knew it. Everybody in the place knew it.

So why wasn't he? It could mean nothing but kudos for Derek Innes as leader—coleader!—of the discovery team. But nothing compared to what he had to gain from an even more convincing tiger sighting in an area this important to the conservation movement. Nonetheless, it was out of character. The Derek she knew would be working to spin this acorn into the granddaddy of all oak trees, not playing it down as he was doing, or at least appeared to be doing.

There's something going on here that I don't understand. And it's something wrong. Very wrong!

Judith was taking unexpected satisfaction from that thought

when she felt the pressure of Bevan's hip against her own, and she turned and looked up to see his mobile mouth twisted into a wry, quirky half-grin. And heard again in her mind the caution he'd uttered about believing nothing of what she'd seen. And she realized from his expression that he was deliberately manipulating this entire conversation, deliberately trying to maneuver Derek in a particular, specific direction, toward a particular, specific objective. But what?

"You're not making much sense, little mate," drawled Bevan in a voice that didn't bother to conceal the sneer it implied. "This may not be much, but it's well and truly the best film evidence that's emerged in recent years, and we all know it."

"We don't know any such thing," Derek asserted, rising to confront his audience, doing his best with bluster and all his considerable verbal skills to dampen their enthusiasm for Bevan's logic. "Just look at what we've really got." He pointed at the now blackened and silent screen. "Images of something that might be a tiger, or might be something else entirely. How could we tell from that? Nobody is going to be satisfied with it, or at least nobody that matters!"

"Oh, come now," was the reply from the usually quiet Reg Hudson, flip-flopping yet again in his support for the movement he clearly believed in. "We all know what we saw, Derek. I mean . . . really! Are you seriously trying to talk us out of believing our own eyes?"

"It could have been a stray dog," Derek insisted. "It was a long way off, the light wasn't that good so early in the morning, and the fog . . . and everybody was excited, stirred up by . . . by . . ." He floundered badly, searching for words but not finding them, an astonishing lapse for Derek.

"By Jan being so overwhelmed by everything," he finally said, and continued speaking, oblivious to the groans of disbelief and—in Judith's and Jan's case—anger the accusation provoked.

Both women looked at one another, then shook their heads, hardly able to credit how Derek seemed so intent on focusing blame anywhere, in any direction, just so it was away from himself. Then Bevan nodded sagely, and Judith was even more surprised. Indeed, she was frankly astonished, because he seemed to be agreeing with Derek.

"A dog, eh?" Bevan said. "Well, it's something we ought to bear in mind."

He surreptitiously nudged Judith with his elbow just as she drew a startled breath and opened her mouth to interrupt him.

She looked up, too stunned to say anything as he blandly continued despite the hoots of derision and objection from almost everyone else.

"Let's not be too hasty," he said. "I don't know what experience you've all had with dogs, but I'd be forced to admit I've seen one or two in my time that could be mistaken for tigers in the right circumstances." He paused long enough to swivel his glance round the tent before focusing again on Derek. "In fact, I once saw a fair-dinkum Queensland pig-dog that would have been a dead ringer for a tiger if somebody had taken the trouble to paint a few stripes on him."

Bull's-eye! Judith couldn't be sure if anybody else noticed, but she saw Derek's eyes narrow in a flicker, saw the way his jaw muscles tensed up. *Bevan's onto something here,* she thought, and wished she knew just what. For some reason Bevan decided not to push any further for the moment, but she could feel the tension in him, too, knew he was all keyed up, ready for something . . . *but what?*

The tension in the restricted confines of the tent seemed to grow almost visibly, to expand like a cloud of smoke until it touched, wrapped, enveloped all of them, and yet Judith realized it was only really there between Bevan and Derek, and with Bevan setting the pace now, inexplicably, unwilling to force a confrontation, it subsided.

The comment about the pig-dog, though, brought a contemptuous snort from Ted Norton, who stomped over to glare up at Bevan and say, "I've been in the bush since before you were a pup, Bevan Keene, and I've never heard such a load of rubbish in my entire life. A dog! My God, man, I can understand *him* . . ." with a sneering nod toward Derek ". . . thinking we're all blind idiots. But you?"

Even for the cantankerous old bushman it was, to Judith's eye, just a bit over the top. Especially since from her position by Bevan's side she could see that Ted's eyes were actually twinkling. He was enjoying this!

It was enough, however, to spark an outbreak of shouted opposition led by Jan Smythe, who was nearly in tears.

"I just don't believe this," she cried. "Next you'll be saying it wasn't even a dog, it was fairies at the bottom of the garden. What are you two trying to establish? That we're all victims of mass hysteria or mass hallucinations? What about my film, for God's sake? I admit that cameras can be made to lie, but you all saw me taking that footage. And whatever else, cameras do not suffer from mass hallucinations!"

"Don't get all frothy, Jan. I'm just sort of playing devil's advocate," Bevan replied, his voice calm now, soft and alluring and even, Judith thought, seductive as he poured on the charm to mollify the angry photographer. "We all know what we all saw, but just how sure are we, I wonder, what it really was? There are feral dogs here in Tasmania, as you well know, and although I'm not saying that's what you filmed, we have to consider every argument and question we might have to face later on. And more important, where's the proof? You have to admit the light and distance factors don't make your film the strongest evidence in the known universe."

"Strong enough evidence for me," was the forceful reply.

"You lot think what you want, but I am staying here until I can get more pictures of that animal. And better ones. If I have to stay alone, I'll do it. I'll sleep with the possums and live off the land if I have to. I'll even eat wallaby!"

That final comment showed her resolve, and Jan capped it by storming out of the tent, her camera bag flinging around her like a battle axe as she shouldered her way past Bevan with a hurt and angry glare.

"Well, I reckon we ought to give this a rest and go check the trap line for exposed film," said Ted, pragmatic to the end. "It has to be done sometime, and the day's half gone already, so let's get to it."

His statement brought Jan back into the tent at a dead run. Nobody, she said angrily, was going to touch those video packs but her.

"Still, Ted's right," she said. "With all this stupid arguing going on, we've forgotten we could have all sorts of better pictures, better evidence, and all we have to do is go and pick it up."

"I disagree." Derek now commanded the floor, and Judith—surprised that Bevan didn't seem disposed to argue with the conservationist leader—fixed her attention on Derek. She watched and listened with avid interest. Derek was up to something. She knew it as sure as she was standing there, but she couldn't figure out what it could be.

Without Bevan to carry any opposition, the rest paused in their discussion to listen to Derek's arguments.

"There is more to this than any of us might realize," he said, sliding into his politician's hat and oily overcoat.

Judith would have smiled if she weren't so immediately suspicious. She'd seen Derek in this role before, all too often, and knew that at his best he could convince almost anyone that black was white and that pudgy pink pigs could fly.

"As Bevan has correctly pointed out, we've planned for just

about everything but success," Derek continued. "And in view of what's happened, I think there are more important things to worry about just now than collecting film that we can always get tomorrow, if it comes to that."

"Wait until tomorrow? With a tiger roaming around out there somewhere? Are you out of your tiny mind?" Jan was fairly livid! She barged to the front of the group and glared at Derek, clearly having lost all patience with him, along with whatever respect she'd granted him earlier in the trip.

There's more to this girl than meets the eye, Judith thought, and glanced up to see Bevan calmly watching the exchange, a curious, speculative expression on his face. He seemed immediately aware of Judith's change in attention, however, and looked down to meet her eyes. He raised one dark eyebrow in the direction of the two protagonists, then grinned mischievously.

The other members of the green contingent had leapt into the fray, now, both of them clearly taking Jan's side of the argument. How could Derek possibly justify doing anything but getting out there now, immediately if not sooner, to see if there was other film of the animal? Now, before the weather decided to change, or the sensor batteries failed, or . . . or . . . ?

Judith listened in frank disbelief as Derek launched into full political mode, turning each person's argument inside out, upside down and backwards, until he had the issue and the people totally confused.

Some of the people.

Beside her, Bevan was silent, listening intently. But he seemed just as intent on watching her reaction to the performance. And across the tent, sprawled on a camp stool with a coffee cup balanced on one knee, old Ted Norton was equally entranced but clearly not convinced by anything he heard. Roberta had retreated to her role as caterer, taking no part in the arguments. She was busy buttering scones and making sandwiches, apparently ignoring the discussion entirely.

Until, finally, there was a pause in the debate at the moment Roberta had obviously been waiting for. “I would just like to point out that regardless of what we do,” she said in a calm, unhurried voice, “somebody is going to have to go and bring in fresh provisions if we’re to stay past tomorrow. Unless,” and she fixed Derek with a stare that Judith reckoned would have brought a more sensitive man to his knees, “we’re all prepared to live on wallaby and bush tucker.”

Now it was Bevan’s turn, and he slid into the conversation so smoothly it was almost as if Roberta had deliberately swept the path for him.

“And whoever goes, it might be wise for us all to have a serious discussion about what’s to be said, or *not* said, about today’s discovery. What, and to whom, and under what circumstances.”

That brought the hubbub to a crashing halt. Bevan had been the first to say anything about what Judith had recognized earlier as one of the major issues in the whole affair. What, indeed, was to be said? And to whom? And—because it was her job to organize whatever was said—*by* whom?

29

Judith looked round the suddenly cramped confines of the tent, realizing that all of a sudden everyone was looking at everyone else, and the looks were looks of suspicion and mistrust. It was like a scene from an old western movie where trusted, trusting partners had just discovered gold and immediately begun speculating how to avoid dividing the spoils.

The impression was so vivid and struck her as so funny that she erupted in a giggle, only to stifle it just as quickly when she realized it had just made her the recipient of some very black looks. Then she suppressed the urge to explain the giggle, but had to wonder which task was the harder.

"Speaking only for myself, I think it's too early to say anything at all," Bevan continued. "We've only been here less than a fortnight. We have all the time in the world to add to our store of evidence, to give Jan a chance for more footage, *better* footage. There's no hurry about making any sort of announcement."

Whereupon he looked directly at Judith, who could do nothing but stare back at him through a wall of silence so tangible between them that she found it impossible to collect her thoughts, much less marshal a reply.

"But . . . but . . . we can't possibly tell *any*body!" Reg Hudson's was the first voice to break the long, speculative silence. And once started, he began to run off at the mouth as if he'd just learned to speak and was enjoying the experience too much to stop. "Well, we must tell the authorities, of course," he said. "Eventually. Not now, of course. Because certainly they'll have to know so the area can have proper protection, and that is of primary importance."

And he went on and on and on, repeating himself, contradicting himself, and making less and less sense as he attempted to explain in scientific and philosophical detail why the elusive tiger had to be protected from all sorts of real and/or imaginary threats.

Containing her need to giggle had become a truly arduous task, and Judith could feel that Bevan, hip against her own, was having similar problems. Reg's pomposity and unrealistic approach to the entire situation, she thought, must strike Bevan as ridiculously as it did her.

Bevan's chuckle rumbled from deep inside him when Reg finally paused for a proper breath, giving Bevan a chance to interrupt.

"You don't reckon maybe we owe it to the backers of this expedition to tell them what's happened?" he asked, his face and voice the very epitome of innocence.

"Certainly not!"

Now it was Ron Peters's turn, and Judith almost laughed as he embarked on a fanatical litany she could have just about predicted word-for-word before he opened his mouth.

"They're only out for financial gain," Ron cried, almost frothing at the mouth in his vehemence. "Vandals, wreckers. They can't be allowed to exploit a discovery as sensitive and important as this!"

He was clearly about to embark upon a lecture even more impassioned than Reg's, but Bevan apparently had begun to lose patience.

"So we just ignore the fact that they've financed this little junket," he said, "and that we wouldn't be here without that finance, much less have the opportunity to see what we've all just seen? Not to mention a simple little thing like contractual obligation, which we all have. What do you expect us to do? Trundle back to civilization and forget the whole thing?"

The sneer in his voice didn't extend to Bevan's mouth, but Judith was certain he was wound up as tight as a watch spring, and could be close to exploding. What surprised her even more was how placidly Roberta and Ted had endured the fanatical ravings of the young conservationists.

"You're one of them," Ron accused, his eyes wide now with clear and obvious fanatical zeal. "You don't care about the principles involved here. You're just out for what you can get!"

He turned to Derek, miraculously transformed from antagonist to champion of the green cause. "You tell him, Derek. Tell him how we've got the numbers, so we can take control of this whole thing. Go on! Explain it to him the way you explained it to all of us the other day."

Derek's face hardened, and he raised a hand in a futile attempt to silence young Ron Peters, but it was too late and he knew it. Bevan had been given his opening.

"Yes, Innes, do tell us about the numbers," Bevan snapped, still not raising his voice, showing no antagonism, no aggression. Just an implacable assurance. "I'm very intrigued by this numbers game," he continued, and smiled a cold, icy smile.

"It's no game," Ron said. "There's four of us—five, counting Judith—and only the three of you. We'll decide things, not you!" And as if to back up his boast, he waved a handful of vehicle keys as if they were some sort of battle trophy.

Judith felt herself go tense. This had gone beyond a joke. Ron Peters was "right round the twist" over this issue, to use an Australianism, and she wondered how much more bizarre the conversation could get. Then she felt Bevan's gaze focus on her, and she almost hunched her shoulders, waiting for the verbal blow she knew had to come.

But when Bevan spoke, it wasn't to Judith, nor was it to Ron, whom he contemptuously ignored. His glance barely touched Judith before striking at Derek like a sword thrust. And yet it was strangely without antagonism, almost as if he actually accepted the Queenslander's leadership role but was refusing to allow that to give Derek any right of dominance over the situation.

"You want to put him back on his chain," Bevan said to Derek in a soft conversational tone. Only then did he turn and confront Judith directly.

"So, what about you, Judith Theresa? Are you really committed to this lot of ratbags?"

He asked the question gently, not as a challenge, and Judith found herself wondering why. She had been expecting a verbal assault, so she was at first unprepared for such calm, didn't have a nondefensive reply on her tongue.

I'm committed to you, which scares the hell out of me. Do you want me to admit that? Or deny it? What DO you want, Bevan Keene?

She found herself mesmerized by his pale eyes, the combination of warmth and challenge she saw there. There was some message for her, some code only the two of them should be able to crack. But in this moment, with everyone's attention focused upon her, only Bevan knew the code, and she had to think long and hard before replying.

"I'm committed to the man who is paying me to be neutral." She finally spat out the words as if they tasted bad. "That's what I'm being paid to be, *neutral*, even if we were to ignore my integrity as a professional. Which, by the way, we *will not* do."

"But Judith. Surely you, of all people, can see the true significance of all this, the importance of it being handled correctly. After all, this is of world-class import." Derek's voice was as calm as Bevan's. It was his attitude that differed. There was an oily quality to it, something that smirked and smarmed.

"Of course I do, Derek," Judith said, fighting for calm in her own voice. Then, suddenly, the words flowed almost without conscious thought, pregnant with sarcasm and a contempt far deeper than she'd ever realized. "I mean, you know I've always been scrupulously neutral, absolutely, totally fair. Haven't I, Derek? You, *of all people,* should know that. But what's fair now? What is it that you want from me? From all of us?"

He opened his mouth to reply, but Judith charged on, giving him no opportunity. "One minute you're trying to talk us all out of believing what we've seen with our own eyes, and the next you want us all to collaborate on some amazing cover-up to protect a creature we're not supposed to believe we've even seen in the first place. And now this ridiculous business about numbers and keys! How childish. What do you intend to do, leave those who disagree with your plans stranded here, while you contact all the media and start putting your own spin on this?"

She flung her hands in the air, waving expansively in a gesture of bewilderment. "I don't understand you any more, Derek. I don't know if you're asking me to compromise my principles or if you're just assuming I don't have any in the first place. But either way, I don't like it and I'm certainly not going to put up with it."

Which was true enough, although she was beginning to believe she had never understood Derek Innes. Suddenly the analogy of a western became too real, and slightly frightening. There seemed no doubt that Ron Peters had come unhinged, and Judith was no longer certain that Derek himself was much more balanced.

"I don't understand any of this, but I'm with Judith." Jan Smythe's voice was hard-edged, raspy and ragged. She moved forward to confront Derek, who, surprisingly, leaned back in retreat from her small but determined presence. "I don't like it one little bit. Just what is going on, Derek? I didn't pay that much attention before, when you were telling us all about how this search would help the conservation movement so much, and how Judith was sympathetic to the cause, and *manageable*. But I can tell you this much. I don't like the way you're acting now, and I don't like the way this whole thing is shaping up. Not one damned bit, I don't. You've been trying to discredit me and my work, and now, well, there's no sense to any of it. So I repeat, I'm with Judith. I'm not going to put up with it, either!"

"Surely it's obvious," Derek said, his voice hot and angry now, filled with bluster. But there was a thread of weakness in his attitude, too, and in the face of blatant mutiny in the ranks, that thread had begun to stretch, perhaps even to unravel.

He glared round the tent, and when his eyes caught Judith's, she saw madness there, a frightened madness that caught her by surprise. Once seen, it was as he'd said, obvious. Derek was a megalomaniac, and very, very close to tipping right over the edge.

Without realizing it, Judith had backed in close against Bevan, and now she felt his tension, knew that he, too, was aware of how dangerous the situation was getting. But when he spoke, it was in that same calm, gentle voice, a voice so soft she could almost see the tension in the room begin to relax in response.

"Some of it is certainly obvious, Derek," Bevan said in that deceptively mild conversational tone. "But I do have one or two questions, if you'd be so kind as to enlighten me."

It was amazing. Derek actually began to puff and preen, affected by the deference in Bevan's voice and attitude. A deference, Judith knew, that concealed muscles coiled and ready for immediate action should it be required. She could feel Bevan's alert readiness. He was playing a game of his own, and ready, just in case, for physical action if it was needed.

His large hands, hands she knew to be so incredibly strong and so astonishingly gentle, took her shoulders, moving her aside and guiding her so that she was behind him, out of his way, allowing him to move to where he was face-to-face with Derek. Not close enough to be threatening, nor was there anything perceptibly threatening in Bevan's manner.

And when Derek nodded, condescending to Bevan's request, Judith could only listen to the questions and answers with growing astonishment as Derek, the politician, was manipulated by Bevan, the grazier, into doing exactly what Bevan had intended should be done right from the start.

Roberta, Ted, and Ron would make a quick run north for new supplies, maybe going as far as Smithton, on the coast, and Judith soon came to terms with the Tasmanian concept of "quick" when it was revealed that it would take most of the day for the return journey.

"Might only need to go as far as Trowutta, or Roger River, or Edith Creek," Ted mused out loud. "We didn't come in on that road, and it's been years since I was up this way, so I don't know what's available, or where."

He got no argument, nor was there any about the real issue: nobody would say one word about what they'd already seen to anyone. Not to anyone at all.

And if anybody seriously believes that, I have this bridge for sale in Brooklyn. The mere thought brought a hint of a grin to Judith's lips, but she kept the thought private even as she looked to the sky, hoping for a vision of flying pink pigs. Still, she thought, there was a chance. Roberta and Ted seemed unwilling to rock the boat any further, and the Ron-the-conservationist could surely be trusted to do whatever Derek instructed.

Or could he?

Could Derek be trusted, for that matter?

Not on any day that ends with "Y."

As Judith glanced into the laughing eyes of Bevan Keene, she determined that it might be more dangerous to trust him than to trust Derek.

30

The rest of that day was, for Judith and everyone else left in camp, little short of a living tension headache, a nightmare of unease and unrealistic expectations that were never met. They went through all the motions, going out and collecting film, checking sensors, but it was all done in a fog of supersensitivity, supercaution, as if what might be out there watching was the boogeyman, rather than the elusive, legendary, almost mythical animal they'd come to find.

They spent the entire day looking over their shoulders, moving like ghosts themselves, or trying to, as they attempted and usually failed to make their way through the thick scrub without noise, without doing anything—whatever that *anything* might turn out to be—to frighten away the tiger they thought they'd seen that morning.

Not that it mattered. By the time the provisioning party returned just before dark, nobody had seen one thing even worth talking about.

And so it went for the next several days, days in which their unrealistic expectations gradually faded as tiredness and, eventually, boredom reclaimed the atmosphere. Only Jan managed to maintain her enthusiasm. She carried her minicamera everywhere, even when "visiting the bushes" and slept with it snuggled up to her like a teddy bear.

Everything fell back into the earlier routine, except in the case of Derek. It seemed to Judith that he spent an inordinate amount of time away from their base, driving out daily. He said it was to check various aspects of the global positioning system he'd brought. Whatever he was up to, it wasn't anything he'd discussed with *his* side of the expedition. They were the ones who seemed most concerned by the apparent secrecy he was displaying. And with every day that passed, he seemed to become more tense, more irritable.

"He's got more than the GPS unit," Judith overheard Ron Peters complaining. The militant conservationist clearly fancied himself as Derek's second-in-command, and he was edgy and nervous as a result of not being asked to share in whatever was going on. He'd taken to following Derek around like a lost puppy but gained only snarls and rebuffs for the effort.

"He's also got a cell phone, for all the good it'll do him out here," Ted Norton remarked. "The global tracking gizmo is halfways logical, I suppose, but a cell phone? Half his bloody luck at getting that to work, with the nearest towers either way up at the coast or over along the Midlands Highway. I can't see the sense in any of it, myself. We know where we are, and who else matters?"

Judith could only agree, although she'd yet to even test her own cell phone, bought at Jeremiah's insistence and never used to check in with him.

Derek was also becoming increasingly paranoid, Judith thought, although she tried, in all fairness, to dismiss that notion as her own reaction to distrusting him so thoroughly in the first place. Still, he kept a small cache of detailed topographical maps and was as possessive about them as Jan was about her cameras. They were with him at all times, and he was suspicious and surreptitious about consulting them whenever any of the others might see him. The one time she inadvertently surprised him in the process of consulting one, he hurriedly folded it closed and shot her an angry glare.

"He's up to something," Judith said to Roberta. "Mind you, he's always up to something, but unless it's my imagination, he's getting more paranoid every day."

"The man couldn't lie straight in bed," was Roberta's reply in typical Australian phrasing. Roberta not only didn't trust Derek, she didn't like him and wasn't shy about showing it.

For his part, Derek seemed content to give the attractive grazier a wide berth. Probably, Judith thought, because Roberta controlled the cook tent and Derek did enjoy his tucker, so long as it wasn't wallaby.

But as the days passed, it was another man whose presence caused Judith the most concern. Bevan's insistence on keeping his own distance from Judith was an attitude that had gone from being confusing to annoying to downright frustrating, not least with her memories of their lovemaking in her own bed. Intellectually, she could understand him wanting to protect her neutrality as official recorder for the expedition, but her emotions refused to be dictated to by her mind. She had only to look at Bevan under some circumstances to feel that too-familiar softness in her loins, to feel her nipples throbbing in response to her emotional urgings.

But what did *he* feel? It seemed impossible to her that he wouldn't be experiencing some comparable emotions, unless he was an even more skilled trickster than she dared believe. Was he merely toying with her? Had he toyed with her from the very beginning? Had she allowed that? Had she, in fact, encouraged it, sought it out, actually wanted it?

Get a life, Judith Theresa. You'll be as paranoid as Derek if you keep this up.

But Derek's erratic behavior was taking a toll on everyone's patience by the end of the following week, except, for some reason, that of Bevan, Roberta, and Ted, who went about their chores in an aura of total calm. If anything, they seemed more amused by his behavior than annoyed by it.

Until the day he returned from his solo trek with a strange, frenetic sort of atmosphere about him, his eyes wild, his every move jerky and slightly out of kilter. They'd all been a bit edgy because of the ongoing drizzly mist that Ted Norton called "west-coast sunshine," but it was obvious there was more than just the weather on Derek's mind.

Judith put her own angst aside and demanded that Bevan accompany her to where they could speak privately. "There is something *really* wrong with Derek," she insisted. "I genuinely believe he might be cracking up, although I can't see why. Do you think he's sneaking off to do drugs or something?"

Bevan's slow grin, normally sufficient to melt her heart and wrap her soul in a sort of security blanket, now served only to infuriate her as he said, "Not to worry. It won't be too long now, I think, and all will be revealed."

Calm. Too calm. Too . . . knowing.

"You know something," she said. "Why won't you tell me?"

"Because you must see it for yourself without my influence or any input from me," he replied, his voice still quiet, still calm, even more infuriating because of it.

"Great! Is this the prelude to another one of those 'Trust Me' pleas? Trust you? I think you're even more deceitful than *he* is!"

"Ah, that's what I love about you, Judith Theresa. Your ability to see things clearly." And now his grin was huge, if predatory. "Haven't you figured it out yet? I don't want you to trust me. I don't want you to trust anybody, especially right now. Just have faith in your instincts and your own integrity. That's all I ask."

"Maybe you ask too much." Her feelings were hurt. He was still toying with her, still leading her around by an emotional leash she had woven herself, and it rankled. She clenched her fist, fighting off the urge to smack him, and managed sufficient control to turn on her heel and march away, back straight, eyes brimming with tears of mingled anger and pain.

By that afternoon, Derek's nervous tension was almost a visible entity, and everyone was on edge as they gathered in the cook tent to avoid the misty drizzle outside. All the work was done for the day, but it was too early to settle, and tempers were exacerbated by sodden clothing, wet feet, and the incessant, ubiquitous mud. Most of the party were content to sprawl where they didn't get rained on, but Derek was constantly pacing, a nuisance in the cramped tent, even without his incessant chatter.

"This is perfect weather for us to see a tiger," he said. "I'd expect one to be on the move early in weather like this. The moist air holds scent well, and there's just enough breeze, and—"

"Just like almost every other day since we got here," said Ted, who kept having to move his feet every time Derek passed where Ted was sprawled near the entrance, carefully plaiting lengths of leather into something or other. "Derek, will you please just settle? Every time I get comfy, you make me move, and I'm too old for that sort of nonsense."

Derek ignored the complaint. He poked his head out through the tent flap, then abruptly jerked back inside the cook tent.

"Jan." His voice was a whisper but his excitement was obvious, and contagious. Even as the photographer moved across the tent to join him, the rest of the group also surged toward the entrance. It was clear Derek had spotted something extraordinary, which could only mean one thing.

This time their tiger was closer. Much closer. Just across the small rivulet that passed by the camp. And this time it was moving, lifting its distinctive head from where it had been drinking, backing away from the edge of the stream in careful steps that couldn't help but be captured on film.

And Jan was filming. She not only had her minicam, but she had dragged out a conventional video camera with a long, bulky telephoto lens. When the animal turned to look back, its attention on something in the scrub behind it, Jan took the opportunity to scuttle over to where she could get a dead rest on the side of a parked vehicle to minimize instability.

Everyone gasped, but the animal appeared not to notice her. Instead, it turned and lumbered back into the dripping undergrowth, moving in the same curious, almost clumsy-looking gait Judith had so often seen on old films from the Hobart zoo. One moment it was there, clear as day, or what passed for daylight in the incessant drizzle. And then it was gone. Just like that.

Everyone exhaled with heavy sighs, as if they'd been holding their breaths collectively.

Then Derek's voice broke the silence. "Well, I guess that ought to be proof enough!" And there was not only smug satisfaction in his voice, but a sort of unholy fanaticism in his eyes that was mirrored in the eyes of his conservationist companions. Derek was positively electrified, his body jerking as if guided by invisible wires.

Judith wondered yet again if he was on some sort of drug, then realized that it didn't matter. He was teetering on the brink of a breakdown, and the reasons were no longer the issue. Why couldn't Bevan see it?

The answer was obvious. Derek had moved so that he was out of Bevan's line of sight.

"You reckon that's proof enough, do you, Derek?" Bevan's question followed a lengthy silence in which everyone else had done nothing but look at each other and at the emptiness where the animal had been. Bevan's voice wasn't overly loud, but the sarcasm in it fairly shouted.

"There has to be three, maybe four minutes of film," said

Ron Peters. "I counted."

"And there'll be tracks, for sure. That sandy place it was drinking should be perfect for getting plaster casts of its tracks." This, surprisingly, came from Ted, which lent a certain veracity to the remark.

His comment drew Judith's attention, and she looked to see that Ted, too, was watching Derek with a cautious, worried look. Glancing around, Judith saw that the others were noticing Derek's eccentric behavior, too. Ted had moved in beside the conservationist, and Reg was watching Derek closely. Ted was trying surreptitiously to draw Bevan's attention to Derek. But he was being too subtle.

Bevan was staring squarely at Judith, who took one look at the devils dancing in his laughing eyes and reared back in cautious surprise. "Right then," he said. "We're all agreed?"

"No!" she cried, and it was an involuntary, unthinking cry. Then she did think, and could only repeat it. "No, no, we are not agreed. There's something really, really wrong here, and I've had enough. I want this out in the open. Now. Whatever it is. Please, Bevan."

She focused on Bevan, flicking her gaze between him and Derek, silently pleading with him to notice, to realize that there might be far more at stake here than a mere agreement about what they had or had not seen.

There was a long pause, during which she knew everyone's eyes had turned to her, during which she knew everyone was confused by her reaction. But she couldn't break Bevan's gaze. She could barely even breathe. Bevan returned her gaze silently, his own confusion apparent. And then, miraculously, he got it. He broke his visual lock with her, turned and ran his gaze over the rest of the assembly. When he got to Derek, there was a perceptible pause, then Bevan turned back to her and visibly shivered.

She caught the change in his expression, could feel the sadness even as he bent his head and shook it in a gesture that was part apology, part self-condemnation.

"You're right, Judith Teresa," he said, this time meeting her eyes frankly, without any guile or amusement. "You're right and you were right earlier. I should have listened to you and I'm sorry. Truly I am."

Reaching into his shirt pocket, he withdrew what looked like a folded-up bit of plastic about the size of a fifty-cent piece, with a piece of string hanging from it. He thrust it in his mouth, then turned and looked across the rivulet for an instant. A piercing whistle stabbed through the drizzle and mist, a unique sound that rose to a crescendo, then dropped into a series of trilling chirps before rising yet again.

The sound of Bevan's New Zealand sheep-dog whistle could as easily have come from some exotic rainforest bird, but the result was even more astonishing. After a minute that seemed like an hour of echoing silence, out of the underbrush across the rivulet poked the head of their tiger, its entire attention clearly focused on the magical sounds from the whistle.

"Come on, Fred," said Bevan with a weary shake of his head. "The jig's up, little mate."

The dog . . . and suddenly it was most clearly, most emphatically, a *dog,* albeit an ugly one . . . how could they *ever* have thought it to be a real tiger?—seemed to smile before plunging its striped body into the rivulet and galumphing towards Bevan. It loped with a lolling tongue and a semaphore waggling of its tiger-like tail.

Bevan bestowed a pat on the animal's head as it reached him, then turned to face the astonished crew of tiger hunters. "Here's your Tassie tiger," he said. "Or at least Derek's version. Bloody oath, mate," he added, turning to stare at the wild-eyed conservation leader who now jerked uncontrollably. "Did you honestly believe we'd be that stupid?"

Then Bevan stepped quickly to help Ted support Derek as the conservationist uttered a mighty shriek and collapsed in a dead faint.

31

"I still have trouble believing you knew all along and managed to keep it so secret." Judith murmured the words from within the safe cocoon of Bevan's arms. Her eyes were closed against the sunlight glowing through the tent roof above them, but she couldn't shut down her mind. "You're even more cunning and devious than Derek at his best."

"If I was, we wouldn't be here, like this, now," he replied. "And I have to say that you repeat yourself an awful lot for somebody who's supposed to be a professional wordsmith. You must have said those very same words at least a dozen times since I got back. And I'm trying to get some much-needed sleep, in case you hadn't noticed."

It was sleep they both needed, having spent most of the night on a mercy dash to get Derek back to civilization and into the much-needed care of mental health professionals. Derek had gone into a frightening, trancelike state after the arrival of Fred and the evidence of Derek's attempted scam had been made clear for everyone to see.

Ted and Reg had also made the journey and were now presumably asleep. Somewhere. Ted had been cornered immediately on their return and informed by Jan and Roberta that Bevan's tent—which he'd been sharing—was now "otherwise engaged." And that Jan and Roberta had already moved Ted's gear out. And that Judith's gear, from the girls' tent, was now stacked neatly alongside Bevan's own.

"If everything's now going to be open and above board with this expedition," Jan had told an astonished and somewhat embarrassed Judith, "then you two might as well be, too. It isn't as if you were really fooling anyone anyway."

So here they were, snuggled into conjoined sleeping bags, with the tacit approval of their companions, and Bevan wanted to talk about sleeping when Judith's mind was fragmented with a million questions that demanded answers, even if he'd already provided them countless times during the journey back from the north coast. Because even with his answers, the whole, entire situation was unimaginable.

"I still don't see how Derek thought he could get away with it," Judith said, reaching out to run her fingers across Bevan's stomach, flicking them above and below the waistline to be sure of maintaining his attention. And his erection.

"He was crazy, that's all," was the reply. "Totally, completely, right round the twist, although he hid it rather well. But there was no real sense in it from the start. Stop that." Bevan wriggled beneath her touch, unable to ignore the effects. "Our little mate Derek wasn't the full quid, and maybe he never has been. But he'd been looking for a real boomer of a conservation issue that would give him a chance to shine, and one day, when he's out organizing some protest, what should he find but a fair-dinkum tiger ring-in. Without the stripes, of course, but stripes are easy.

"So Derek fronts up to the owner of this wondrous beast, and starts sounding him out about conservation issues, doing a real snow-job on this kid, or so Derek thinks. But what he didn't know, and this is where coincidence defies all logic, is that the kid with the dog is young James McShane, formerly of Tasmania, and by further coincidence, the baby brother of my beauteous and favorite motor mechanic."

"She of the monster truck," Judith interjected. "Yes, I'd like to meet her, one day."

"I'll bet you would. Anyway, young James, who's all of nineteen and smart as a whip, and who's been up there working as a jackaroo during university vacation, is about as antigreenie as . . . as . . ."

"As you and Ted and Roberta," Judith concluded for him.

"Yes, that," he said unashamedly. "Judith, darling, I wish you'd move your hand. I'm trying to concentrate here."

Which she did, although Judith doubted that her hand's new location would improve Bevan's thinking. Nor did she care much. She was enjoying herself immensely.

"Anyway, young James let Derek convince him to bring the dog to Tassie for this 'joke' Derek wanted to play. I suspect an all-expenses trip home had something to do with it, but the boy swears he was only doing his duty to the state, as he saw it. You heard him say that, I believe."

She had. Right after Derek's collapse, a tall, rawboned, tow-headed youth had splashed across the rivulet, eyes ablaze with laughter at his delight in tricking the trickster. In fairness to young James McShane, the pleasure had turned to concern when he saw Derek's condition, but he remained unrepentant about his role—and Fred's—in the whole tiger deception game.

"Only first, James phoned and told his sister, and she told you, and you arranged a double cross." Judith wriggled against Bevan's warmth, reached down to stroke the muscles of his thigh. She was getting bored with the tale now, and other temptations beckoned. She reached higher.

Bevan groaned, the effectiveness of her ploy rigid within her fingers.

"Tell me again why you didn't blow the whistle on him right at the start," she whispered. "You could have. You knew what was going on even before you accepted Jeremiah's offer to become involved."

Bevan groaned again, this time with a combination of frustration and feigned annoyance. "You know damned well why," he said. "Because I wanted to lead him all the way down the garden path first, and make him suffer, like he made you suffer with that nonsense up in Queensland. And, okay, I was maybe a teensy bit jealous of him having known you first."

"He didn't *know* me first," Judith said with a sigh. "He didn't, for instance, know this." And she guided Bevan's free hand to her breast. "Or this." And she guided it lower, wriggling against the sheer delight his touch created, thrilling to the sensations his fingers immediately provoked.

"And I didn't know just how far round the twist he really was," Bevan said, his voice soft in her ear, his fingers equally soft against the center of her femininity, which pulsed at his touch, flooding her loins with pleasure. Bevan rolled over, pinning her with his body, all thoughts of sleep clearly gone now, as her fingers guided him within.

32

It was much, much later when they resumed their conversation.

"And you're sure everybody will agree to just let this die?" Judith said. "I mean, there's no good purpose in creating a public scandal over Derek's illness and . . . well . . . everything." This, too, was a question she had asked before, and although she knew Bevan's view, she was less sure than he about what the rest of the party would say.

"Nobody would believe it anyway," Bevan said. "You hardly believe it, and you were there . . . here. Besides, what's to be gained by making a meal of it? We mightn't like old Derek, but none of us would ever have wished him the problems he's got now, much less those that would be caused by blasting this all over the media."

Judith felt much the same. There was a story there, but it was too bizarre, and would cause too much hurt to too many people to make it worth the telling.

"Ignoring the story doesn't say much for my journalistic integrity," she said. "I know people who'd literally kill for a story like this, regardless of who got hurt."

"But you're not one of them, which is one of the reasons I love you. There are more important things in life than destroying somebody for a news story. Even a twit like our poor little mate Derek. Besides, we've still got the story you signed on for."

"So you say. But how? Derek is the one who convinced

Jeremiah it was worthwhile in the first place. Without him, well . . ." Then she reflected for a moment. "But of course! Jeremiah doesn't even know yet, does he? And I suppose I get the fun job of explaining to him how he's been conned. You'll end up looking for your tiger without me if he decides to take it out on the messenger."

"No chance. I'd just flatly refuse to go without my wife, or fiancée, or whatever you'll agree to," Bevan said, then laughed at the reaction that provoked. "Hear me, Judith Theresa. I am not going bush alone with that Smythe woman, and that's for sure. She's too tough for me."

"But you'd have Roberta to protect you." Judith couldn't help that little jibe, now that she knew Bevan's exquisite neighbor was only, in Bevan's own words, "a wonderful friend and a better neighbor."

"But there was never anything between Roberta and me, like you've obviously been imagining. Never. So believe it." He sealed the statement with a kiss, then added, "Besides, despite the fact that Roberta could face a mob of wild cattle without batting an eye, she told me right from the start she's not fussed about what she calls 'stressful interpersonal relationships.' You mightn't get her within a bull's roar of another trip involving greenies or vegetarians or anybody else she couldn't totally dominate. She only came along to check you out. You do realize that, don't you?"

Now Bevan's grin was thoroughly wicked.

"She was afraid you wouldn't be a decent cook, not being a proper Tasmanian farm girl and all, and I might have to fend for myself, or starve, or—"

"But how could she know that I . . . we . . . ? She hadn't even met me!"

"Because I told her, you goose. I knew, right from the first taste of your cousin's burnt offerings. You did too, only you weren't game to admit it, in case your journalistic integrity might be compromised or something."

Judith tried not to blush at the truth of his comment, and swiftly changed the subject.

"I still think you let Derek go on far, far too long," she said.

"I wouldn't have had to if he hadn't been so bloody incompetent. I mean, think about it, Judith Teresa. He had a cell phone to communicate with James, but it only worked on very rare occasions and not well even then. His walkie-talkie wasn't much better and his map reading . . . well, let's just ignore his map-reading skills. Young James said it took him three days on the road to get close enough to know where to start trying to find us. And do you know how far he and that damned dog had to travel, bush-bashing all the way, to actually get to us? He'd have gotten here faster if he'd walked back around by road, and that's about thirty miles."

Bevan rolled over and stared thoughtfully at the patterns of sunlight on the tent roof. "He's a damned fine splendid bushman, that boy. A credit to his upbringing. But he told me he could hardly believe his luck when he finally did locate us, and if Derek hadn't peeked out at just the right moment, young James was afraid he'd be spending another night in the bush before Fred would get his chance to . . ." Bevan paused, then quickly leaned over to try and repair the damage with a kiss. But it was too late.

Judith reared up out of the sleeping bag as if she'd been stung. "But . . . then . . . that means . . ." She was incoherent as the time line scurried through her brain, as the logic of it all became apparent. "So the first time, that very first sighting, that was . . ."

She gulped, had to fight for breath as she suppressed the urge to throttle Bevan right there on the spot. Except that she couldn't believe what he was implying. And she couldn't *not* believe it, either.

So she merely said, "That first sighting *wasn't* Fred?"

Bevan didn't reply, didn't even move. And wouldn't meet her eyes.

"Tell me!" she insisted.

"That I love you? I'd have thought that was obvious enough, Judith Theresa, but okay—I LOVE YOU. The question is, do you love me as much, or more, or am I just a holiday fling, or . . . ?"

"TELL ME!"

"I just did. Your turn now." Bevan punctuated his words with slow, gentle caresses along her naked, far-too-sensitive thighs.

Judith melted, lost focus, closed her eyes so as to better savor the idyll. But eventually, his clever, delightful fingers pried the words from her.

"I love you too, and you know it, you sly devil. And yes, since you asked so nicely, I'll probably even marry you. But *only* if you tell me—what, exactly, *did* we see?" Her mind still sought the answer, but her body was—once again—betraying her.

Judith succumbed to Bevan's caresses, shifting to ease his access to her supersensitive areas, then reveling in the touch of his lovemaking. It was a while before she could even *think* what the question had really been all about.

"Was it really a tiger? Tell me the truth, dammit! You know, Bevan, you have to know."

"We saw what we wanted to see," said the man she'd fallen in love with. "What we *had* to see." And he laughed before he pulled her into his arms and stilled her protests with kisses and promises of dreams past and dreams yet to come.

ABOUT THE AUTHOR

Victoria Gordon is the pseudonym under which Canadian/Australian author Gordon Aalborg has written more than twenty contemporary romances, including *Finding Bess* (Five Star Publishing, 2004).

As himself, he is the author of the western romance *The Horse Tamer's Challenge* (Five Star Publishing, 2009) and the Tasmanian-oriented Five Star suspense thrillers *The Specialist* (2004) and *Dining with Devils* (2009) as well as the feral cat survival epic *Cat Tracks.*

Born in Canada, Aalborg spent half his life in Australia, mostly in Tasmania, and now lives on Vancouver Island, in Canada, with his wife, the mystery and romance author Denise Dietz.

More on www.gordonaalborg.com.